My Mother's Kitchen

MEERA
EKKANATH
KLEIN

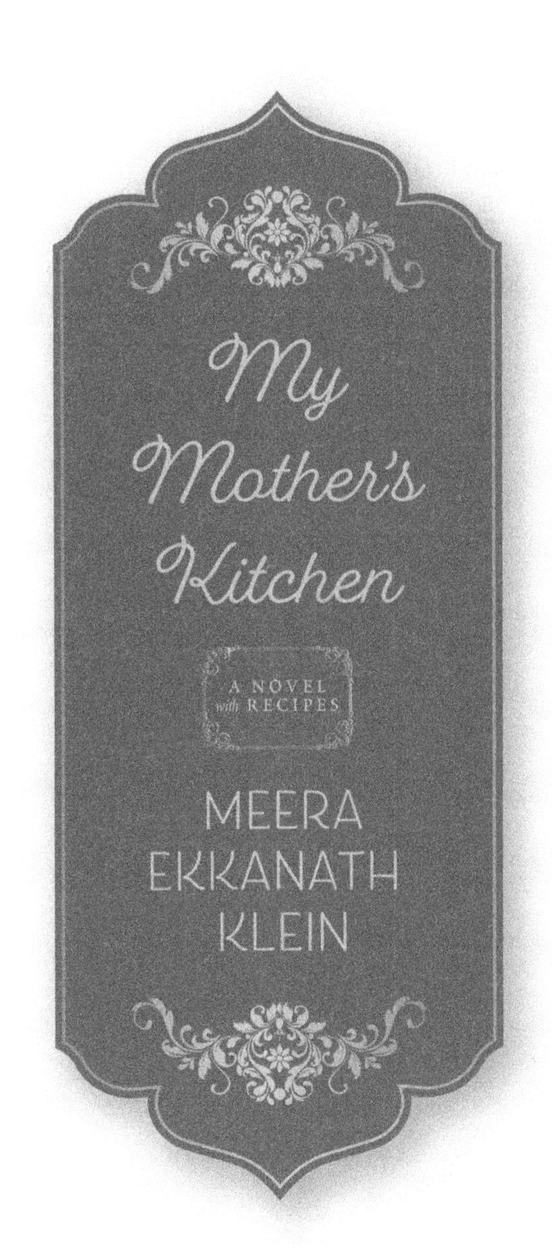
My Mother's Kitchen
A NOVEL with RECIPES
MEERA EKKANATH KLEIN

PUBLISHED BY HOMEBOUND PUBLICATIONS

Quantity sales and special discounts are available on quantity purchases by corporations, associations, bookstores and others. For details, contact the publisher or visit wholesalers such as Ingram or Baker & Taylor.

Visit us www.homeboundpublications.com

Second Edition ISBN: 9781938846700
Book Designed by Leslie M. Browning
Cover Images by © Jag_cz (Shutterstock.com)
Interior Images by © Bariskina (Shutterstock.com)

Library of Congress Cataloging-in-Publication Data

Klein, Meera Ekkanath.
My mother's kitchen : a novel with recipes / by Meera Ekkanath Klein. — first edition.

pages cm
ISBN 978-1-938846-29-8 (pbk.)
1. Food--Fiction. 2. Domestic fiction. I. Title.
PS3611.L4495M9 2014
813'.6--dc23

2014005784

10 9 8 7 6 5 4 3 2

Homebound Publications is committed to ecological stewardship. We greatly value the natural environment and invest in environmental conservation.

To: Meg

Happy Reading

Meera

Nov. 2022

Dedication

This book is dedicated to the pair of noisy Mockingbirds nesting outside my kitchen window. The tiny gray and white mama and papa birds spent weeks tirelessly feeding their hungry babies and defending them against a stalking cat, the extreme heat and a freak summer thunder storm. One day the nest was empty, without a word of thanks the babies were gone. A wise mother knows when to let her baby fly away. My mother, Leela Sadasivam, was one of these wise mamas. Thank you for letting me soar.

~

Chapter One

Kashi's Story

• • • • • • • • • •

Kashi's day follows the rhythm of the sun. She can hear the far off sound of a rooster crowing and the final notes of the nightingale. It is still dark outside; the only hint of the coming dawn is the faint tinges on the horizon, a pale suspicion of light. Kashi wants to burrow her head into the pillow and keep the day at bay. But before long her father will be asking for his first cup of coffee, and besides it is almost time to get ready to go to work at the Big House. Spending time with Meena and her mother is the highlight of her day. She loves the walk up the slope, past the meadow filled with wild mustard, and through the dark cavern of trees. The trail leads through the raspberry brambles and past wild crabapple trees. Coming up the hill and seeing the Big House for the first time, as it is called by the villagers, is always a thrill. The house or bungalow is not the biggest home in the hilltop village of Mahagiri but somehow it seems to occupy a lot of space with its creamy-colored walls and bright red tile roof. The front entrance is a welcoming riot of brilliant bougainvillea blossoms and yellow roses. Her mistress, Little Mother, loves roses and the front yard is a riot of neon orange, red, white, blinding yellow, pale pink and deep almost black red blooms that fill the air with their intoxicating fragrance. The smell of roses is a haven of peace for Kashi.

Since the death of her mother two years ago, Kashi and her father have lived in the small white washed cottage with Kashi taking care of the kitchen and the inside chores. And today is no different.

So she gets up and goes outside to wash her hands and face. Next, it is time to light the fire in the kitchen hearth. She fills the earthen fireplace with bits of twigs and a piece of pre-cious newspaper and starts a feeble flame. Using an iron pipe, she blows gently on the struggling fire and soon the twigs begin to turn orange. She quickly adds a few more dry sticks and then a small log as the fire grows brighter and hotter. She sets the aluminum pan of water on the open flames and goes outside with a brass pot. She balances the round brass pot on her head and walks a few yards down to the public water pump. The sun is still low on the horizon, the first rays peeking shyly over the hills. Even though Kashi can hear the sounds of the waking villagers, there is no one at the pump and she quickly fills the brass pot with the icy cold water. The vessel is cumbersome on her head and she walks a little un-steadily, almost tripping over a large rock.

"Steady there, miss," a voice calls behind her and a warm hand closes over her elbow, helping her keep balance. She can't quite turn around to see who is helping her. Then the figure, a tall one, comes into her line of sight on the right side and she sees it is a villager named Raman. She's aware of the warmth of his fingers on her bare elbow and wishes she could ask him to remove his hand. As though he read her thoughts,

Raman removes his support and she nearly topples over. This time he doesn't offer any help and Kashi looks up the path to see her father and his friend Thimban walking toward them.

"Kashi, can you make an extra cup of coffee here for Thimban?" her father, Bhojan, asks. He looks at Raman suspiciously.

Kashi walks as quickly as she can back to their house. She can't wait to get inside the protection of the thick mud walls. Her house like all the others in the village is whitewashed with a clay tile roof. Each house faces the village square. A large banyan tree with gnarled old roots stands guard in the center of the square. This wooden guardian provides shelter for the wizened men who like to gather under its dappled shade as well as for giggling young girls and boys who play tag. Kashi remembers sitting under the tree with her mother when she was too weak to walk across the small square to the village temple. It seems as if it was just yesterday that her mother's frail body was wracked with a deep cough. The cough pounded her thin frame until she had no more breath left in her lungs. Each time Kashi passes the shady tree she can imagine her mother sitting beneath the dark canopy, laughing and healthy, her face lifted up to the warmth of the early morning sun. This morning her mother's image is not laughing, instead she looks worried.

Kashi shrugs off her absurd imagination and keeps walking. She grunts as she lifts the heavy brass water pot from her head and places it down. She enters the kitchen just as the pot of water is nearly boiling. From a small cupboard, she removes the day-old milk and measures two cups of milk and hot water into a small saucepan and places it on the warm hearth. Within minutes the milky mixture begins to boil and Kashi opens another cabinet door and reaches inside for a jar of instant coffee. Carefully she measures four level teaspoons into the now boiling milk and water. She removes the hot milky coffee from the fire and drops three large lumps of brown sugar. The sugar melts in the hot liquid sending out a deep sweet fragrance that mingles deliciously with the coffee. Next, Kashi uses a steel tumbler and pours the coffee back and froth from the tumbler to the sauce pan until the brown liquid is frothy and uniform in color.

"Ah..I can smell the coffee," a voice says from the front of the house. It is Thimban, her father's companion. He enters the kitchen with Bhojan right behind him. Both men squat on low stools, moving close to the hearth for heat and light. Wordlessly, Kashi gets up and hands each man a steel tumbler of hot coffee. The tumbler is placed inside another small round container to protect the men's hands from the hot metal.

"This is excellent coffee Kashi," Thimban says, smacking his lips after each sip. His moustache quivers every time he takes a drink from the metal cup. "Well, Bhojan, can we get to business? I have to travel to Mahagiri this morning to buy some supplies."

Bhojan glances nervously at Kashi and places his empty coffee cup on the ground beside him.

"Ur ..yes. Of course. Kashi, Thimban as you know owns the land east of the temple where he grows cabbages and potatoes. He also has a tea plantation on the hill outside of Mahagiri."

Kashi has no idea why her father is listing all of Thimban's assets just nods her head.

"Well, yes. So he has come to me to ask your hand in marriage and knowing him to be a man of character I have agreed to the match."

Bhojan looks at Kashi from the corner of his eye. Ever since her mother's death, his fifteen-year-old daughter has developed an independent streak that sometimes frightens him and sometimes surprises him. Right now he isn't sure what her reaction will be but he doesn't think it will be good. Kashi's eyes are downcast and she doesn't look up or say anything.

"Come on Kashi, say something," Bhojan urges.

"Yes, girl can't you talk?" Thimban asks in an annoyed tone.

Kashi raises her head and looks at her father. Her glance is filled with despair and a sense of betrayal and Bhojan winces inwardly.

"Whatever you say father," Kashi says in a soft, defeated voice.

Bhojan wants to say something comforting but he can't find the right words.

"Good, good. Then it's all settled. We can arrange the date after speaking to the temple priest," Thimban says, rubbing his hands together in satisfaction. "I'll come back in a few days to talk to you both about the dowry."

It is the practice in the village for the groom to give the bride a dowry, a gift, before the wedding. The dowry can be anything from a few cows to a goat or even a warm woolen blanket, depending on the wealth of the groom. Kashi knows that Thimban's dowry will be grand and feels a sense of hopelessness grip her chest. For some reason at that moment she recalls Raman's warm fingers on her bare elbow. She rubs the spot now, imaging his callused hand supporting her.

Chapter Two

Kashi's Story Continued

• • • • • • • • • •

MAHAGIRI, SOUTH INDIA, 1955

The peace is shattered by someone hammering on the wooden doors. I'm almost asleep on my mother's lap lulled by her soft voice, and I sit up startled, blinking the sleep out of my eyes. Devi, our housekeeper, and my mother walk to the door.

"Stay in here," mother says in a firm voice over her shoulder to me as she walks through the open doorway to unlatch the door.

"Who's there?" Devi asks through the crack of the door.

"Please Devi sister, open the door," says a pleading voice. "It's me Kashi."

"Kashi," mother exclaims. She unlocks the door and pulls it open. "What's going on?"

I can't resist peeking out and almost yell in surprise when I see Kashi tumble into my mother's arms. Her face is bruised and one eyelid is swollen and closed tight.

"Come in the kitchen," my mother leads an exhausted Kashi inside.

"Meena, get up and pull out the mat from behind the door."

I run to do as I'm asked and soon Kashi is curled up on the bamboo mat. Kashi looks very different from her usual smiling self. She is the daughter of our cowhand, Bhojan, and during the weekdays she takes care of me and helps Devi in the kitchen with light chores. But now her round face with smiling dimples is drawn and thin and her lips look like they would never smile again, they are so swollen and red. A cut on the corner of her mouth is leaking a string of blood.

Devi pushes me aside to kneel beside the girl and wipes her face with a rag dipped in warm water. My mother is rummaging in a wooden box for her first-aid supplies when there is another violent banging on the kitchen door. Mother turns with a questioning look at Kashi, who tries to sit up. She looks frightened and her voice is all squeaky. "It's him, little mother, don't let him take me away."

My mother gets up and lays a reassuring hand on Kashi's forehead.

"Lie back down and don't worry. I won't let anyone take you away."

She doesn't ask Kashi any more questions. She strides to the door and flings it open. Her back faces me and I can see she holds herself so straight and stiff that she looks taller than her five feet.

"What's the meaning of this racket," she asks in a cold voice. "Is this the time to come knocking on a door and waking up a woman and a five-year-old child?"

I peer around the kitchen wall, through the half-open doorway, and see a group of men. Bhojan is in front of them,

his face apologetic in the dim light. The re are fiv e men behind him with flashlightsandonecarriesastoutstick.

Bhojan steps toward my mother, “Little mother, I’m sorry to cause you such worry,” he says in a careful and polite voice.

All the villagers and our neighbors call my mother “little mother” as a sign of respect. Her real name is Sudha Lakshmi.

“Tell her to return the girl,” a voice shouts from behind him.

Bhojan turns and motions to the speaker to be quiet.

“Please little mother. My daughter has to come with us. She has shamed me and my family and needs to be punished.”

My mother draws herself up taller and although I can’t see her expression I know her lips are probably drawn thin in anger and her black eyes flashingintemper .

“Bhojan, you know better than to come knocking on the door at this time of night. Yes, your 15-year-old daughter is with me and she stays here until she is better. Have you seen how she looks with a swollen face and black eye?”

“But, little mother, you don’t understand…” Bhojan says when he is rudely interrupted by a man’s voice.

“Let me up front,” he says. He pushes Bhojan aside. He is tall with a thick woolen scarf wrapped around his head and he looks like a giant next to my petite mother. His eyes are bloodshot and his big moustache quivers every time he yells. His voice is loud and I wince when he steps closer to my mother.

“Thisgirlismine.G ive her to me.”

My mother does not step back from his belligerent face. “Oh, and who are you? I know Bhojan is her father. But what right do you have to be here?”

“Th at girl is promised to me. I agreed to the marriage and just today I caught her with another man. I demand she come with me. I know what to do with such girls.”

Bhojan steps up to my mother, in front of the aggressive stranger, "Little mother, this is Thimban. He is engaged to my daughter. She has disgraced him and my family."

My mother looks over her shoulder and sees me peering around the corner and then she looks back at Bhojan and Thimban.

"If I agree to listen to your complaint tomorrow will you leave me and my daughter alone tonight?"

"We have to come back tomorrow? Thimban asks. "I don't know…"

"If you take the girl right now and something happens to her, I will make sure you will regret it for the rest of your life. The chief constable is a friend. Now, it is late, and I think you should all go to bed and sleep off your toddy drink."

She stops Bhojan's protests with an impatient gesture. "I can smell the alcohol on your breath, so go home before you all do something you'll regret. I will meet with you here tomorrow morning."

"You give me your word that I can take the girl tomorrow?" Thimban asks.

My mother shakes her head. "I said I'll listen to you and we can decide on a course of action."

Bhojan pushes Thimban aside and says, "Little mother, thank-you. We'll come back tomorrow." Grumbling a little, the men turn around and leave. Thimban turns back as if he wants to say something, but Bhojan pulls him away. He knows that my mother will keep her word for he respects and trusts her.

My mother closes the door, bolts it and leans on it for a moment with her eyes closed. She then walks over to Kashi and pulls up a low wooden stool. She sits down and takes one of Kashi's small hands in her own. I scoot along the floor and come to rest beside my mother. The blood has been cleaned off Kashi's face. Devi applies an herbal ointment on her cheek and swollen chin.

"Devi, warm some milk with honey for Kashi and make up the spare mattress so that she can sleep on the floor in my room. Also, bring a couple of aspirins from my room."

Devi goes to light the small kerosene stove and places an aluminum saucepan with milk on the blue flame. She walks out of the room through the back door, avoiding the front door which is now bolted and locked.

My mother turns back to Kashi. "Now Kashi, I need to hear from you what happened. Th en you can drink the milk and take some medicine for the pain. I want you to rest, but tell me what happened."

"Oh, little mother, it's all my fault." Kashi wails, tears streaming from beneath her puff y eyelids. "I know my father wanted me to marry old Thimban. But every time I'm near the well or by myself he tries to grab me. I hate his hot smelly breath. A few weeks ago he tried to stop me while I was on my way here. I was surprised and screamed so loud that Raman who was nearby came over to help. When Thimban saw him, he went away, cursing Raman. I was so grateful to Raman that I took him a bowl of my sweet rice payasam. He was by himself in the house and was so nice to me that I sat down and talked to him. Tonight I was going to his house with some leftover rice when Thimban came out from behind a tree and asked me where I was going. I tried to run away but he grabbed me and said all kinds of bad things about me. When he slapped my face, I fell down. He tried to reach for me but I hit him on the head with the rice bowl and ran away as fast as I could. I had nowhere to go, so I came here."

"Kashi, what were you thinking?" my mother sighs. "I know it's hard to understand, but your father did what he thought was best for you."

Kashi cries quietly. I feel sorry for her. She looks so sad and worn down like the puppy my mother found on the side of the road after a truck hit it.

"I don't know what to do. I wanted to ask for your help but I knew everyone would be angry with me. Please help me."

My mother is quiet for such a long time that we can hear the pan of milk sizzle and the hoot of an owl outside.

"Meena turn off the stove," she tells me. "Kashi, I will try my best to help you. Do you want to marry this Raman?"

Kashi's tears stop. She tries to sit up and the eye that is not swollen is filled with happy tears. "You'll help me? I don't want to marry anyone right now."

Just then Devi comes in with a jar of eucalyptus honey. Soon Kashi is sipping the hot milk and honey. We walk across our tiny courtyard to the bedroom and I watch my mother tuck Kashi in and speak to her in a low, reassuring tone. I can't hear what she says even though I strain my ears.

"Come, miss big ears," my mother tweaks my ears. "You've heard more than what's good for you tonight. It is way past your bed time, Meenakutty."

I wake up next morning and lie in bed for a moment thinking about everything that happened the night before. I lean over to see if Kashi is still in bed but the mattress is neatly rolled up and pushed to the side. I hop out of bed. I hope I'm not too late for the meeting.

The morning is a busy time in the kitchen with the cow hands bringing in pails of fresh milk. My mother and Ayah strain the milk and pour it into big tin cans, ready to be delivered. Everyone wants to buy milk from our cows because our milk is never watered.

"Little mother, we are ready for the clean milk cans," says Bhojan. My mother is definitely in charge of our cows and tells the cowhands when to milk the cows and how to take care of them.

"Today, my sister will be here to help in the vegetable garden," Bhojan tells my mother as he collects the milk cans.

"That is good because we need the help, Bhojan. It's past time to plant the tomatoes."

People from the village come and help plant her garden. We grow potatoes, beans, cabbage and carrots in neat rows.

The kitchen gets crowded with people and animals. Our three cats and dog try to force their way into the room and beg for a taste of the fresh milk. My mother always feeds them.

I walk in and my mother looks up and smiles.

"It's my sleepyhead. Go, get something to drink. Kashi is in there," she gestures with her head toward the kitchen.

Kashi sits on the floor, shelling sweet peas. I dip into the bowl of green peas. I pop the fresh sweet peas into my mouth. Kashi stops me before I grab another handful.

"Stop that little one. Your mother has some warm milk for you right by the fireplace."

She gets up and brings me a steel tumbler of warm milk. I sneak another handful of peas. I watch Kashi as she sits back down. Her face is still puffy and looks lopsided and her lips are raw and chapped. I feel sorry for her again.

"What's going to happen to you?" I ask.

She shrugs her shoulder and sighs, "Your mother has promised to look after me and I know she'll take care of me."

"Did you have a meeting yet?"

"Yes, it was scary to see Thimban again. But I sat next to your mother and didn't look at him. He was yelling and screaming, but your mother invited the chief constable. When he arrived everyone was much quieter. I couldn't listen to everything because I was so nervous."

"Will you have to marry Thimban?"

"No, your mother said I could live here. When I turn seventeen she said she will arrange my marriage. Until then I don't have to marry anyone." Kashi smiles, and even with her discolored lip and bruised face she looks like the old Kashi I know.

I smile back. I'm happy she won't have to marry an old man with smelly breath.

"When you get married, I'll ask mother to make you some lemon rice for the wedding feast," I say to Kashi, who giggles, and gives me a handful of peas. I knew my mother would take care of Kashi.

I take a sip of sweet milk and look around the smoke-darkened kitchen walls. I love this place with its warmth and its rich aromas of spices and cooking. There is no place like it.

My mother's kitchen is a miracle-working spot, a place of transformation. Here a handful of rice, a pinch of turmeric and a splash of fresh lemon juice are magically transformed into mouth-watering lemon rice. A slice of cucumber and tomato with a sprinkle of salt and pepper becomes a tangy relish. This special place not only brings about change in food but in people too. But like all changes it can sometimes be painful.

For being such an enchanting place, the kitchen is actually very ordinary. It consists of two rooms, connected by an open doorway. The first room has three pieces of furniture, all large and made of wood. There is a long teak table with measuring cups and milk strainers on it. The china cabinet occupies another wall, filled with pieces of fine china as well as stainless steel pots and pans. Against yet another wall is a large cupboard with a mesh covering. I loved to open this door and take whiffs of the buttery tang of yogurt and the biting aroma of dried chilies.

The second part of the kitchen is where the cooking takes place. A large open-fire hearth occupies most of the room.

The cooking hearth is made of river clay and every few weeks Devi walks to the river bank and brings back a plastic bucket filled with moist, red clay. She uses this clay to mend any cracks and smooth the edges of the open fireplace. On the wall opposite the cooking fireplace, there is a window with a wide ledge where ripening tomatoes, mangoes and other seasonal fruits and vegetables stand in a row, attentive as soldiers on parade. Baskets of pungent onions and garlic, impossibly perfect red potatoes, orange-fleshed yams and long tubers sit in a corner. Bunches of red chilies, garlic and herbs hang from the low wooden beams and their fragrance add pungency to the already aromatic kitchen. There are several low stools and a bench placed in front of the window. This special kitchen and my home are on hilltop in the outskirts of the town of Mahagiri in south India. The house with its red tiled roof and smooth whitewashed walls is surrounded by hundreds of tea bushes. From my backyard the hillsides look like they have been carpeted in green.

As the first fingers of dawn light up the sky, the kitchen comes alive with the rich aromas of cooking and the cacophony of sounds. During the cool, foggy evenings, the kitchen is warm and cozy. Twilight has come and gone, the cows bedded down and the only sounds in the still kitchen are the voices of mother and Devi, idly gossiping about the day's events. A few embers glow in the fireplace and my mother rests her aching back against the warm hearth. I join her, loving the comfort of her sturdy body.

My mother's presence makes our house into a home. I have lived in this old house my whole life—all five years of it—with my mother and Ayah. I was born in this house and Ayah says she was right there to catch me. But now I'm almost as tall as Ayah even though she is a grownup. Her face is all crinkly like old paper. The best part of her face is a small diamond nose ring. I like to watch it flash in the sun and want one too.

Ayah's hair is all white and she always wears tied back into a knot at the base of her head. Her hands are twisty and on cold days she says her knuckles are on fire with pain. She is the only woman I know who likes to smoke Indian beedis when she is alone. My mother says it's a bad habit and makes your breath smell. But, I like the way Ayah smells. Ayah drinks her tea black with lots of raw brown sugar. She always uses a huge brass cup with no handles and if the cup is too hot, she wraps the end of her sari around it before she takes noisy gulps from it. I think she makes this noise because two of her front teeth are missing. I can't make a loud noise like she does. I tried it with my milk, but I just ended up with warm milk dribbling down my chin.

One day I try to drink from Ayah's cup but she gets very angry.

"This is my cup, little one," she says. "It was given to me by a priest because I saved his son's life and the priest blessed the cup. But the blessing will wear off if someone else drinks from it."

So, now I don't touch her brass cup. My mother bought me my own steel cup with a built-in sipper. I like my cup better.

My mother is always there, just like Ayah. She is taller than Ayah and always stands up very straight. She has thick, black hair and her face is always smiling. But when she gets angry, her lips get thin and her face gets dark as a thunder cloud and like the thunder cloud when she bursts with anger, there is a lot of noise and a lot of water, usually my tears. Even the tough cowhands who take care of our six cows, one bull and two calves are frightened of her temper.

My mother likes to dress in lovely silk saris that are cool to touch. She drapes the long pieces of smooth silk or crinkly cotton material around her waist and lets the end dangle over her left shoulder. She manages to wrap the sari so quickly that I can never see how she makes those neat folds in the front.

"When you are a little bit older I'll show you how to put on a sari, Meenakutty," she says to me when I complain.

She always wears flowers in her hair and a big, red dot on her forehead. She wears a bindi dot because she is married, unlike Ayah who is not married.

I like to wrap my mother's silk brocade saris around me and push her gold bracelets and glass bangles up my skinny arms. I admire myself in the long mirror and see my pointy chin, brown eyes and thick black braids. My knees look funny because they are so bony, but the silk sari covers them up. The clothes smell of sandalwood and my mother.

Our house is big and filled with enormous pieces of furniture so that I feel like a midget when I sit in the huge wooden chairs in the living room. The large rooms are always cold and damp when the air outside is chilly. On most days I have to wear a sweater to go outside and only in summer does the sunshine wash away the fog and cold.

There are 4 bedrooms in my house and all of them have enormous dressing rooms and bathrooms. The bedrooms have fireplaces, but we never light a single log in any of them because firewood is scarce and expensive.

I sleep with my mother in one of the dressing rooms because it is small and cozy. The room has a huge, wooden cupboard for my mother's silk saris and clothes. My clothes are stored in a small drawer under our bed.

Ayah says, "The people who lived in here were foreigners from a faraway place called England. They left in a hurry because look at all the furniture and plates they left behind, even the chair you like so much, Meena."

The big rocking chair is my favorite place to sit. I found a box filled with a stuffed camel and wooden statues of strange looking animals. The little brown and white camel is beloved toy.

Mother's Lemon Rice

1 cup basmati rice
2 cups water
1 teaspoon salt
3 tablespoons ghee, unsalted butter or vegetable oil
1 teaspoon brown mustard seeds
1 small onion, minced, about ½ cup
3 tablespoons minced bell pepper, any color
½ teaspoon turmeric powder
1½ tablespoons lemon juice
1 tablespoon minced cilantro, for garnish
¼ cup dry roasted cashew bits

Preparation: Wash and drain the basmati rice. Bring water to boil, add salt and washed rice. Cover and simmer on low heat for about 15 minutes. The rice should be tender and the water fully absorbed. If necessary, let rice simmer an additional 1 to 3 minutes. Set aside.

Heat the ghee in a saucepan with a lid. Add mustard seeds and cover. Listen for the mustard seeds to pop. When the popping sound starts diminishing, add minced onion and bell pepper, and sauté for 2-5 minutes. When the onions and peppers are soft, add turmeric and stir until the spice is thoroughly mixed. Add cooked rice to turmeric mixture and fold in until the rice is a uniform color. Remove from heat and add lemon juice. Fold in cashews and cilantro. Serve hot or warm with plain yoghurt.

GHEE: Ghee is clarified butter and made by heating unsalted butter and skimming off the bubbling whey. The process takes about 15-20 minutes and the liquid butter should be a warm, yellow color and smell slightly nutty and aromatic.

Serves 2-4 as a side dish.

Chapter Three

Sudha's Story

• • • • • • • • • •

Her sister Rukumani was five years old and she was barely two when their parents were killed in an accident on their way to sell fresh coconuts at the local market. Sudha can still remember watching her father's skinny legs hugging the coconut tree trunk as he shimmied up to the very top of the tree to knock down coconut after coconut. With just a piece of jute rope tied between his ankles he could climb the tallest tree in just a few seconds. The coconuts from the tall trees were tender and filled with sweet water. Their fresh taste was popular and so once a month her parents made the trip into the next village to sell the coconuts and buy rice and vegetables. But this night they never returned. When Sudha was much older a neighbor would tell her that the bullock cart driver had fallen asleep and let his bullocks lead the cart into a ditch. The wheels were stuck in the thick mud and the driver just managed to jump out of the cart before it flipped over into the ditch which was filled with water from the recent monsoon rains. The bulls fought for a foothold but the cart overturned and her parents were later recovered, their bodies bloated and filled with muddy ditch water.

Th at day changed their lives. Suddenly they were the orphan girls. The people of the little village of Kottapali were a tight knit group and most of them were related to each other, either by marriage or birth. A distant uncle and aunt with no children of their own agreed to give the two sisters a home. Sudha missed her mother's voice and soft touch. She was a frightened little girl when she first met her aunt.

"Come Sudha you don't have to be shy with me," said a voice and a pair of arms lifted her up. She gazed into the big brown eyes of her aunt Sita.

Her aunt sat down on a chair and drew Rukumani close to her.

"Both of you are welcome to live with me and your uncle Ramu," she said. "I know it's hard to lose both your parents but maybe we can find something to help you two."

She put Sudha down and took each girl's arm, "Come with me to the kitchen."

Sita's kitchen would have been a dark and smoky room but for the large skylight on the roof. Sunlight poured in and turned the small homely space into a warm and inviting area. There was a wooden table for chopping vegetables. A large hearth where huge logs were burnt. Bunches of herbs and gourds hung from the overhead rafters.

Sita led the girls into the kitchen and asked them to sit on low wooden stools.

"Now, whenever I feel sad or lost, if I keep my hands busy then I find that everything always works out," Sita said, washing her hands in a sink. She then took down a stainless steel container and scooped out two cups of some white grain.

"This is suji," she said. She poured the cream of wheat into a wide saucepan and placing it on the hearth. She added several spoonfuls of golden ghee and soon the kitchen was filled with the toasty smell of wheat and brown butter.

"Soon I'll add some sugar," she said. "Rukumani, come here and keep stirring the suji so that it doesn't stick to the pan."

"Sudha, I need your help. Can you peel these cardamom pods and crush them in this mortar and pestle?"

She showed Sudha how to peel the pale green pods and take out the tiny wrinkled seeds. Sudha thought it was a miracle that the tiny dark seeds could contain such a heady fragrance, a powerful scent that filled the room and her heart. The sweet spice mended two broken hearts as it permeated the room with its aroma.

When the cream of wheat turned a pale golden color, Sita added some sugar and then a cup of hot water from a pot on the hearth. The sweet mixture immediately formed a thick pudding. She kept stirring the pudding until it was tender and smooth. She took down a small stainless container and pried open the lid.

"This is special saffron coming all the way from the snowy slopes of the Himalayan Mountains."

Sita placed a small pinch of the bright orange strands into a spoonful of warm water. Immediately the water turned a bright orange and the air was filled with the exotic smell of the spice. As the saffron was softening, she took time to heat a saucepan on the flame. When the saucepan was warm, she added a generous amount of golden ghee and waited for the liquid butter to warm.

"Sudha, you can bring the cardamom powder and Rukumani can you get that container for me?"

Sita took the container from Rukumani, opened it and pulled out a plastic bag of plump cashews and another bag of dark red raisins. Sita added a handful of nuts and raisins to the warm ghee and using a wooden ladle stirred the mixture. The raisins seemed to drink up the butter and turned large and juicy. The cashews were more restrained, retaining their beautiful shapes but turning a golden brown. The delicious sweet smell of frying nuts and raisins filled the kitchen. Sita took the saucepan off the fire and added the powdered cardamom to the cashews. Next, she added the aromatic mixture and the saffron threads into the thick wheat pudding. Using a wooden spoon she made sure the pudding was a uniform orange color and the nuts and raisins were evenly distributed. She placed generous scoops of the fragrant pudding on two steel plates. She handed one to each of the girls. Sudha took a bite of the creamy pudding, rich with ghee and cardamom and sighed in pleasure.

"Aunty Sita, I want to learn to make such a delicious pudding."

Sita laughed, "Of course you do, and everyone who tastes my kesari pudding wants to make it. I will be happy to teach you."

The kitchen became Sudha's refuge. She learned to make stews using bitter melon. "Good for diabetes and high blood pressure," Sita pointed out as she chopped slices of the wart-like vegetable. Sudha learned the secret of spices and the wonder of working with fresh vegetables from pale green eggplants to brilliant orange pumpkins.

Over time the ache in heart for her parents was filled with the pungency of coriander seeds, the sweetness of cinnamon and the bite of fresh chili peppers. So she sautéed, fried, boiled and chopped in the little kitchen.

Chapter Four

Second Saturday Husband

• • • • • • • • • •

"Long ago in ancient India there lived a famous king named Pandian. He ruled a powerful kingdom of Madurai in south India. He was a happy man but his only sorrow was that he had no children. So he performed a sacrifice called yagna and when he lit the sacrificial fire a three year old girl stepped out of the flames. The girl was very pretty but had three breasts. This worried the king until he heard a divine voice whispering to him that the child would grow up to be a beautiful girl and the extra breast would disappear when she set her eyes on her true bridegroom. King Pandian named his new daughter Meenaskhi because she had beautiful eyes shaped like fish or meen. She grew up to be a bold and lovely princess. While traveling she set eyes on Shiva in the mountains of Kailash and her third breast disappeared. For the princess was none other than goddess Parvati, Lord Shiva's wife. The couple was married in a splendid ceremony and they happily ruled over the kingdom of Madurai for many years."

—the story of Meenaskhi as told by Devi

My name is Meena short for Meenaskhi, the goddess who has her own temple in a faraway city.

My father, Unnikrishnan, owns a cashew and spice plantation near the small city of Chandur about 200 kilometers away, and we don't see him much. He works long hours, even on weekends, because "a plantation doesn't take a vacation," he always says. But once a month, he comes to visit us in our hill-top town.

"Ahh," he always says, taking a deep breath. "This air is like a health tonic, so pure and cool. It's so muggy in Chandur that I can't sleep."

When my father married my mother nearly eight years ago, he bought her this house and the cows as a wedding present.

"He was so in love with your mother that he wanted to give her a special wedding gift," Ayah tells me the story. "He had come to the bank where she was working as a clerk and he took one look at her and fell in love with her. She was only 20 years old."

My mother and her sister were orphaned when they were very young and grew up in our ancestral home in the village of Kottapali in Kerala.

"Your father came to your great-uncle and asked to marry your mother. Your great uncle didn't want to give your father any dowry money for your mother. But that didn't matter to your father. He bought her this house and two cows and a bull.

"Your mother was supposed to live here only a year or two until your father built her a nice home on the farm. But it took nearly three years for the house to be built and by then your mother loved Mahagiri and so your father agreed to let her live here with me for company.

"I came here looking for a job and your mother was kind to me even though I was too old to be of much help in the kitchen. But I know about healing and sickness and so I help her."

Every second Saturday is a festival, a special holiday, for my mother. Preparations for my father's arrival begin on Friday evening when my mother has the entire house dusted, swept and cleaned. Devi is kept busy in the kitchen, chopping vegetables, or sorting through platters of pearly white rice, looking for tiny stones and pieces of rice husk.

I run into the kitchen, my nose twitching at all the enticing smells.

"Amma! Amma!"

"Ah, there you are, you little sleepyhead," my mother says. "You can help crush the cardamom pods after your breakfast."

I love peeling the pale green cardamom pods and crushing the fragrant spice in a small mortar and pestle. The pungent spice is an essential flavor in the rice pudding. I can already taste the creamy smooth pudding, flavored with bits of cashews and raisins, and plenty of sugar and fresh milk.

"We're having payasam too?"

"Did you forget today is second Saturday?" my mother teases. "Tomorrow is also a special day."

"But, today is your mother's day," Ayah says with a grin. "The second Saturday husband is coming to visit his bride."

She cackles over her joke and my mother blushes.

"Go on, Ayah, go about your work. You have much to do and no time to sit and chat," my mother affectionately scolds her old confidant. "You have to go buy the flowers for Vishu."

Vishu! How could I forget my favorite holiday? On Vishu day, we celebrate the start of the Malayalam New Year.

"Does that mean I can help you make the Vishu kani tonight?"

"Of course, Meena, I'm counting on your help tonight, but first we have a special lunch to make for your father."

"Will there be aviyal?"

"No feast is complete without aviyal. Go on, hurry up and finish your breakfast."

Aviyal is vegetable stew that was delicately flavored with turmeric, yogurt and fresh coconut. My mother's aviyal is rich and colorful with all kinds of vegetables and has a subtle taste. The dish is even more delicious the next day. I love the tangy, mild taste of the dish and could eat it every day.

I gulp down my breakfast of milk and the whole wheat chapattis with honey and get to work on the tiny cardamom pods.

"The bus is coming up the hill, little mother," says Kashi, walking as fast as she can into the kitchen. "The master will be here soon."

My mother rushes to her bedroom to wash her hands and comb her hair. She pats sweet-smelling powder on her cheeks and neck and makes sure that the bindi dot on her forehead has not been smudged in the kitchen heat.

My mother and I wait at the front door for my father to arrive. I can hear his booming voice before I see him.

"Bhojan, careful that bag has all the papayas and mangoes. Kashi, you can carry this small bag, it's not too heavy."

I peer out from behind my mother's cotton sari, holding the cloth in front of my face, and soon see him coming down the path to our house, carrying a cloth bag in each arm. A black suitcase hangs from his right shoulder and makes him walk bent over as if he is an old man.

He sees my face and drops all the bags and opens his arms wide.

"Meenakutty, come here and give your Achan a hug," he says, kneeling down. When he kneels down, his knees poke out from the folds of the dhoti cloth that is wrapped around his waist. I run down the path and fling my arms around his neck which smells of shaving cream and mangoes.

"You are so big now, kutty, that you must surely be nearly 10 years old," he says, holding me away from him and looking at me.

I grin at him and touch his bristly black moustache. My father is tall with a big stomach and hairy arms and legs. His eyebrows are thick and make him look scary, but his eyes are kind and large and brown, just like mine. His hair is wavy and thick with lots of white strands in it.

"I'm only five years old, Achan," I say. "I don't start school until next year."

He laughs his booming laugh and hugs me again.

My father stands and turns toward my mother. I watch them look at each other and then my mother starts to bend down and touch his feet, a respectful greeting of a wife. My father stops her from bending all the way down and rests his hands on her shoulder for a moment. He drops his arms and turns back to me.

"Come along Meena and help me unpack all the bags. I have many good treats for you."

I skip behind my father, my heart bursting with joy to have him home again. He has brought all kinds of fruits and vegetables and the living room, filled with bags and bulging sacks, smells like a marketplace. There are pale yellow mangoes, their fruity fragrance filling up the room, as well as orange papayas. I touch the skin of the prickly green jack fruit, the outside hard and scratchy, but the inside is thick and fleshy. Each fruit is shaped like a cone with a large pit in the middle. Th e jack fruit has a strange taste. The first time I took a bite of it, it tasted strange. But now I love the unique jack flavor, a combination that tastes a bit like banana and pineapple and something else that is hard to describe. Ayah has to use plenty of oil on her fingers when she cuts open the jack fruit because the white sap is very sticky.

My father hands me a piece of bright orange candy.

"Have a piece of halva," he says with a smile.

I bite into the gooey candy. The halva is a chewy fudge, made of sugar and coconut oil, and flavored with small crunchy bits of cashew. I lick my oily fingers and sigh with satisfaction. My father laughs when he sees me sucking my fingers, trying to get the last bit of sticky fudge.

"I also have your favorite banana chips, kutty," he says, holding out a greasy brown bag.

I dig out a handful of banana chips and enjoy their salty crunch. These are special chips, made out of semi-ripe plantains, rather than bananas. I particularly like the ones that are slightly burned because they taste sweeter and crunchier.

* * *

That evening after my bath, I help my mother and father decorate the kani. The kani is an important part of the celebration of Vishu or New Year. On the eve of Vishu, my mother and father put together the kani, a beautiful display of fruit, vegetables, jewelry and coins arranged around a mirror. On Vishu morning I look in the mirror and see the lights and sparkling jewelry.

Last year was the first time I had stayed up to help and my father had protested.

"Sudha, you know that children aren't allowed to decorate the kani. It must be a surprise, a wonder for them when they first see it on the morning of Vishu," he had said.

"I know that, but I want her to learn how to make the kani. She loves arranging everything. It is still a wonderful sight in the morning when all lamps are lit," my mother had replied.

So now, I help my mother with the decorating. I watch her take out the big silver tray and small round mirror with a stand. The tray is wiped clean and placed on a table which is set up in the middle of the second bedroom. My mother arranges her creamy white silk sari that is threaded with gold on the tray. I place a small sandalwood statue of Lord Krishna, playing the flute, next to the silk sari. My father props up the mirror in the middle of the tray. Ayah has brought in two fresh coconuts that have been split open to form white-fleshed bowls. Each coconut "bowl" is filled with grains of rice and white beans. A small yellow squash, bananas, mangoes, jack fruit and a large pineapple are all arranged on the tray. Huge bouquets of flowers, mostly yellow because it is an auspicious color for Vishu, are placed all around the idol, mirror and fruit.

"Meena, bring me the oil lamp from the other room," she says.

I run into the living room and bring back the lamp which is bright and shiny. My mother fills the tall brass lamp with oil and places five cotton wicks in the oil. The wicks will be lit tomorrow morning.

My father has brought special red "bindi" powder and yellow sandalwood paste. The table is laden with fruits, vegetables, and flowers. Finally, my mother brings out her fancy jewelry and places the strands of shiny gold on the table. My father drops handfuls of change on one corner of the table. This change, along with pieces of fruit, will be given out to anyone who visits our house on Vishu day.

Whenever my father visits us, I'm moved out of my mother's bed and into the third bedroom. Ayah keeps me company tonight on a mattress at the foot of my bed. I fall asleep, listening to her soft snores.

It seems like I have just fallen asleep when my mother's hand shakes me awake. One of her hands is covering my eyes so that I can't see anything.

"Wake up Meena. Come see the kani," she whispers.

I groan and sit up. She keeps my eyes covered and helps me off the bed and guides me into the second bedroom. As we approach the bedroom, I can smell the sweet scent of burning incense and the oil from the lamp.

"Keep your eyes tightly closed," she says. She wipes my face with a warm cloth.

"Place your hands right here," my father says. He takes my hands and places the palms on the table.

"All right, little one, open your eyes and see what a prosperous new year is in store for you," my mother says. "See the Lord in the mirror."

I look up at my mother, disappointed, "Amma, it's just me in the mirror, where's the Lord?"

My father smiles at me, "Oh, Meenakutty, look carefully and you'll see the Lord shining in your eyes because He's inside you."

I stare at my face in the mirror. The lights from the oil lamp are reflected in my eyes. I open them wide at the enchanting sight in front of me. It is like a magical scene with all the fruits, flowers, gold and jewelry glittering in the light of the oil lamp.

"Look carefully at everything Meena. See the flowers, the fruit, the grains and jewelry?" my father says. "Now place your palms together and pray to Lord Krishna for a wonderful year."

I put my palms together, close my eyes and murmur my prayers. My mother smears some sandalwood paste on my forehead. The paste is cool on my skin and my father places a pinch of red powder in the middle of the sandalwood paste. My mother tucks a red hibiscus flower petal behind my right ear and turns me around.

"Come, get your kani present from us," she says.

I hold out my hand and she places a banana and a shiny coin in it.

"May your new year be filled with fruit and blessings," she says.

I turn to my father, who is hiding something behind his back.

"Here is your Vishukanattam, a present from me," he says with a smile.

I place the banana and coin on the table and eagerly tear open the plain brown package which contains a new skirt and blouse. I bury my face in the soft silky material. It smells of my father's shaving cream and something fruity. The skirt is a soft pearly grey with flecks of silver and pink and the blouse is a pale pink with flecks of silver and grey.

"I love them Acha," I say and run into his arms.

"I'm glad little one. Wear them in good health."

Aviyal Stew

1 cup dried unsweetened shredded coconut
1 cup yogurt room temperature
1 cup green beans cut into approximately 2-inch pieces
1 ½ cup potatoes, cut into ½" x 2" pieces
1 cup carrots cut into ½" x 2" pieces
½ cup zucchini, cut into ½" x 2" pieces
½ cup peeled cucumbers, cut ½" x 2" pieces
¼ cup water
1 teaspoon turmeric
1 teaspoon salt
Optional: 1 small green chili chopped (to spice up yogurt-coconut mixture) 1tsp. to 1 Tbs. lemon juice (to flavor yogurt-coconut mixture)1-2 Tbs. coconut oil (as a drizzle topping for stew).

Preparation: Using a food processor shred coconut to coarse powder. Add yogurt (and chili if desired) to the food processor and pulse to mix. Set aside.

Cook beans, potatoes, carrots, turmeric and salt with water in a covered pan, over medium heat 5-8 minutes. Stir occasionally to keep the potatoes from sticking.

Add salt, zucchini and cucumber, and continue to cook, in a covered pan, over medium heat for another 5 to 8 minutes. Stir occasionally until vegetables are just cooked.

Turn off heat and stir in yogurt/coconut mixture. Add additional salt, and lemon juice to taste.

Drizzle coconut oil on top of stew, if desired, before serving over warm rice.

Serves 2-4

Chapter Five

Ayah's Story

• • • • • • • • • •

Ayah's childhood was a jumble of smells and sounds. Her family lived in a small village at the edge of a nature preserve and at night Ayah could hear the lonely trumpeting of an elephant or the wild cry of a peacock. She would shiver at the night sounds, terrified the animals would escape from their enclosure and find her in bed. Ayah's name was Rani. Her father owned a small tea stall near the bus station. She spent her days helping her mother with her younger brothers and sisters and on occasion lending a hand at the tea stall. She enjoyed sitting in the tiny shop, serving tea and making change for the villagers. When she turned sixteen her mother decided working in a tea stall was not a proper job for a young girl. So at 17 she went to work at the nature preserve, first as a maid to the foreign manager and later as a nanny to his two small children. Rani loved the two boys with their fine silken hair that shone like gold and their milky white skin. Rani thought their eyes looked like chips of sky just after the monsoon rains had washed the air clean. The boys' mother was a sickly woman who kept to her room with her maid. Rani rarely saw her. But the person she did see often was the manager, a lean man with ginger colored hair and a band of freckles across his long nose and cheeks. His eyes were a startling blue and he never left the house without his broad-rimmed sun hat. He was busy from the early hours to late at night making sure all the animals were safe and that tourists didn't get too close to the tall wire mesh fences.

Rani started answering to Ayah or nanny when her two charges started calling her Ayah instead of Rani. Before long Ayah became her name and no one remembered her name was Rani, except for the manager who noticed the small dark girl with big eyes and a bright nose ring. The manager's name was Timothy and he found the nursery with Ayah and his two boys to be a peaceful place. Every evening, before his late-night rounds of the preserve, he washed his face, combed his ginger curls and made his way to the nursery. Here he found Ayah giggling as she fed the boys milk toast or soothing puddings. He watched the young girl tickle and play with his boys, bathe them and sing songs in her native language. When the boys were finally asleep and twilight had come and gone, he felt himself relax into the big comfy chair. He must have fallen asleep when a gentle touch on his forehead woke him up. It was Ayah leaning over him, brushing a strand of hair off his face. In the dim light he found that her dark skin was soft and that she smelled of baby powder and vanilla. He inhaled her subtle fragrance and found comfort in her arms. For the few moments he was buried in her warm flesh, he forgot about his sickly wife and the problems of the nature preserve.

The next morning Ayah was filled with regret. What had she done? She turned to the one friend she had on the estate, an old woman who had a reputation as a healer. The old woman made Ayah drink a bitter concoction to ensure that her one night with the manager would not result in a baby.

"Herbs are like magic. They can cure or kill," the old lady said. She lived in a one-room apartment on the far end of the estate compound.

"I'm still here because everyone needs my help just like you did today," she cackled.

The rafters of the little room were hung with all kinds of herbs. The air was pungent with the scent of sweet mint, the sharp smell of lemon verbena and the tang of other bitter herbs. The old lady pounded bits of herb in a marble mortar and pestle and mixed them in hot water or in nutty coconut oil. Every surface of the small room was filled with tiny glass bottles with cork stoppers. Some of them had herbs floating in pale oil and others were empty, waiting to be filled as needed.

After that one night Timothy never came into the nursery again. Perhaps he was racked with guilt or perhaps he didn't want to endanger his position in the community. Ayah was happy to play and sing to the boys.

Ayah was fascinated by the herbs, their textures and smells. She loved the sweet flavor of coconut oil and watching it turn bitter or sour with the addition of a particular herb. Whenever she had a moment of free time she went to the healer's one-room shack. She helped clean bottles, pick herbs and pound dried seeds into fine powder. Every day she learned more about the healing power of herbs, plants and seeds.

"Everything you need to make yourself better is right here in front of your eyes," the old lady told her. "You just have to learn to open your eyes and look."

When the estate manager left for England with his two boys and sickly wife, Ayah remained at the estate. She lived with the old woman in the tiny shack. She slept in front of her hearth, and continued to help the old woman with her herbal cures. A brand-new government hospital was built on the outskirts of the town and gradually less and less people came to the little hut asking for help for a sleepless night or for stomach pain. Ayah and her companion were comfortable in their room surrounded by the musty aroma of herbs, fresh and old. One cool December morning Ayah tried to wake up the old lady for her morning herbal tea but she had died in her sleep.

In the passing years Ayah didn't notice it but she started to resemble the old lady with her grey hair and sharp eyes that pierced the heart of each patient so that they were forced to tell the truth.

A new manager took over the nature preserve and he didn't appreciate the old hovel on his property. Ayah was asked to move. So she packed all her herbs and bottles in a large bag and headed out the estate gates. She had no wish to return to her family. As she was passing the bus station she heard a conductor call out, "Next bus to Mahagiri leaves in five minutes."

Much later Ayah would tell Sudha that something, a higher power perhaps, propelled her to that bus. Before long she was bouncing her way up the hill, past mango groves and banana plantations, to Mahagiri.

The bus driver wanted a cup of hot tea and stopped at Vasu's tea stall and Ayah decided to join the driver. Vasu was an old gossip and when he learned that Ayah had no place to stay, he told her that the lady at the big house needed help. He even offered to show Ayah the way after he closed down the stall for the night. Making sure the padlock was secure; Vasu beckoned Ayah and started walking down the hill toward a large white house. Evening was well on its way and sky was a deep purple but Ayah could see the bright roses in the front yard. She took a deep whiff of the night jasmine and honeysuckle. The lights glowing inside the big house were warm and inviting. For Ayah the house looked like a refuge from the cool breezes and darkening skies.

Vasu took her to the back door and rapped on the wooden door.

"Who is there?" a voice called out.

"It's me little mother," Vasu replied. "I have someone you might want to meet."

The door cracked open and a woman looked out at them. Her face was obscured in the dark but Ayah could make out her white teeth. *At least she's smiling.*

"Who is with you?"

"This is Ayah; she came on the last bus from Greater Mahagiri. She's a healer and needs a place to stay the night."

"Vasu, you know this is not a motel. I can't have strangers coming in at night."

"Little mother..."

"Stop calling me that..."

Ayah could hear the temper in the voice and spoke up, "Miss I have no wish to intrude. I'll be on my way. Vasu thank you for your help."

She turned and started down the dark path back to the bus stop.

"Wait. You can't go out at night. Come back and let's talk in the kitchen where it's warm."

Ayah followed the woman inside.

"Vasu you can go home. I can take care of Ayah here," Little mother said.

Vasu took leave and Ayah looked around the spacious two-room kitchen. The space was clean and tidy. The dishes were draining in the sink and the hearth fire had been almost extinguished. Now the woman went back to the hearth and poked it until it started to come back to life.

She put a pan of water and milk to heat. She turned around and looked at Ayah in the light of the fire. For the first time Ayah could see that she was very young just a girl.

"I'm sorry to intrude like this," Ayah began.

But the woman waved a graceful hand, "It's no bother. I have to be firm with the villagers because otherwise they are here all the time to check up on me."

Ayah was curious about this young woman living in a spacious house by herself. Before she could say anything, the woman indicated she should sit down on one of the low wooden stools. She then handed her a cup of warm milk after stirring a generous spoonful of honey that smelled of flowers and wind.

Ayah accepted the hot drink and wrapped her fingers around the steel tumbler.

"Thank you little mother."

The woman shook her head and smiled. "Not you too. Everyone calls me little mother even though I tell them not to call me that name."

Ayah smiled as she sipped the milky honey drink. "It suits you perfectly."

"So Ayah will you me your story and I'll tell you mine."

The two women sat by the dying embers until late into the night and in that darkness found a common bond of sisterhood.

The next morning Ayah moved her things to the small room next to the kitchen. Before long villagers were coming by asking for help with a cough, a fever or measles.

"You know little mother," she told Sudha years later. "The first time I saw this house the lights were glowing through the window. I thought it was my imagination but I felt the house was welcoming me. I felt like I was home when I came into this kitchen. You and this house are a refuge for people like me."

Chapter Six

Going to the Temple

• • • • • • • • • •

"Long ago, when the world was young and gods and goddess roamed the land, Lord Ganesha with his elephant face liked to visit the local temple and taste all the sweets that were served. He especially liked the round rice balls flavored with brown sugar and fresh coconut. One night he ate too many rice balls. His stomach was so huge that it made him walk unsteadily. He was toddling home under the full moon when he heard snickering and laughter. He looked up at the dark sky and saw the pale orange face of the full moon. The moon was laughing at him and his big stomach. Ganesha became angry and without thinking he pulled out his ivory tusk and threw it at the laughing face of the full moon. The light of the moon disappeared and world turned dark. Finally, all the other gods and goddesses came to Lord Ganesha and begged him to bring back the moon. He refused at first, but after everyone kept pleading with him, he finally relented. But he allowed the moon to come back in full glory only one day a month. And that is why the moon gets small and grows bigger every month."

—the story of Ganesha as told by Ayah

For the past few weeks my mother has not been feeling well, but I know it's not serious when I hear Ayah teasing her.

"You must be missing your second Saturday husband," she laughs. "Are you still thinking of him from his last visit?"

I couldn't hear my mother's reply, but whatever it is, it has Ayah laughing uproariously.

"What's so funny, Ayah?" I ask, running into the room. "Tell me so I can laugh too."

Ayah dabs her eyes with the end of her sari, "Well, little one, your mother is…"

She is rudely interrupted by my mother, "Meenakutty, I'm not feeling too well. I thought it might be a good idea to go to the Ganesha temple and do a little pooja ceremony."

"What's wrong with you, Amma?"

"Nothing, a little pooja won't fix. Be a good girl. Go take your bath and put on a nice skirt so we can go to the temple."

I hear Ayah snickering. I want to hear what the two women are discussing, but my mother waits until I leave before speaking again. A few hours later, Ayah is ready for the outing, dressed in one of my mother's old silk saris. Her hair is slicked back with coconut oil and even her nose ring is sparkling. My mother has dark circles under her eyes, but her face is radiant with an inner glow. She looks even more beautiful than usual in her dark blue and gold sari. Her gold necklace reflects the pale December sunlight and lights up her face in its glow. Her gold bangles jangle on her arms as she fusses with her sari pleats.

Today Kashi is also coming with us.

"Little mother, the taxi is just leaving the village. Would you like to go in it to the temple?" Kashi asks. She is dressed in a red and yellow silk sari that rustles as she walks. "The driver said he will charge us only for one way, if we want to take the bus back."

"Kashi, the car is a good idea. I'm not sure I can sit in a bouncing bus," my mother replies.

I step closer to her and slip my hand in hers. She looks down at me." It's all right Meena, my stomach is upset and I'll drink some ginger tea before we go. I'll be fine."

The taxi is a black and yellow Ambassador car. The driver, Babu, is a young man with curly hair and twinkling eyes. He keeps the old car in good condition and the inside smells of incense and leather polish. The shiny seats squeak as I shift my bottom across it.

"Meena, you sit in the middle, next to Babu and your mother can sit next to you in the front," Ayah says. She gets in the back seat with Kashi.

Since I am too short to see over the dashboard, I look at the little pictures and photographs Babu had pasted all over the front dash of the car. There are colorful pictures of several gods and goddess, including one of the elephant-headed god Ganesha who is supposed to bring good luck. The pictures are smeared with golden sandal wood paste and draped with small garlands of fresh flowers. One of the photographs is a black and white picture of a smiling old lady with no teeth. Babu notices me staring at the photograph.

"That is my mother who passed away a year ago," he says, touching the photograph with a respectful gesture. "She sits right there and looks after me when I'm driving, especially in the rain or at night."

As soon as we are all settled in the car, Babu turns on the engine and after a bit of coughing and sputtering, the old car comes to life with a bang. We are on our way to the temple.

I notice that my mother holds a cotton handkerchief to her mouth. Every time the car drives over a rough patch on the road, she raises the cloth to her nose.

"What's in the kerchief, Amma?" I ask.

"Just a slice of lemon," she says, "The smell of the lemon helps settle my stomach."

I promise myself that I will walk seven times around the Ganesha temple if my mother feels better soon. I don't like to see her so pale and tired.

The Ganesha temple sits on a high hill in the town of Mahagiri and is about thirty minutes from our house. When we arrive at the hilltop temple, Babu stops the car in front of the temple entrance and goes around to open the door for my mother and Ayah.

"Little mother, I'll go park the car in the shade. When you are done, just come out and wait for me here, and I'll bring the car."

We make our way up the twenty-four granite steps. At the top I wait for Kashi, my mother and Ayah to catch up to me. Our first stop is at the slipper stall where we take off our slippers and sandals. We hand them over to a tired-looking lady behind the counter. She gives us a little piece of paper with numbers on it.

"I'll keep the receipt," Ayah says. "We need it to get our slippers back."

She puts the slip of paper in a cloth bag that hangs from the waistband of her sari. I take my mother's hand and we walk down the narrow street in our bare feet. I step over some dark looking liquid and a pile of rotting fruit. I wrinkle my nose at the smell of fresh cow dung. The narrow lane leading up to the temple is not paved. During the rainy season the street is a mud puddle, but today the dirt is packed down hard to form a clean surface. I don't like walking down the street in my bare feet, but no one is allowed to wear shoes on temple grounds.

The passageway is usually a busy place especially on special holidays, but today we are able to move freely. All along the narrow pathway, there are many little shops and vendors selling everything from clothes to flowers. The flower shops have huge piles of roses, marigolds and jasmine blossoms. Men, women and even children sit in the stalls and string the blooms into long colorful garlands. I watch a man's fingers magically transform a few bright orange marigolds and fragrant holy basil leaves into a garland beautiful enough for a god or goddess. A little girl painstakingly threads creamy jasmine blossoms on a string to make a garland that looks like a strand of pearls.

There are other vendors hawking fresh coconuts, bunches of yellow bananas and bundles of sweet-smelling incense. Another shop is selling calendars with colorful pictures of Lord Ganesha. There are several shops selling photographs of the elephant god. A young girl with a wicker basket balanced on her head stops my mother.

"Please mistress, buy some lucky charms," she says pointing to a pile of saffron yellow and black threads. "This will ward off the evil eye and keep you safe."

She holds up a delicate string bracelet. I tug on my mother's silk sari. "Please Amma, can I get a charm?"

"Really, Meena, you don't need anything to keep you safe." She frowns at me and then looks from my pleading face to the hopeful eyes of the young girl. "All right, we'll get you one. But remember all this won't keep you safe if you don't listen or behave."

"I promise to behave Amma," I say, jumping up and down in excitement. The girl gives my mother a yellow and black thread bracelet. My mother ties the charm on my right hand.

"Wear it in good health, little sister," the girl says with a smile.

Ayah stops at a stall to buy a coconut, some bananas and garlands of fresh marigolds and jasmine.

"Please Amma, give us alms and be blessed," an old man pleads with us. He is so bent over and thin that his ribs and backbones seemed to poke out of his skin.

My mother slips him a coin and we make our way to the temple. The iron gates stand open. I can hear the chanting of priests and smell of the oil-burning lamps. The temple consists of a large open outer courtyard with a huge stone sanctuary in the center dedicated to Ganesha. Along the outer courtyard, there are small shrines, each dedicated to different gods and goddesses including Lord Shiva and Goddess Parvathi. Before entering to the main shrine, we make our way around the courtyard, paying homage to each small shrine and statue. The air is thick with the smell of sweet incense, fresh flowers, cow dung and people. I stop to look at a beautiful and colorful statue of lord Muruga, Ganesha's brother. Muruga is seated on a peacock and the tail feathers of the bird are painted in bright blue and green. I watch as an old lady pays respect to the statue by bowing down and touching her forehead to the ground in front of the shrine. Her lips are moving in silent prayer and her hands are folded together. She finishes her prayers and places a coin in the strongbox that is next to the statue.

I follow my mother and Ayah around the courtyard. We enter the main shrine and stand behind the steel railings. I peer from under the railing into the narrow doorway of the sanctuary. My eyes adjust to the dimness of the sanctuary and I can make out a gleaming shape of Ganesha, with its huge belly, draped in bright orange silks. The god's many shiny necklaces, bracelets and other jewelry reflect the light of the lamps. The oil lamps flicker and cast shadows on the god and the young priest who stands inside the inner sanctum. The priest wears the traditional white dhoti cloth around his waist and a holy thread is draped on his bare chest. His hair is tied back into a small, neat knot. He has holy ash marks on his chest, forearms and forehead. He holds a platter of fruit, flowers and a bit of burning camphor. His eyes are closed and his lips move in prayer. We wait for the priest to finish chanting and ring the temple bell hanging from the ceiling. The melodious note echoes in the stone temple and everyone shouts out, "Om Ganesha! Om Ganesha!"

The priest steps out of the sanctuary and hands out bits of fruit and flowers to everyone. He stops and smiles at me and places his hand on my forehead in a gesture of blessing.

"Little one, your prayers will be answered today," he says in a soft voice.

I look up at him and say, "I want my mother to feel better and I want a baby sister."

"Well, you are not asking for much are you, little one?" he smiles.

He tucks a jasmine blossom behind my right ear and again blesses me.

My mother drops some coins in the priest's platter and accepts a small banana from him. Ayah gives the priest the coconut, bananas and flowers as an offering to the temple. The priest takes the gifts and goes back inside and closes the doors of the shrine. It will open after the priest performs another "pooja" or service.

People wander back to the courtyard. It is close to midday and is starting to get warm. Families with children sit on the ledge surrounding the courtyard, enjoying the bananas and other fruit.

"Amma, can we get some chickpeas?" I ask.

The temple sells small paper cones of chickpea snacks. Tiny chickpeas are cooked in salty water and then flavored with bits of onion and coconut. I love the salty taste of the peas and could devour handfuls of the snack.

"Meena let me go sit down and rest a bit. You and Ayah can buy chickpeas," my mother says.

Ayah and I walk to a small stall at the corner of the courtyard. We buy several paper cones filled with the chickpea snacks. We join Kashi and my mother on a stone ledge. I dangle my legs over the ledge and happily munch on the treat.

I finish the last of the salty snack and sigh in satisfaction at the savory food. We stop at the public tap and wash our greasy hands in the cold water. I cup my hands and drink handfuls of the refreshing water. We make our way to the slipper stall. Ayah pulls out the wrinkled receipt and carefully smoothes it out before handing it to the lady behind the counter. We pay her and put on our slippers. We climb down the giant stone steps to the main road. Babu has pulled the car next to the stone steps and is wiping down his taxi. He puts away the red cloth and opens the doors.

I lean my head against my mother's shoulder and smack my lips, savoring the nutty taste of the chickpea snack in my mouth.

Chickpea Snack

1 cup cooked garbanzo beans or chick peas.
(If using canned beans, drain and rinse them.)
1 small onion, red or white, minced
2-3 tablespoons vegetable oil
1 teaspoon mustard seeds
1 tablespoon fresh lime juice
1 teaspoon salt
Fresh black pepper to taste.

Preparation: Heat the oil in a saucepan with a lid. Add mustard seeds and cover pan. The mustard seeds will pop and turn grey. As soon as the popping slows down, add onions. Let the onions soften (3-4 minutes). Add cooked garbanzo beans, salt and coconut. Stir until the beans are well coated with the onions and coconut. Turn off heat. Stir in the fresh lime juice and black pepper.

Serve with rice, Indian flat bread or just by itself for a healthy snack.

Chapter Seven

Big Sister

• • • • • • • • • •

One evening a few weeks after our visit to the Ganesha temple, we are seated in front of the kitchen fireplace, waiting for Devi to finish her supper. I am curled up by the warm hearth, drowsy and comfortable.

"Meenakutty, are you asleep? I want to tell you something," my mother's voice interrupts my nap.

I yawn so wide that my jaws crack. "No, I'm not asleep yet."

"Do you remember what you wished for at the temple?"

I sit up, no longer drowsy. "I asked for a baby sister and that you would be better. You are better, aren't you Amma?"

"Yes, don't worry Meena. I'm fine. I've been tired because I'm going to have a baby."

I am wide awake now. "I'm going to be a big sister?" I grin down at Devi who is listening to us. "Did you hear that Devi? I'm going to be a chechi."

"Yes, I heard little one."

Everyday my mother's stomach grows rounder and bigger. She looks like she has swallowed a fat pumpkin. Ayah massages herbal oil on her back and shoulders and rubs her feet and fusses over her. Devi is always busy in the kitchen preparing foods to tempt my mother's finicky appetite. Along with my mother, I enjoy the spicy foods and soothing stews. I watch Devi prepare a spicy mango relish. She peels a mango that is slightly unripe. The green smell of the mango fills the kitchen as Devi slices the fruit and then carefully cuts each slice into small bits. She tosses the freshly cut mango in a mixture of salt and fiery chili pepper powder. Next, she heats some oil in a small pan and when the oil is hot, she adds a small handful of mustard seeds. The seeds sizzle and pop and their nutty aroma are mouthwatering. Devi removes the oil from the fire and pours it over the mango and mixes it all together to form a tangy relish.

My mother loves this pickle with every meal and even though it burns my tongue I can't stop eating the spicy fruit. I soothe my burning mouth with sips of cold buttermilk.

Devi also prepares mellow and soothing stews for my mother. A favorite potato stew or Ishtu has thick chunks of potato, onions and tiny slivers of fresh ginger. The vegetables are cooked until everything is velvety smooth. The stew has fresh coconut milk which Devi makes by pouring hot water over freshly grated coconut and then squeezing out the milk. The Ishtu is a perfect sauce for rice and I gobble up bowls of this calming stew.

One sunny spring afternoon I am busy playing hopscotch with Kashi in front of our house when a bus comes to a hissing stop at our gate. The black diesel fumes float our way and Kashi and I look up to see a stranger get down from the bus. She is an older woman dressed in immaculate white robes. As she comes closer I see that she has bright eyes filled with curiosity.

"Is this Sudha amma's house?"

She has a soft clear voice and I follow Kashi to the gate and look up at the stranger, whose only ornament is a pair of large gold earrings. The earrings tangle from her ear lobes that are round and hang half-way down her neck. I have never seen anyone with such big earlobes or such large earrings and I stare at her with my mouth open.

"Yes, we call Sudha amma little mother," Kashi says. "Does she know you?'

"Yes, I had sent a letter saying that I was coming. My name is Muthu and I'm a cousin of hers."

"Come on in and I'll get little mother. Meena, can you go tell your mother that her cousin Muthu is here."

I nod and run as fast as I can to the back of the house. My mother is sitting in our courtyard with Devi and Ayah.

"Amma. Amma. There is someone named Muthu to see you."

My mother gets up slowly. "Muthu is here? Why didn't she tell us she is coming?"

"Amma she says she sent you a letter."

"She did? Well, never mind. Devi, go make some tea, and Ayah make sure the room next to the second bedroom is cleaned and ready."

My mother issues these directions as she walks toward the front of the house. I run alongside her. We meet Kashi and Muthu at the front door.

"Come in Chechi. Come in," my mother says, using a respectful greeting of big sister. "We didn't know you were coming."

"Oh, Sudha daughter it has been very difficult these past few months. Losing my husband so suddenly and then finding out that the house didn't belong to us but to my husband's sister and having no place to go."

Muthu's voice breaks down and she starts to cry. My mother murmurs in a soft voice and drapes her arm around Muthu's shoulders and leads her into our living room.

"I already told you the last time I saw you that you are welcome to come stay with us as long as you like."

"I don't want to be a burden. I want to help."

"We'll talk about what you can do after you take a bath and have some hot tea."

A few hours later, Muthu joins us in the kitchen where Devi is sorting through a plate of rice and my mother churns milk into butter. Every evening, my mother churns the leftover sour cream into butter. She pours the rich cream into a narrow ceramic jar with a long-handled wooden churner. She rolls the wooden handle between the palms of her hands. The churner has a three-inch wooden ball with a spiky carved edge. As the round ball swishes the cream around, the butter separates and sticks to the spiky edges. As soon as all the edges of the ball are coated in butter, my mother takes out the churner and scrapes the butter. She forms the butter into a small ball and places it in a pan of cold water. The cold blob of butter floats and bobs on the water's surface. Later, Devi melts the butter to form nutty ghee.

"Here, let me do the churning," Muthu takes the churner out of my mother's hands and starts to twirl the wooden handle between her flat palms. Her hands are a blur and within a few minutes she is scraping a small round ball of fresh butter.

"Muthu is my mother's cousin," my mother explains to us. "She has no family and when I saw her last year I asked her come stay with us. Her husband was very ill at the time and I wanted her to know that she has a home with us."

Muthu smiles at us and says, "It was a shock when my sister-in-law came the day after my husband died and told me that the house belonged to her. I thought it was ours but I knew it was no use arguing with the woman, so I packed up all my belongings and went to visit your sister. She said she would write you a letter to let you know that I was coming."

"We didn't receive your letter because it takes the post a long time to get up the hills to us," my mother says "In any case, I'm glad to see you. As you can see we can use the help."

"Amma, is Muthu going to stay with us?"

"Really Meena, you know better than to call elders by their name. Muthu is a granny to you and you'll call her Muthi from now on," my mother's voice is firm.

"Don't be too hard on the girl, she is still only six years old," Muthu smiles at me and I smile back at her. She looks so cheerful that I can't help liking her.

"You can call me Muthi or patti," she says.

"I'll call you Muthi because it's just like Muthu," I reply. "Muthu means pearl, doesn't it? Why don't you wear pearls to match your name?"

"Meena..."my mother says, ready to stop what she thinks is my rude behavior.

"It's alright Sudha, let the girl ask questions because that's how youngsters learn. I don't wear pearls because I could never afford them and now I can't wear them because I'm a widow. The only jewelry I have is my thoda earrings."

"Why are you ear lobes so big?"

"She will ask endless questions if you let her," my mother says, frowning at me. I know she isn't really angry at me because her eyes are smiling.

"My ear lobes are big because when I was a child it was fashionable to have long ear lobes so we could wear huge gold earrings. All of us children wanted dangling earlobes like Lord Buddha's to hold our beautiful thoda earrings."

"But how can it get so big?"

"It's a long process. First, the barber comes and makes a hole and then he sticks a small twig in it. Each day he comes back and pushes in a larger twig and when he can't push anything more, he dabs some herbs on the earlobe. Soon the earlobe becomes infected and huge and while it is swollen he makes the hole bigger."

I touch the small gold studs in my ear and shiver at the thought of pushing bigger and bigger twigs into the tiny hole. "Didn't it hurt?"

"Oh yes, it hurt a great deal but all my girl friends and I thought the lobes looked so beautiful that we were willing to suffer."

I open my mouth to ask another question but my mother interrupts. "You have asked enough questions Meenakutty, time to take a bath and get ready for bed."

Muthi soon becomes part of our household and helps Devi in the kitchen and even Bhojan with the cows. She seems to know how to do everything from cooking and cleaning to milking cows and churning butter.

The weeks pass and my mother's stomach gets bigger. She is now so large that she walks very slowly and complains of a backache. Every evening Ayah prepares her bath, mixing bitter-smelling herbs with the steaming water and pouring the herb-infused hot water over my mother's body. Ayah then massages warm oil on her back and legs. My mother is uncomfortable at night and can only lie down for a few hours at a time. She takes up most of space in the bed and I find I am more comfortable on a mattress on the floor beside her bed. No matter how early I get up, my mother is always up before me. She sits in the kitchen with her legs up on a bench drinking milky tea. She dips Britannica tea biscuits in the warm drink and enjoys the soggy snack.

One morning when I open my eyes, I find Muthi sitting next to me. She is patiently waiting for me to wake up. I rub my eyes and look at her.

"Meenakutty, your mother has gone to the hospital to have her baby. When the taxi comes back we can go see her."

"Can't we go now?" I ask, upset that my mother has left without saying goodbye. "She didn't even say anything to me and I was sleeping right here."

"Kutty, she wanted to wake you up but Ayah and I thought you should get your rest because soon you'll be busy helping your mother. She left in the middle of the night and you were fast asleep."

"Can't we go by bus now?" I ask again.

"No little one. We need to wait until the car comes back. You don't want to wait in the hospital. Besides, your mother asked you to do something for her."

"What did she say Muthi?"

"The tinker is coming by this morning and your mother wants you to pick out a toy for the baby."

The tinker is an old man who visits us once a month. He pushes a little cart filled with all kinds of odds and ends. There are pots and pans for sale and he can sharpen the even bluntest knife. Sometimes he has small toys for sale. These toys are discards that he fixes and sells. Once he gave me a wooden car that had a piece of string attached to it that I could pull along. He had painted it in bright colors and it is one of my favorite toys.

"Alright, we'll wait for the tinker to come before going to the hospital."

A few hours later, I am dressed and ready. There is no sign of the tinker or the taxi car and I am just about to go inside and ask Devi to take me to the hospital when I hear the familiar clanging of pots and pans. The tinker is here.

I run to the front of the house and look through the gate. The tinker has pulled into our front yard and he is already surrounded by a crowd of people. He sees me peering out from behind the gate and waves to me. I wave back and wait for Muthi to come unlatch the gate. Muthi must have also heard the tinker's cart because she comes to the gate and pushes open the latch and we step outside. Bhojan is admiring some big blue and white beads.

"They will be perfect for the cows," the tinker says in a coaxing manner.

He is a skinny man with a bright plaid cloth wrapped around his waist that reveals his skinny brown legs. The cloth is held in place by a huge leather belt and a large dirty cloth bag hangs from it. I know he keeps his money and coins in the bag that is usually tucked away under his belt. A red and white turban is wrapped around his head and his tattered old shirt is full of holes. Ayah says he dresses in old clothes because he doesn't want to be robbed on the road by bandits who might think he is rich. His bloodshot eyes light up when he sees me.

"Little one, I have just the right thing for you."

He hands me a jump rope.

"This is a latest fancy rope. Do you see the little beads on it? They will make a nice sound when you jump."

I admire the rope. "I need a present for my baby sister."

"So you are big sister now? Let's see what I have for a baby."

He walks around to the back of his cart and rummages through the pile of newspapers and old clothes.

"I have just the thing for a little girl."

He hands me a bundle wrapped in a rag and I unwrap it to find a perfect little doll. The doll has long black hair with a cheerful smile and big black eyes painted on a soft cloth face. She has a colorful skirt and blouse and there are bangles and anklets painted on her hands and feet. She is just the thing for a baby girl.

"Now, Meenakutty we don't know if you have a baby brother or sister," Muthi says.

"Not to fear. I have a perfect gift for a boy. Here it is."

The tinker hands me a stuffed bear. Its little body is made up of a patchwork of colorful pieces of material. He is soft and cuddly. The bear will be a perfect toy for a boy.

I look up at Muthi. "I'm ready to go see my mother."

Just then we hear the familiar spluttering of the taxi car and soon the black and yellow car comes up the hill and stops in front of our house. I am ready to jump in and go to the hospital right away, but Muthi makes me wait while she goes inside and changes her white robes. She comes back carrying a bundle of blankets and sheets and a Horlicks jar filled with the creamy white Ishtu stew.

I hug the stuffed doll and bear to my chest. I bounce up and down in the taxi car seat. I am impatient and can't wait for the car to reach the huge government hospital. We finally arrive and I follow Muthi down a narrow hallway. A nurse in a starched white uniform shows us the way and I rush into the room and see my mother lying on a narrow cot. There are two cribs beside the iron bed. Did someone else have a baby at the same time?

My mother lifts her head and looks at me. She has dark circles under her eyes but her face lights up with a smile when she sees me, "Meenakutty, you are a chechi. Come meet your brother and sister."

Two babies? And both are mine? I am so glad I bought a doll and a bear from the tinker man.

Ishtu

4 medium red or yellow potatoes,
peeled and cut into 2 inch chunks
2 medium white or yellow onions
1 inch piece of ginger, grated
1 teaspoon salt
2 cups water
1 can coconut milk

Preparation: Peel and cut potatoes into 2-inch chunks and peel and cut the onions in half and then quarter each half. Place vegetables in a pan with a lid, add 1 ½ cups of water, ginger and salt and cook for about 15 minutes. Make sure the onions and potatoes are completely cooked but not mushy. If necessary, cook the stew for another 5 minutes.

Pour the can of coconut milk into the cooked vegetables. Stir thoroughly. Rinse the can with the remaining water and add to the stew and warm the stew on low heat. Don't boil. Taste for salt. Serve over hot rice.

Chapter Eight

The Naming Ceremony

• • • • • • • • • •

The twins are nearly a month old and today they will receive their formal names. The house is bustling with cousins, uncles and aunts who have arrived for this auspicious ceremony. The babies have pet names: We call my sister Thangam or precious and my brother Appu or little one. Even though everyone calls me Meena, my formal name is Meenakshiammal.

"Amma, why do Thangam and Appu need new names? I like their pet names."

My mother doesn't reply right away as she is busy sorting through a pile of baby clothes.

"All children need formal names that will be used on special occasions. We can continue to call them Thangam and Appu. But it might change when they get older. Did you know we used to call you Baby until the day after your naming ceremony?"

"Can you tell me what their new names will be?'

"Meena, you know better than to ask. It's considered bad luck to say the names out loud before the priest whispers them in the babies' ears. You and everyone else will know the names in a few hours. Now, please go give these clothes to Devi so that she can iron them for me."

My father has just arrived. I can hear his booming laugh in the kitchen. I run toward the welcoming sound.

"Acha, you came," I yell running into his arms.

"Of course I have come, Meena. I couldn't wait to see what kind of big sister you are. You know this is a special day for big sisters too? And I have just the thing for you."

He hands me a small box. The package is too tiny for new clothes. Nestled in the black velvet-lined box is a thin gold chain with a little star pendant. I lift out the delicate golden strand and hold it against my neck.

"Acha, it's a beautiful necklace. I'll wear it for the ceremony today. I can't wait to show this to my friend Kumari"

"Here, let me fasten it for you."

I can barely wait for my father to hook the gold necklace around my neck. I run down the hall to my bedroom and to look at my reflection in the mirror. The chain sparkles around my neck and I twist my head from side to side to admire myself.

"Well, well, look at big sister admiring herself," I turn around to see my aunt, my father's sister, come into the bedroom. She has a towel wrapped around her head. She removes the towel and starts to pat her long hair dry.

"Look, Valiaamma, look at what Achan gave me."

She admires my necklace and says, "I was waiting to give this to you after the ceremony. Since you are almost seven years old I think you are ready to wear these today."

She drapes the wet towel over her shoulder and walks over to her suitcase.

She, too, hands me a tiny box. Inside the grey satin-lined box is a pair of gold earrings shaped like miniature stars.

"Oh, Valiaamma, they match my necklace."

I'm so excited that I can barely stand still while my aunt removes my gold studs and replaces them with the new star-shaped earrings.

I run into the kitchen where Devi, Ayah and Muthi are busy chopping, stirring and cooking.

"Look Ayah, at my new earrings and necklace."

"They are beautiful kutty," Ayah says. "You look like a young lady."

Devi and Muthi stop what they are doing and admire my jewelry. I sit on the wooden bench and finger the star pendant around my neck and watch all the activity around me.

The kitchen is steamy and pungent with the aromas of cooking. I take a deep breath of the sharp scent of ginger and sweet tang of tamarind which means our family's favorite condiment 'injeepully' is bubbling on the stove. Devi is cutting vegetables for Aviyal, a vegetable stew flavored with coconut and yogurt. Muthi is churning rich cream into sweet butter which will be melted to make flavorful ghee. The ghee is used in the sweet rice puddings.

Ayah lifts a lid off a pot and the steamy scent of iddlis or rice dumpling fills the air.

"Yum, iddli," I say, getting a whiff of the fragrant steam.

Ayah squints at me through the steam. "Yes, little one, we are having iddlis today. They are the perfect baby food. Would you like a taste?"

"Yes, please Ayah."

Ayah lifts the tiered iddli tray out of the pot and places the steaming cakes on the table. Iddlis are usually steamed in a special iddli pan called an iddli tree. Each tier consists of four disks, each holding four molds, which are about 2 inches apart on a central trunk. Ayah can cook 12 or 16 iddlis at a time.

She now uses a clean knife to carefully scoop out the delicate dumplings. She places two of the steaming cakes on a plate and hands it to me.

"Kutty, here is a dab of sweet butter for your iddlis," Muthi says as she places a knob of creamy white butter on the spongy cakes. The butter melts into a warm golden puddle on the steaming rice cakes. Ayah sprinkles a spoonful of white sugar on top of the melted butter which glistens like ice crystals on the dumplings. I bite into the warm rice cake and the taste of butter and the sugar melts deliciously in my mouth.

We have iddlis most days for breakfast. I know it takes Devi several days to make the batter. The batter is made from a mixture of white rice and urid dal, a special white lentil.

First, Devi sorts through rice and lentils and then rinses and soaks the grains in cold water. The next morning, she grinds the rice into a coarse paste and the dal into a smooth mixture with an old stone mortar and pestle. The pestle is a hole in a block of granite stone and is so heavy that I can't lift it. Devi is very skilled and keeps the grains inside the hole with her right hand and uses her left hand to move the pestle around to crush the soft lentils. The lentil mixture is ready when it looks like heavy cream. The rice and dal are then well mixed together with a small spoonful of coarse salt. The batter is then allowed to rise and rest for another day. Finally, when the batter is puffy and filled with air, it is ready to be made into spongy cakes. Ayah uses a bit of ghee to grease each iddli mold before ladling spoonfuls of the creamy liquid into it. The iddli tree is then placed in a pot of boiling water. Each dumpling is steamed until it is light, moist and perfectly cooked. My mother likes to eat the dumplings with spicy sambar stew and my father likes them with tangy aviyal. I like them best with sugar and butter.

"Kutty, you better go ready for the ceremony," Ayah says to me as I lick the last of the butter and sugar from my fingers.

"Ayah, will you send my friend Kumari to the bedroom when she comes?"

I had started school a few months ago and had invited my best friend Kumari Sen to the naming ceremony.

I wash my hands in the sink before walking to my mother's bedroom. She has just finished giving the infants a ceremonial oil bath. Each squirming baby is rubbed down with warm fragrant coconut oil and then scrubbed with a paste of freshly ground mung beans. My little sister smells deliciously of coconut oil and the clean scent of mung bean paste. She opens her mouth and blows a bubble at me. I smile and wipe her delicate chin with my knuckle.

"Meena, go take a quick wash and get dressed."

A little later, dressed in a silk skirt and blouse, I accompany my mother to the living room. I see Kumari is sitting on a sofa with her mother. She waves and I wave back. The chairs and sofa have been pushed to the side to make a large empty space in the center. A bamboo mat is spread out in the center of the room and there are many silver trays of fruits, flowers and incense near the mat. A small terracotta bowl with camphor, ready to be lit, is on the mat. The priest, an old man, with large grey hairs sticking out his ears, is sitting cross-legged on the mat. He is re-arranging the flowers and fruits around the terracotta bowl while muttering prayers under his breath. I can't understand what he's saying but everyone is quiet, watching his fingers and listening to his chanting.

When we enter the room, he gestures for us to sit beside him on the mat. I move close to my mother and lean on her. My father looks very regal in a brand-new white dhoti cloth, trimmed with gold threads and a pure-white shirt. He has my baby brother in his arms. His sister, my aunt, follows him with the other baby. They sit with us on the bamboo mat. The priest lights a match and drops it in the camphor which immediately bursts into orange flames. The priest's chanting grows louder. He pauses for a moment and leans close to my mother and asks, "Which is the older baby?"

"The girl is older by three minutes."

My aunt moves closer to the priest and holds the little girl so that the priest can tie a black and gold thread on the baby's chubby wrist. My sister's eyes are wide open. She looks like she is enjoying all the attention. The priest bends down and blows on the baby's head. She jerks back and her face puckers up as if she is about to cry. My aunt soothes her and gently bounces her in her arms. The priest blows three times on the baby's face and then dabs a bit of reddish powder on her forehead. He then does the same with my baby brother who lets out a sharp scream. My father shushes him and he calms down.

"He's blowing all the evil spirits out of the way," my mother whispers in my ear.

"What is the girl's name?" the priest asks my parents. My father whispers in priest's ear.

The holy man chants several words in Sanskrit and then leans down and whispers in the baby's ear. His breath must have tickled her ear because she squeals and turns her head away from his face.

"Bless our baby girl Subhalakshiammal," he says. He tucks a small orange marigold behind her right ear and sprinkles her forehead and face with holy water.

He asks my father for the boy's name and again leans over to whisper the name into the baby's ear. "Bless our baby boy Govindaraman."

"The gold smith can now pierce the ears," he tells my mother. The gold smith has been waiting at the edge of the mat. He rises up from behind me and comes to squat beside us. He is a middle-aged man with a serious expression. He has gold-rimmed glasses and carries a small cloth bag.

"Are you the baby's aunt?" He asks my aunt, who nods her head. "You are the baby's father's sister?"

"Yes, I'm the girl's Valiaamma," my aunt replies.

"Is the boy going to be pierced too?" he asks her. My aunt looks over at my mother who shakes her head no.

"Well, hold the baby's head and I'll pierce the girl's ears."

I peer around my aunt and try to see what he is doing. My aunt's body blocks my view. A few seconds later, my sister cries out in pain as the gold smith pierces both her ear lobes.

As soon as he is finished my mother takes my sister in her arms and soothes away her tears. I look down at her little ear lobes which now have small twigs in them.

"Why doesn't she have gold earrings?" I ask my mother.

"The neem leaf twig will help heal the opening. In a few days we will put some small gold earrings in her ears. She will look as beautiful as you, Meenakutty."

I smile and touch the golden stars in my ears.

"I'll go feed and change her. We'll join you in the dining room," she tells the relatives, watching the ceremony. My sister starts whimpering. Her wailing grows louder and it's a relief when she and my mother disappear into the bedroom.

My brother is quietly sleeping through all this noise. My father now hands him to Muthi and takes my hand.

"Let's enjoy some iddlis and tomato chutney, Meenakutty, and celebrate this day."

Tomato Chutney Recipe

2 large red onions, peeled and sliced into eighths
1-2 tablespoons vegetable oil
5-6 fresh tomatoes cut into quarters
1-2 spicy green chili (optional)
¼ cup hulled mung beans or chana dal (optional)
1 teaspoon salt or to taste
2 tablespoons vegetable oil
1 teaspoon brown mustard seeds
1 bay leaf or curry leaf (if available)
1-2 dried red chili (optional)
Minced cilantro leaves for garnish

Preparation: Toast hulled beans in a skillet until golden brown. Remove the toasted beans/peas and use the same pan to sauté onions with a bit of oil until they are charred and tender. This can take about 10 to 15 minutes. When the onions are done, remove them from the pan. Use the same pan and add five or six fresh tomatoes, chopped thick. No need to peel them. Add one or two green chilies, if using, to the tomatoes. Let the tomatoes wilt in the heat and soften. Remove from the pan.

Use a food processor to chop the beans/peas, onions and tomatoes into a thick sauce. Add one teaspoon of salt or more as needed. Heat remaining oil in a saucepan and add mustard seeds. Cover and let the seeds splutter and turn grey. Add processed chutney to the oil, along with a bay leaf or curry sprig, if using. Garnish with minced cilantro leaves.

NOTE: Add one or two chopped dried red chilies to the oil for a spicier chutney.

Chapter Nine

Picnic in the Park - Flower Show

• • • • • • • • • •

We hear the exciting news from the postman who doubles as the village telegraph officer.

"Its official," he tells us one sunny May morning. "I have it on good authority that the PM is coming for a visit."

"The prime minister is coming to Mahagiri?" Devi asks, her voice pitched high in excitement.

"Yes, Devi sister, that is what I'm telling you. I accepted the official telegram from New Delhi addressed to our local commissioner with the news that Pandit Jawarlal Nehru himself is coming to the Flower Show."

He pauses to take a sip of cool buttermilk and wipe his sweating brow. "The PM will be the guest of honor at the Flower Show and stay at Glyngarth Villa."

The Flower Show is an annual event at the local botanical garden in Mahagiri. During the Flower Show, the lawns are hidden under huge white tents and the paths filled with vendors and noisy families. Display tables are set up in every spare inch of the garden and the locals show off their best fruits and vegetables.

Visiting the annual Flower and Fruit Show is like a pilgrimage for my mother. She loves to look at the displays of cut flowers, the different varieties of roses and hibiscus. We taste jams made from plums, pears and my favorite, golden raspberries. I sniff so many kinds of roses that my nose is itchy and I keep sneezing into my pocket handkerchief

My mother, Devi and Ayah constantly talk about the important visitor coming to our hillside town. There is a photograph of the prime minister in the local magazine and I stare at the black and white image of the tall man. He wears a long white jacket and a narrow white Nehru cap on his head. Even in the photograph I can see he has bright eyes and a kind smile.

On the day of the event, Ayah and my mother take the early morning bus to Greater Mahagiri. The bus station is already crowded and I see police cars and motor cycles along the main road. Ayah pulls me along and we stand in line to get into the gardens.

We stop at a wooden table where different kinds of beans are on display. There are mounds of purple beans, waxy yellow beans and delicate beans that look like pieces of wiggly green string.

"Here, ma'am, is the latest kind of bean. It's called the French String Bean and it is tender and tasty," the vendor tells my mother. He looks a little like a brown string bean himself, tall and thin.

I try a sample of the bean he hands me and I like the crunchy taste.

"How much for a kilo of the French beans and the purple ones?" my mother asks the vendor.

I walk over to the next stall while she bargains with the bean man. Here a tired looking woman is standing behind a display of small baskets of gooseberries. Some gooseberries are tiny and hard like the marbles I like to play with, but others are round and shiny like small green rubber balls.

"Go ahead, taste one," the woman says to me. But I look around for my mother before taking a berry.

"Go ahead Meena, try the big gooseberry," my mother says.

I take a bite of the berry and my lips pucker, I am ready to spit out the sour tasting fruit.

"No, don't spit it out," the vendor says. "Chew on the berry and take a sip of water."

My mother hands me a plastic bottle of water and I take a sip, anything to get rid of that sour taste from my mouth. But I'm amazed that the sour fruit now tastes like sweet nectar.

"Is this magic?" I ask the vendor. "The gooseberry is so sweet."

"That, little one is not magic but what gooseberry tastes like when it's mixed with water," she smiles at me.

I take another bite of gooseberry and wash it down with water, a mouthful of liquid honey. I love this new taste.

"That's quite enough of that," says Ayah. "You'll get a tummy ache if you eat too many raw gooseberries. I'll cook them and make a pickle for you."

We meander down a path toward a small artificial pond when I hear the sound of the organ-grinder's music. I let go of Ayah's hand and run down the hill. There is a small crowd of people watching the monkey perform. The creature is dressed in toy-size pants that fit him perfectly with his little tail poking out of the back. He wears a dark green vest that hangs open with the most adorable fez hat on his head. There is a tiny bunch of artificial red flowers pinned to the vest. The hat tassel moves back and forth as the monkey prances and dances to the music.

"Say your prayers like a Christian," the monkey's owner commands the little creature. Immediately, the monkey kneels down and makes the sign of the cross. The crowd claps and murmurs in admiration. The organ-grinder gives the monkey a bit of banana as a reward.

"Now say them like a Muslim."

The monkey again kneels down and then turns east toward Mecca and prostrates itself. The crowd claps as the monkey chews on another piece of fruit.

"Now do it the Hindu way."

This time the monkey folds his palms together and bows down to an imaginary deity.

"Now ask for alms," the organ grinder tells the monkey.

The creature takes off its cap and walks around the crowd with it in his hand. Many people toss coins and rupee notes into the tiny cap. I look up at Ayah who unties her cloth money bag and hands me a rupee note. When the monkey stops in front of me, I kneel down and slowly drop the rupee note into the tiny fez. The monkey freezes for a moment and stares at me with curious button eyes and then he tears off a red rosebud from his vest and thrusts it at me. The crowd laughs at my surprised expression.

"The rascal must really like you, little miss," the organ grinder grins at me, showing off a mouth filled with blackened teeth. "He hates giving away anything."

Ayah insists we go meet my mother in the greenhouse but I want to stay and watch the monkey perform all over again. My argument with Ayah is drowned by an announcement on the loud speakers.

"Please join us in the main pavilion for the opening ceremonies with Panditji Jawarlal Nehru," a disembodied voice blares through the speakers. "Ceremonies begin in less than 30 minutes."

"Come on Meenakutty, let's see if we can get a glimpse of the prime minister," Ayah grabs hold of my hand and pulls me along.

It is crowded near the main pavilion and we try to find a way to the entrance. Just then I spot a monkey's tail disappearing behind the tent. I twist my hand away from Ayah and follow the monkey. I catch a glimpse of the creature as it lifts the tent flap and goes inside. Without pausing I follow the hairy tail into the tent. I stand up and look around. I am on what looks like the stage area of the pavilion because there are many electrical wires and several microphones in front of me. On one side of the stage I can see the backs of several men sitting on folding chairs. I hear a commotion and look around to see the monkey running across the stage. It is chattering and looking around wildly. One of the men from the crowd darts up and tries to grab the monkey.

"Please don't hurt the monkey," I yell and run toward the man who looks over his shoulder at me. He lets go of the monkey's tail. The frightened creature leaps over a table and knocks down the microphone.

"Its all right little monkey," I whisper and try to get the animal to come toward me.

Meanwhile the crowd in the pavilion is getting restless and I can hear murmurs and whispers.

"What's going on?" a man asks.

"It's an angry monkey," another man replies. "It's running around and jumping on people's heads."

The monkey slowly moves toward my hands and I hold out the little red flower he gave me. I can see the animal's nose sniffing the air.

"Where is that naughty animal?" a man asks, running up the aisle.

It is the organ grinder and he looks sweaty and hot. He reaches up and grabs the little monkey by the tail. "Come here, you rascal. You'll get no food if you don't dance."

The man snatches the monkey and walks back down the aisle.

"Meena, what are you doing?" says Ayah's voice from the back of the tent.

Suddenly I realize there are hundreds of people in the tent looking up at me and I can feel my face getting hot and tears burning in my eyes.

"You are fine, little one," a voice says above my head. "Come on let's get you to your family."

The voice belongs to a tall man in an immaculate white suit and he has such a kind face that I smile back at him.

Ayah hurries up to the stage, "Please excuse my girl. She didn't mean to cause any harm."

"It's quite all right," the man says with a smile. "She's very brave to try and save the monkey. What is your name, little one?"

I hang my head, suddenly tongue-tied. "It's Meenaskhi, sir and I'll take her now so that the program can begin," Ayah says, grabbing my hand. We start walking down the steps of the podium. I tug my hand from Ayah's and run back to stage.

"I like to be called Meena," I say to the man. "This red flower was given to me by the monkey and I'm sure he'll want you to have it as a thank-you."

I hold out the little red rosebud to the man who laughs and bends down and swings me into his arms. "You know Meena, this white jacket could use a bit of color and that flower is perfect."

He hugs me tight and puts me down and I walk toward Ayah. Walking down the aisle, I glance back and see that the man is at the podium starting to give a speech.

"Really Meena, do you know who that was?" Ayah asks peering down at me. "That was the prime minister of India and you gave him a plastic flower."

She starts chuckling and later while we unpack our picnic lunch she tells my mother the entire story. My mother also laughs and then bends down to give me a hug.

"Somehow you keep getting in trouble, don't you Meenakutty?"

"Amma, next year we should bring the twins," I say and avoid answering my mother's question.

My mother's picnic luncheons are a feast for the eyes and mouth. For today's picnic she has packed foods that travel well. First there is tomato rice—rice cooked in a broth of garlic and fresh tomatoes and topped with crunchy cashews. I scoop up mouthfuls of the flavorful dish with small rounds of poori. The bread is soft and perfect with the tasty grains. We finish up with curd rice—rice mixed with mild yogurt, sharp ginger flecks and bright-red pomegranate seeds. We end our finger-licking feast with slices of golden ripe mangoes, dripping with juice and flavor.

I can barely move after all the food, but our day at the flower show is not over yet. My mother and Ayah pack up and urge me to follow them. We make our way to the judges' tent which is hot and crowded. But no one seems to mind the heat in this canvas cave. We find seats in the middle row and wait for the judges to announce who has won the best of show. I don't hear the announcements because I fall fast asleep, full of tomato rice, poories and sunshine.

A few weeks later I can't helping smiling when I see a photo of the prime minister in the local paper with a red flower pinned to his white jacket.

Tomato Rice

1 cup basmati rice, washed and drained
1 cup water or as needed
4 medium ripe tomatoes, chopped (about 2 cups chopped)
1 small onion, any color, minced
6-8 cloves of garlic, peeled and then sliced
3 tablespoons vegetable oil or ghee
1 teaspoon mustard seeds
1 teaspoon turmeric powder
1 teaspoon salt or as needed

Optional: One fresh green chilly minced; curry leaves (a small sprig);
Garnishes: Toasted sunflower seeds and minced coriander leaves.

Preparation: Heat oil in a pan. Add mustard seeds. Wait for the seeds to pop and when the popping sound fades, add onion (optional chili pepper) and garlic.

Sauté over low heat so that the garlic does not brown and when the onion is soft, add turmeric powder, chopped tomatoes and salt. Let the tomatoes soften and become sauce-like.

Add 1 cup water and rice. Let the water come to a boil, and simmer the rice and tomato mixture for 15 to 20 minutes. Check to make sure the rice is not sticking. When all the water is absorbed and rice is cooked, remove from flame and stir in garnishes. Serve with yogurt.

Chapter Ten

Visiting a Friend

• • • • • • • • • •

"Lord Krishna's best childhood friend was a boy named Kuchela. Kuchela, a very poor Brahmin boy, and Krishna, a royal prince, both attended the same school. After their schooling was over the boys went their separate ways. Krishna became the king of Dwaraka while Kuchela remained a poor man. He married a good woman and had many children. Kuchela and his wife lived in great poverty, hardly able to feed their children. One day Kuchela's wife suggested that he seek the help of Krishna, his childhood friend. At first Kuchela was reluctant to ask Krishna for help, but his wife pressed him and he finally made up his mind to go visit his old friend. Kuchela was very embarrassed that he had no gift to take to Krishna. His wife knew that Krishna loved pounded rice or avil, so she found a few handfuls of avil and wrapped it in a small cloth for Kuchela to carry to his friend.

Kuchela became very anxious as he approached Krishna's palace in Dwaraka and was worried that his friend would not recognize him. But when Krishna saw Kuchela, he ran to him and hugged his friend. The two companions spent many happy hours together reminiscing about their childhood. Kuchela presented Krishna with the avil and Krishna grabbed the pounded rice and ate it with relish. Finally, Kuchela took leave of his friend and on the way home he berated himself for not asking for Krishna's help to take care of his family. He was worried about how he would explain everything to his wife. Deep in thought he walked past the place his hut used to stand. He stopped and looked up and saw a huge house. Thinking he was on the wrong street, he started to turn around. His wife ran after her husband and explained to him that by the grace of Lord Krishna their old hut had turned into a beautiful mansion. Kuchela knew that his childhood friend had taken care of him without him asking for his help. Krishna always helps his friends and devotees."

—as told by Ayah

A few months after the naming ceremony, Kumari invites me to her house and I can hardly wait for the school day to come to an end. We bounce and jump with impatience while waiting for Kumari's dark blue Ambassador car.

"That's Chelappan, the driver," Kumari says, tugging on my hand and pulling me toward the waiting car. "Chelappan, I have a friend with me."

Chelappan is an old man who moves very slowly. He wears a fancy hat with a wide brim and bows slightly as he opens the car door for us.

"Well, little one, does your friend have a name? Or is she a princess just like you?"

I giggle, "I'm not a princess. My name is Meena and Kumari is my best friend."

Chelappan has one hand on the door and pauses to consider my words. "Well, I think you are a princess just like Miss Kumari here. Did you know she has a crown?"

"A real crown?"

"No, it's not a real crown," Kumari says, climbing into the back seat of the car. "It's a fake cardboard one but it has some shiny stickers on it."

Chelappan laugh sounds like a bark, "I always said a crown doesn't really make you a princess and cardboard is hard to come by right now and so it's precious."

I move next to Kumari and Chelappan closes the car door and climbs into the driver's seat. Kumari's house is on top of a very high hill and the car groans as it makes its way up the long curving driveway. Chelappan pulls into a garage, right next to the main house, and starts to get out, but we don't wait for him to open the door.

"Come on Meena and I'll show you my house. We have to take off our shoes in the hallway because we have nice carpets."

Kumari's house is bigger than mine and the front hallway had a thick yellow carpet that leads into a grand living room. A shiny piano sits in one corner and on the floor there is a huge bear skin in front of the fireplace. I can see the bear's glassy eyes staring at me and the animal's mouth is open in a perpetual snarl. Kumari must have seen the look of fear on my face because she rubs her bare toes on its hairy paw.

"That's just an old bear skin, not a real animal. My father says it took him three shots before he killed it in the jungles of Kashmir. You can feel it if you want, it's really soft."

I shake my head no. Just then Kumari's mother comes, "Beti, you have come with a visitor," she says and bends down to hug my friend. "Welcome Meena to our home. How are your brother and sister?"

I feel shy and answer in a soft voice, "They are fine, Aunty."

She is very tall, much taller than my mother, and has smooth white skin. She wears a simple cotton sari that is draped in the Bengali style, over her right shoulder, not like my mother's sari which goes over the left shoulder. Kumari's mother is elegant in the simple sari. She smells like a rose garden and has many jangling gold bangles on her slender arms. I think she is beautiful. She looks at me with kind eyes and says, "Come on in Meena, I'm glad to have you visit us. Let's go into the dining room for a snack. Tell me about your day. After a snack you two can go outside and play."

I had always thought our dining room table as big, but Kumari's table is much longer and the wood is so brightly polished that I can see reflection of the huge glass chandelier on its surface. There are twenty-four chairs around the table with beautiful brocaded seats. I try to move the chair closer to the table but it is too heavy and Kumari's mother has to help me.

"Lalita, please bring the girls a snack," she calls out to Kumari's housekeeper.

Lalita is small and dark with very white teeth. She beams at us and brings in a huge silver tray filled with stacks of sandwiches, tiny cakes with bright pink icing and a pot of steaming tea.

"An English tea for the two misses," Lalita says, plopping the heavy tray down on the shiny table.

"Be careful with that," Kumari's mother's tone is sharp.

The sandwiches have a salty filling with tomatoes, bits of lettuce and cucumber

"Do you like the sandwiches?" Kumari asks.

I nod my head, my mouth full of bread and tomatoes. I swallow the tasty mouthful and say, "It's delicious. What is it?"

Her mother replies, "This is cheese, a tasty delicacy made from milk. Kumari's father bought us the cheese from New Delhi. This cheese is from Canada and is quite good on toast."

We finish our snack and wander into Kumari's room to wash up. Kumari shows me her doll collection and we play with the dolls, changing clothes and pretending to give them a bath. I want to explore the house.

"Come on Kumari, let's see the rest of your house. Where does your granny live?"

"Alright, I'll show you granny's room, but make sure you don't touch anything. Granny can get angry if someone touches her things without asking."

"I promise not to touch anything Kumari."

I follow her down a long corridor and out of the back door. We walk through a small garden filled with roses, marigolds and dahlias. The flowers are all blooming and the air is thick with the sweet scent of roses and jasmine. I take deep breaths of the fragrant air. Kumari's grandmother lives in a small cottage at the far end of the garden. There is a stone bench in front of her door. Kumari knocks on the wooden door using the brass knocker shaped like a monkey.

"Coming, coming," a voice says from inside. I step away from the doorway, suddenly shy and a little frightened.

After the bright sunlight, it is hard to see inside the dark house but I can make out a figure, all dressed in white. She walks out into the sunshine and I see an old lady with sparkling brown eyes. She is very short, just a little taller than me, and looks like a wrinkled fairy godmother. She wears a flowing white sari that billows around her in graceful swirls. I like her kind eyes and smile at her. She smiles back, her pink gums glistening in the sunlight.

"Is it my favorite granddaughter coming to visit me?" she asks peering at Kumari who is almost as tall as her grandmother. "And you have a friend with you. Good, good. Come in both of you. Kumari, show her what she has to do before entering the house."

Kumari leads me to a small pump next to the garden bench.

"Granny likes us to be really clean before coming inside her house. We need to wash our face, hands and feet."

We dry ourselves on a towel that is hanging on a flowering bush. I drape the towel back on the bush and follow Kumari into Granny's house.

For a moment I think I'm in a dollhouse because everything is so small. I love the tiny rocking chair, miniature table and wooden chairs. Granny motions us to sit in one of the miniscule chairs and bustles into the kitchen.

She brings back a small plate heaped with round white balls. "Here Kumari and Meena, you both have to try this Bengali sweet I made today. This is sandesh and anyone who eats one will only speak sweet words. I used milk and just a little sugar and plenty of cardamom to make these sweets."

I bite into the silky soft Sandesh. The sweet melts in my mouth and is a perfect flavor combination of milk, sugar and spice. I love the elegant taste.

"Granny, this is the best sweet I've ever had. Will you show me how to make these sweets? I think my mother would like them too."

The old lady grins so wide that I can see her pink gums. "Of course, I can show you how to make sandesh Meena. I'm so glad you are interested in cooking. Kumari likes to eat but never wants to learn how to make anything. You must bring your mother next time. I'll show you both how to make Sandesh and other fine Bengali treats."

We finish our plate of sweets and thank Granny before heading outside.

"Come on and I'll show you our summer patio," Kumari says after we leave Granny's little cottage.

We walk around the house and through the garage to the front of the house. The front yard is on a long gentle slope and from here I can see all the way down into the valley. The hillside is blanketed with green tea bushes and from a distance it looks smooth as a green carpet. We walk down the well-worn dirt path to the part of the hillside that has been leveled. Here Kumari's family has built an open-air summer house. The breeze blows in from all directions, bringing in the cool evening air. I can see the wisps of fog creeping up from the valley. A circular wooden bench allows us a breathtaking view of the distant mountains. It was a wonderful feeling standing on the mountain with the whole world spread beneath me, just waiting to be explored. I can't wait to grow up and travel the rolling hills and endless plains stretched below me. Over on the horizon, against the setting sun, I can make out an airplane. I imagine what it must feel like to be on that plane, high above the orange-gold clouds, flying to a faraway place.

"I feel like a world explorer from here," I say. "We can pretend to be lost in the mountains of the Nile. Do you see the crocodiles below us, waiting to snap our feet?"

Kumari giggles, "You make up the best stories Meena. Next time, we can wear my rain boots and pretend."

"Or we can pretend this is the summer palace of a famous king. He's here to escape the heat of the valley. But he doesn't know that his life is in danger here."

"What's going to happen?"

"Well, one of the neighboring kings is plotting to overthrow him. He has sent some bad men who will try to kill the king."

"Let's play that story," Kumari says. "We can use my cardboard crown and I will be king. You can try to sneak up and kill me."

"I can think of other stories," I say.

"Meena, its time for you to go home," Kumari's mother's voice floats down to us. "Chelappan will take you home."

"Next time, Kumari we will play all kinds of pretend games in this summer palace," I promise my friend.

We walk up the hill to the waiting car.

"Meena, my mother sent this plate of sandesh for you," Kumari's mother hands me a silver tray heaped with the delicate milk sweet.

"Thank you Aunty," I say. "I'll share these with my mother."

I wave good-bye and carefully climb into the back seat of the car, ready to go home and sample the delicious dessert again.

Sandesh

First make the chenna cheese:
Chenna Cheese recipe

8 cups whole milk
4 tablespoons fresh lemon juice

Preparation: Bring the milk to a rolling boil in a large saucepan. Keep stirring the milk to prevent sticking and burning. As the milk boils, heavy foam will form. When the foaming subsides, add the lemon juice, remove the pan from the heat and gently agitate the milk for about 1 minute. Large clots should form as the milk and lemon juice interact. Using several layers of cheesecloth, draped over a strainer, strain the whey. Squeeze excess whey out of the cheese by twisting the ends of the cheesecloth. Let the cheese rest in the strainer over the sink with some kitchen weights or a brick wrapped in plastic. After about 25 minutes, remove the cheese from the cloth and place on a clean cutting board. Using the heel of your hand, press bits of cheese onto the board. Gradually gather all the cheese and knead into soft pliable dough. This can take up to 10 minutes. The Chenna cheese is now ready to be made into fudge.

Fudge recipe

1 recipe Chenna cheese from 8 cups of milk
½ cup sugar, brown sugar, superfine white sugar
or maple sugar
Optional: 4 tablespoons of dried fruit puree such as
apricot, dates or figs

Other flavoring ideas: A tsp of vanilla, almond or coconut.

Preparation: Knead the sweetener into the prepared Chenna cheese, until it forms a grainy paste. Heat a heavy-bottomed sauce pan and add the Chenna cheese fudge. Use a wooden spoon to stir the mixture and let it cook for about 10 minutes. The fudge would be slightly glossy. It will thicken as it cools. Spread the fudge on a buttered cookie sheet and let it cool. Either cut the fudge into squares or roll into logs or balls. Makes about two dozen fudge squares. Store in an airtight container up to 2 days or in the refrigerator for 4 days.

Chapter Eleven

Shopping with Ayah

• • • • • • • • • •

The monthly Bazaar Day in the town of Greater Mahagiri is a popular event. Greater Mahagiri is a sprawling town that spreads across two small hillsides. At the bottom of the slopes is a large meadow and this is where the monthly market takes place. Makeshift stalls and tents are set up and the grassy area is transformed into a huge outdoor marketplace selling everything from green bananas to cows, goats and sacks of grains.

My family has been going to the monthly market as long as I can remember. I loved going to the market with my mother and Ayah and coming back home late in the evening, munching on sticks of chewy sugar cane.

Ayah is older now and moves more slowly but these shopping trips are the highlight to her week. I help her gather the baskets and bags to take with us. Our day starts early and I shiver in my cotton skirt and sweater. In the kitchen, the fire is lit and milk boils in a pan. I hold a steel tumbler of warm milk and sugar close to my body. The hot drink takes away the morning chill and I feel better. Today, Raman is coming with us while Kashi is going to stay home to take care of the twins who are more interested in playing than in shopping.

Raman's curly black hair and face are completely covered by a thick woolen scarf.

"Everyone ready?" he asks in a muffled voice. "The bus is coming down the hill. It will be here in a few minutes."

I wrap my favorite purple shawl around me before following the adults to the front gate. The sky is turning a pale pink and the birds are twittering in the jacaranda tree. The morning breeze stirs the leaves and drops a faded lavender bloom at my feet. I pick up the flower and blow into it. It puffs up like a miniature purple balloon. I squeeze the opening shut with my fingers and admire the perfectly shaped blossom for a moment. Then I gently tap it on my cheek and it pops with a satisfying fizzle of air. As I bend down to pick up another fallen flower the headlights of the bus washes over us. The huge vehicle comes to a stop in front of us with a hiss. The oily diesel scent fills the air. I can no longer smell the delicate scent of the jacaranda flowers.

"I guess even at eleven you are never too old to blow jacaranda balloons," Ayah teases me as we get into the bus.

I know she needs help to climb up into the bus and I hold her hand. "Get in, little one," Ayah says, clinging to my hand.

I clutch several bags in one hand and Ayah in the other and slowly climb up the three steps into the bus. The interior is lit by dim bulbs and smells strongly of cigarette smoke, human sweat and diesel fumes. There are quite a few early morning shoppers in the bus but we find an empty seat near the back. The conductor, dressed in his khaki-colored uniform, stops to collect our fare.

"Going shopping, little mother?" he asks.

My mother nods and hands him the money for the tickets.

"How is your wife?"

"Oh, the wife is fine," he replies as he balances himself against the steel pole and writes the fare in his book. He tears out the tickets and gives the stubs to my mother.

The bus picks up speed and I turn to look out through the dirty windows. I push open the window and the cool air stings my cheeks and makes my eyes water. The vehicle makes several stops and soon there are no more seats. People start crowding the aisles.

The trees are just a green blur as the vehicle speeds along the narrow highway. We drive by the dhobi village where the washer people live. I can see them standing in the muddy-brown water, beating the clothes on the large stone slabs. I can almost hear the thud, thud of the clothes on the stones. Soon the grassy slopes will be a colorful mosaic of clothes drying out in the noonday sun.

When the bus slows down on a sharp curve I see a small boy standing by the roadside, his naked body shivering in the early morning air. He looks like he's ready to go down to the river for a bath. For a second our eyes meet and we smile at each other.

The diesel engine struggles up the hill and comes to a stop. The conductor yells, "Last stop. Bazaar day today."

We stand. Raman and my mother collect all the baskets and bags. We wait our turn to get down from the bus and Ayah grabs my hand.

"Hold on Meena," she says. "Walk with me."

"Shall we get some breakfast?" my mother asks. "I know that Anjalie will have something tasty for us."

"Little mother, I prefer to go to the Woodlands Hotel for breakfast," Raman says. "Shall I meet you at the grain store in about an hour?"

"Of course Raman, go ahead and have your meal. Here, take a couple of rupees so that you will have enough for coffee."

My stomach grumbles reminding me that I haven't had breakfast this morning. The sun is warming the cool air and the dew on the grass glitters—tiny diamonds in the sunshine. I smell Anjalie's food even before we see her little stall. My mother's friend Anjalie is known for her flaky pastries and tasty sauces. Her food stall is really a make-shift shed with a thatched roof. The narrow wooden counter serves as a table. There are about six stools in front of the counter. Anjalie cooks her food in the darkened interior of the stall using two small kerosene stoves. She has a long wooden table for her serving utensils and containers of spicy sauces.

"Come and sit down Didi," she greets my mother. She calls my mother Didi because she says she is like an elder sister to her.

"What do you have for us today, little sister?" my mother asks her friend.

We all wash our hands using water from a plastic bucket by the side of the stall and sit on the high stools. I wrap my feet around the stool legs and lean on the counter to peer at Anjalie who is busy in her little kitchen. Anjalie is comfortably plump and whenever I sit on her lap, I feel like I'm sinking into a pillow. She has lovely smooth skin like the picture of the woman on my mother's face cream jar. Her thick gray hair is pulled back into a long braid. She likes to wear big gold earrings and her diamond nose ring is shaped like a small flower. I call her Anjalie Aunty and we stop at her stall for breakfast every Sunday before shopping.

"You sure have grown since the last time I saw you," she says to with a smile. "A few poori masala will plump you right up."

I watch Anjalie pinch a knob of dough from a bowl and using her palms she rolls and kneads the dough into a perfect ball. She dusts a cutting board with a sprinkle of flour. She then rolls the ball of dough into a round shape. Meanwhile, a pan of oil is smoking hot, ready for the bread. Within a few seconds, Anjalie has made half a dozen poories and begins frying each one in the pan of hot oil. The poories puff up into round balls that float on the oil. She drains them on a newspaper. She then slides the cooked bread onto a green banana leaf which she places on a bamboo plate. The hot poori and a spoonful of masala potatoes are served with tangy yogurt. The aroma of the nutty fried bread mingles with the gingery spice of the potatoes. I carefully tear a piece of piping hot bread and scoop up the yellow potatoes with it. The flaky bread and creamy potatoes melt in my mouth. I can taste the bite of ginger and freshness of the cilantro leaves in each mouthful. I finish several poories before I'm finally satisfied. Anjalie pours us glasses of strong coffee, creamy with buffalo milk and sweetened with brown sugar. I blow on the hot liquid and sip the delicious brew. My mother and Anjalie are busy catching up on the all news. I turn around and watch the crowd of shoppers. Already a long line of hungry customers wait for us to get up so that they can have some breakfast at Anjalie's open-air kitchen.

We throw our used banana leaves in the overflowing trash bin and wash our hands. A dog comes up and starts to dig at my leaf which has fallen out of the full trash bin. I hand the bamboo plate back to Anjalie and thank her for the delicious breakfast.

"That was very tasty aunty," I say. "Next time I'll bring my friend Kumari."

"Come again, Meenakutty," she says and turns back to her stove.

We make our way to the market where vendors sit on bamboo mats with their wares spread out in front of them while others have make-shift stalls made of tarp and bamboo poles. The market is already crowded with shoppers and the sounds of vendors and bargain hunters fill the air.

My mother and Ayah know many of them and we stop to chat. I wish we could keep moving but market day is all about visiting as well as shopping for bargains. Ayah stops in front of a vendor who sits behind a huge mound of dried chili peppers. The air is spicy hot with their smell and I feel my nose trembling with the need to sneeze.

"Are these hot?" Ayah asks, fingering a long, fiendishly red pepper between her fingers.

"Big mother, I only sell the freshest and hottest peppers in Mahagiri," the vendor says. He has a big bushy moustache that wiggles when he talks. "See how they snap? They are the best."

Ayah haggles over the price of the chili and I turn and look around. Right next to the pepper merchant, another man sells plastic pots and pans from his bicycle. Bright orange, green, red and yellow jugs of all sizes and shapes are tied to the bicycle. There are even small jugs tied to the handle bars and I wonder how he can ride with his heavy load. Across the narrow street from us, there is a merchant selling all kinds of nuts and dried fruits. Mounds of almonds, wrinkled raisins, pale cashews, and sugary dates are arranged in neat piles on a bamboo mat. The man shoos away flies with a large white handkerchief.

"Sweet jaggery for sale," a woman cries out.

I turn and see a woman balancing a basket on her head without using her hands.

"Here, let me see what kind of jaggery you have," my mother calls to the woman.

The woman lifts the basket off her head and squats down on the ground. She pulls back a cloth and shows my mother neat rows of small cakes of brown sugar. Flies buzz around the cakes attracted by the sweet scent of the sugary treats. The woman tries to brush them away but they are persistent.

"I'll take three of the light brown cakes and four of the dark ones," my mother says. "Get me the ones from the bottom of the basket away from the flies."

The woman wraps the sugar cakes in pieces of old newspaper and hands the bundles to my mother.

As we pass the fruit stand, a voice calls out, "Ayah, little mother, stop here for a minute."

It is Mohammed, the fruit man and his fruit stand is filled with bunches of red bananas, baskets of sweet limes, tiny orange tangerines and bunches of green and red grapes.

Mohammed is a tall man with a pock-marked face. I never know if he is looking at me or not because his eyes look in different directions.

"Little one, do you want to try a grape?" he asks.

I wish he wouldn't call me little one. The vendors see me nearly every month and treat me like I'm two years old.

I nod my head and Ayah nudges me to answer.

"Yes, please," I say to the eye looking in my direction.

Mohammed laughs and hands me a bunch of dark red grapes. They are tiny and have a flowery perfume.

"Here, try these," he says. "They are called rose grapes because they have a nice flavor. Spit out the seeds, little one."

The grapes are sweet as nectar and the papery skin tastes like rose petals.

"They are sweet and taste like flowers," I say to Mohammed, who grins at us.

"Your daughter has a discerning palate, little mother," he says. "So can I pack a few kilos of grapes and sweet limes?"

My mother and Mohammed start to argue about the fruit. I finish the last of the grapes and wipe my sticky hands on my skirt.

After buying the fruit, we make our way down the hill toward the grain merchants. We pass the fish market and I hold my nose and try not to breathe in the pungent smell. The grain merchant's store is large and filled with huge cloth sacks of different kinds of rice.

"Come in little mother," he says to us. "The best parboiled rice has just come in this week."

"Little mother, while you buy the grains, I think I'll go check on Perumal's grandson. I heard he was not doing too well," Ayah says to my mother.

"Meena and I will go ahead to the vegetable stall after we finish here," my mother says.

A car horn startles me and I look over and see Kumari leaning out of car window, waving and yelling my name.

"Meena, I'm so glad I found you. Chelappan and I have been going up and down this road looking for you."

Kumari jumps out of the car. "Namaste Sudha Aunty. Can Meena and I go with Chelappan to look for a new skirt for me?"

"Hello Kumari. You have grown so tall since the last time I saw you. Are you going to Lalchand's Cloth store to buy a skirt?"

"Yes, Aunty and then we'll take the cloth to the tailor next door. After shopping, can Meena and I go to the tea room and have vegetable cutlets? My mother gave me money."

"Of course she can. That was nice of your mother. Can you bring her back to the bus station?"

"I can give her a lift home and that way you won't have to look for her at the bus stand."

"Thanks for letting me go with Kumari, Amma," I hug my mother. "Please buy me a piece of sugar cane."

Mother smiles at me and hugs me goodbye. I can't wait to go shopping with Kumari.

Anjalie's Poories

2 cups whole wheat flour
½ teaspoon salt
2 tablespoons melted butter, ghee or vegetable oil
2/3 cup warm water or as needed
Vegetable oil for frying

Preparation: Place flour and salt in a bowl and mix well. Add the melted butter/oil and rub it into the flour mixture until it well incorporated. Add warm water, a little at a time, until the dough is formed into a sticky mass. Place the dough on a clean, floured cutting board and knead until it is smooth and pliable. This may take a few minutes. Cover with a damp cloth and let it rest up to 30 minutes. Divide the dough into 16 portions. Roll each portion into a ball and using a rolling pin roll the ball into a 10 inch round. Place the rolled out bread between sheets of wax paper so that they don't stick together.

Meanwhile heat the oil over moderate flame until it reaches about 350 F. Carefully slip one poori into the hot oil. The bread will sink into the oil and then rise to the top. Gently tap the poori with a fork or slotted spoon. Cook each side for about a minute. If the poori is just the right thickness, it will puff up like a ball. Let the poori cook until golden brown and gently remove it from the oil without puncturing the bubble. Drain on paper towels.

Makes 16 poories. Serve warm with masala potatoes (see chapter 13) and plain yogurt.

Chapter Twelve

The Bathhouse

• • • • • • • • • •

During the summer months the skies are a bright blue and the sunshine is warm and the house is full of guests. We call our summer months the "tourist months."

One summer, my mother's sister, Rukumani, visits us. She is a much taller than my mother and looks a little scary with her thick glasses and frowning face.

She has 7 children, all boys. She pinches my chin and says, "You are going to be a beauty. Just remember to stay out of the sun and keep smiling."

She sighs, "Even one girl can brighten up my life. But the good lord only gives me boys." I overhear her talking to my mother one afternoon. "You are lucky Sudha; you have two girls and a boy. But I have borne so many children that my body is tired. I don't know what I'd do if I have to give birth one more time."

My mother murmurs something I can't hear.

"Yes, yes, I won't do anything foolish but I don't think I can go through with yet another delivery."

She has brought three of her boys, my cousins, with her on this trip and they are a lot of fun. The boys, ranging in age from seventeen to twenty-one give me a lot of attention. They play games with me, read to me and give me piggyback rides.

* * *

Every night Ayah helps me take a warm bath in the bathhouse behind our house. Here the water is heated in huge brass pots on an open fire. The bathhouse is a spooky place. There is no electricity here and the small windows don't let in much sunshine. The open fire has baked the walls to a smoky black and when I was younger I was never allowed in this room because of the hot pots and open flame. But now that I am nearly twelve, Ayah lets me come in and wait for her.

Ayah carries a small bucket of steaming hot water and mixes it with cold water in a red plastic bucket and douses me. She then scrubs my back with a grainy paste made from mung beans. The paste stings my neck and I hate it when she tries to clean my face.

"I can wash my own face," I tell her.

"I forget how big you are now," Ayah says. "You used to yell so loudly when I scrubbed your neck."

Kashi and Devi bring the twins who do yell and splash. I am glad to have finished my bath. We go into the prayer room after our bath and I sit on the cement floor and take in the scent of fresh jasmine, incense and burning oil. But soon the twins join me and there is no time for quiet solitude.

"Now say your prayers," Ayah says.

The twins argue about who gets to ring the tiny brass bell. I am too tired to listen to them. Ayah comes in and tucks me in and rubs my back. I murmur a thanks and start to fall asleep. I sit up when I hear the sound of weeping, coming from outside. "Amma," I call.

But there is no answer. The house is still and dark. My cousins sleep in the other bedrooms and share mats in the dressing rooms. My mother and twins are down the hall in the third bedroom and I don't want wake up the three-year olds. So I go into my bathroom and stand on an upturned plastic bucket and look out the screened window. The big jacaranda tree and its branches cast scary shadows on the tiled roof of the bathhouse. The bathroom's windows are covered in fine mesh to keep bugs out and in the moonlight the shadows outside are like monsters in one of Ayah's stories.

I rub my eyes and stare into the gloom, but I can't see anything. I listen and in the warm silence I think I hear faint moaning and weeping. I know I should go back to bed, but I want to find out what's going on. Ayah is always telling me that I'm a brave girl. I slip the latch off the wooden door of the bathroom and step outside into the moonlight.

There is a faint flickering glow coming from the narrow windows of the bathhouse. I stand in the shadows trying to decide where to go when I see a ray of light coming toward me from the direction of our kitchen. The beam gets closer and I see it is Ayah with a kerosene lantern in one hand and her medicine bag in the other.

Ayah is a healer and people come from all over to ask for her help. Sometimes I go with her when she has to visit an ill person and she lets me carry her cloth bag of dried herbs. My mother doesn't let me go if the sickness will make me ill too. I want to call out to her, but I know I'm not supposed to be wandering around at night, so I stay silent and slip back into the unlit doorway.

She quickly walks past me into the bathhouse and when she opens the door, I hear the moans and cries clearly. As soon as Ayah shuts the door, I step out from the shadows. The bathhouse windows are too high for me to look through, but there are small, narrow slits, the size of bricks on one side. I creep to the side of the bathhouse and squat down and peer through the narrow opening. I'm protected in the pitch-dark here, surrounded by night shadows.

My bare feet make no noise on the soft cold earth and I wish I had worn my slippers. Inside the bathhouse, illumination from an oil lamp and two kerosene lanterns casts a warm mellow glow. My aunt lies in front of the fire on an old mattress that had once been on our bed. She is naked and her body is covered in sweat. Her head is propped up and her face twists with pain. Her breasts hang low on her chest, her nipples dark and big. Her stomach quivers and is covered with a network of pale, stretch marks.

Ayah gets in my way for a moment and I can't see what's happening. When she moves away, I can see my mother kneeling beside my aunt. She raises my aunt's head to give her a sip from a small brass cup.

"Why did you do this to yourself," she asks. "Ayah here could have helped you."

"Instead of coming to me for help she went to that old woman in the village and that old fraud used a sharpened oleander stick to get rid of the growing baby," Ayah says.

"You don't understand," gasps my aunt. "I knew I had to do something. I couldn't go through with it again. Seven is more than enough."

She gasps and a flood of blood and liquid pour out from between her bare thighs. Ayah uses rags to wipe up the blood and says to my mother, "Give her more tea to drink and pour some of that herbal medicine in it."

More fluid flows from between my aunt's legs. Ayah changes the rags and my mother gives my aunt sips of herb tea.

My limbs are starting to cramp and my bare feet are cold, but I don't want to leave. I stand up and stretch my tired legs and back.

"Ahhh," a loud screech makes me jump. I bend down and peer back into the dim bathhouse. My aunt is doubled over in pain.

"A little baby, even another boy, can't be as bad as this," my mother says to Ayah, who shakes her head. I see my aunt is almost asleep, her face pale and exhausted.

Ayah pours a tiny amount of herbal oil into her palms and then she massages my aunt's belly with sure firm strokes.

"If she's up to it, let's wash her," she says to my mother. "Then she can go to sleep."

My aunt wakes up and nods her head. Both women roll her off the mattress onto a bamboo mat. Ayah takes out a pouch of dried herbs and sprinkles them in a large bucket of steaming hot water. I wrinkle my nose when I get a whiff of the bitter smell of the herbs. Ayah and my mother pour the herbal water over my aunt, dry her and tie clean rags between her legs.

They wrap her in a clean sheet and lead her to another mat.

"Let her sleep, that's the best thing for her now," Ayah says. "You go to bed, little mother. I'll stay here and keep the fire burning so your sister is warm."

My mother nods wearily, "Wake me up, if there is any change. Tomorrow she can have some of the rasam Devi made today."

Rasam, a spicy broth rich with garlic, cumin and black peppercorns, is my mother's answer to all ailments. The dark and tangy soup is part of every meal because my mother believes it aids digestion. I love to mix the flavorful stock with rice and creamy yogurt. Thinking about the mouth-watering soup, I almost miss hearing my mother close the bathhouse door. I quickly wipe my feet on the coarse coconut fiber doormat and get in bed.

"Oh, no. Who left the door open," I hear my mother mutter.

I crawl deeper in the covers and wait for her to come and scold me. Even as I wait I fall asleep.

The next morning when I'm in the kitchen, sipping my warm milk and sugar, I ask my mother, "Where's Big Aunty?"

"She has a fever and is not feeling well," she says.

"Can I go see her? Is she…."

I almost ask if she is still in the bathhouse. Instead I say, "Is she going to die?"

My mother looks at me with a strange expression. I tremble at her sharp look.

"No, Meena, she won't die. Instead of asking foolish questions, go make yourself useful and see if Bhojan has come to get the milk."

Bhojan arrives early every morning to milk the cows. I search for him in the fields behind our house. As I walk back I see the doctor's car pulling into our driveway. I find one of my cousins playing marbles in the inner courtyard.

"Hey, brother, can I play too."

"Here," he tosses me a bright blue marble. "You can keep it."

"Thanks," I roll the smooth marble between my fingers. "Why is the doctor here?"

He looks up at me. I see dried tears on his cheeks.

"Oh, brother. Your mother will be fine," I say and throw my arms around his neck. He hugs me close.

"OK you two. Is that the way you play marbles?" Ayah asks.

I laugh and sit back.

"Look, Ayah. Look what brother gave me."

She peers down at the shining marble in my hand.

"That's a very nice marble. Brother, the doctor said your mother will be well soon. Her fever is already gone."

My cousin's eyes are bright with happiness.

"Come on Meenakutty. I'll show you how to shoot marbles."

I don't like being called kutty anymore because only babies are called kutty, but I don't mind when my cousins call me by that name.

A few days later, my aunt and her sons leave. She is pale and moves slowly. I hear my mother tell Ayah that my aunt will never have children again. I remember that night in the bathhouse and my mother's words, "No son can hurt this much."

Rasam or Pepper Water Broth

4 cloves of garlic peeled or sliced into thin slivers.
½ teaspoon cumin seeds or powder
½ teaspoon black peppercorns or coarsely ground pepper
1-2 tablespoons of oil or ghee or unsalted butter
1 or 2 tomatoes cut into large pieces
1 teaspoon turmeric powder
½ teaspoon salt
2 teaspoon tamarind concentrate
½ cup red lentils, rinsed
2 cups water
1 tablespoon brown sugar
1 tablespoon fresh cilantro/coriander leaves, chopped finely.

Preparation: Crush the garlic cloves, cumin seeds and peppercorns in a mortal and pestle or use the optional powders. Heat the oil or butter in a large saucepan. Add crushed garlic and spices and let the mixture sizzle. Add chopped tomatoes, stir well. Add turmeric, salt and lentils. Add water, tamarind concentrate and let mixture boil. Simmer covered for about 20 minutes or until lentils are soft. Taste for salt. The broth should be faintly sour and pungent. Add sugar and cilantro leaves before serving over warm rice.

Serves 2 as a side dish.

Chapter Thirteen

Lakshmi and Gopal

• • • • • • • • • •

My mother is a gentle person who rarely yells, screams or throws a tantrum. She leaves all the drama to me. She is always telling me that my lungs are like giant balloons that fill up with air and that my screams can be heard all the way across our valley. I know she disapproves of my emotional flare-ups by the way she presses her lips together. In our small town my mother is known for her generous nature and compassionate heart.

Just like her soothing presence, my mother's kitchen is a place of comfort and solace. The once white-washed walls are discolored by the smoke from the kitchen hearth and if I press my nose against the grey walls I think I can smell all the curries, pilafs and vegetables my mother has cooked in that room.

She helps mend broken spirits and bodies in this humble room. That is exactly what she tries to do for Lakshmi and Gopal. The couple, who is practically ancient in my twelve-year-old eyes, lives in a small house on the Lane, a row of 12 houses just across the street from our rambling bungalow.

The simple cottages on the Lane are built close together and have only a single wall separating them from one another. This morning I'm with Ayah when she visits Janaki's sick baby. Janaki's house is small, compared to mine. There are only two rooms, one for sleeping and a kitchen with a wood fireplace for cooking. At the back of house there is a small washing and bathing area. In some houses, the bathing area is hung with bamboo mats so that it's somewhat private, but Janaki's house has no privacy.

"Thank you for coming Ayah," she says to us. "The baby is not sleeping well."

"Do you have any fresh water?" Ayah asks her.

"I have to go get it from the tap."

"You go ahead and get me some water," Ayah picks up the whimpering baby. "I'll take care of the little one."

Janaki picks up a round brass pot and makes her way to the public tap. Since there is no running water in the Lane, everyone has to use the public pump near the bus stop. This is a busy place and some days I sit on the stone wall that surrounds our house and watch the children splash in the muddy waters. They look like they are having so much fun and wish I could join them. But I know Ayah would say I live in the Big House and cannot play with street urchins.

"They are not of our class, Meenakutty," she says when I question her. "They work in the fields and tea plantations just like their parents before them. You are born into a family that is blessed with many privileges. Like your mother you must learn to use these privileges to help people, but that doesn't mean you can socialize and play with them."

The twins always beg Ayah to let them jump in the water puddles. I don't ask her anymore because I know it upsets her, but that doesn't keep the twins from pleading.

But as I watch the children and their mothers, big sisters and grandmothers fill round brass vessels with clean drinking water and carry the full pots on their heads to their homes on the Lane, I sometimes wish one of my own privileges would be to play on the street. The women make many trips to the pump every morning and evening. The sound of the water mingles with the voices of the women raised in song or gossip.

When Janaki comes back with the water, Ayah washes her hands, and peers into the baby's eyes and throat. When Ayah presses the baby's tummy, he starts to cry.

"Janaki, I think your baby has gas. I'll leave some herb oil to rub on his stomach and make sure you do a good job burping him."

Janaki promises to do as Ayah says and we head back home.

"How would you like to get a cup of hot tea, little one?" Ayah asks me.

"Can we go to the tea stall?"

I like to visit the tea stall with Ayah who is very fond of the milky tea and salty snacks. The tea stall owner makes the tea frothy by pouring the hot liquid from one container to another so that it looks like a long piece of silky ribbon. Ayah always buys me a small treat—a lentil cake or bit of bread and mashed potatoes. My mother doesn't like me or the twins to eat the greasy food from the road side vendor. I know there are flies sitting on the wooden counters, but I think the food is delicious. My mouth waters with anticipation as Ayah hands me a small container of yellow potatoes. The creamy mixture is smooth on my tongue and melts in my mouth. The small bits of crunchy pepper, the zing of fresh ginger and the lemony flavor of the mashed vegetable all meld into an irresistible and tasty snack. Sometimes there are green peas or bits of carrots in the potatoes. I use a piece of bread to carefully scoop a bit of the bright yellow mixture. The flavors explode in my mouth and even my mother's tasty potatoes stew can't compare to the tangy flavor of the tea stall dish. Now that my hunger is satisfied I look up and see that Gopal is seated on the other end of the wooden bench.

He is thin and his arms are all knotty like the pear tree in our garden and I think he must be old as that ancient tree. He is always smoking beedis and smells of smoke and sweat. I'm not surprised to see him at the snack shack because I've seen him here every time we walk to the bus stop. He must spend most of his day sitting in the sun, talking to the tea stall owner or reading a newspaper.

He lights a beedi and the foul-smelling smoke from the cigarette creeps into my nose. I wrinkle my nose at the pungent scent.

I think Ayah would like to smoke a beedi too but I know she doesn't smoke in public. She watches Gopal inhale the pearly grey smoke and says nothing.

Gopal winks at me.

"Here miss, go buy yourself a lentil cake," he says and gives me a small coin.

"Hey, she doesn't need any more oily food. Her mother will give me trouble," Ayah says with a glare.

Gopal smiles, "So, let her buy it next time. You know just now you sounded just like my Lakshmi. That woman has a sharp tongue."

The vendor hears Gopal and chuckles.

"And sharp claws too, eh," he says with a funny laugh.

Gopal gets up and stamps on his beedi stub on the earthen floor.

"Time for me to go," he mumbles and leaves quickly.

"Why did he leave Ayah?" I ask.

Ayah says nothing. Her expression is sad and she shakes her head wearily

I can't help thinking how different he is from his wife Lakshmi. She and Gopal are one of the older couples who live in the Lane. Lakshmi looks very old but I think she is a lot younger than Ayah, who has only one or two teeth in her mouth. Lakshmi wears nose rings in both sides of her nose. She has a black tattoo mark on her forehead which is long and wavy like a snake. It disappears into a wrinkle on her forehead and weaves into her hair. She is a day laborer and works at a construction site a few kilometers from our house. Every morning, she leaves for work with a small basket on her head containing her tin lunch pail wrapped in cloth. Ayah says her work is to cut up big stones into smaller pieces. When there are no more rocks to break up, she spends her time on the tea plantation picking the tender green tea shoots. Our house is surrounded by gentle slopes of tea bushes and workers are always needed to pick the tea leaves and carry them to the sheds for processing into black tea.

A few days later, I'm sitting in the branches of an old poinsettia tree in our front yard when I hear shouting and yelling from across the street. I hurry down and climb on to the stone wall to see what the commotion is all about.

"What's going on?" I yell to a girl who is standing close to our gate.

"It's Lakshmi and Gopal. They're fighting."

I hear footsteps behind me and see Ayah hurrying out.

"Ayah, Ayah. Where are you going?"

"Meena, you need to stay right here. I'll be back. Let me go see what the fuss is all about."

I have no intention of staying behind and missing all the excitement. I follow her across the street to the Lane.

"You are a good for nothing old bag of bones. You're not worth feeding. I should break your miserable head," I hear Lakshmi's voice yelling.

I don't like the sound of her angry voice. I look around at the crowd gathered in front of the Lane.

They don't look frightened. In fact, one of the men laughs and a woman giggles and shakes her head. I begin to feel a little better. Perhaps it's all a joke and Lakshmi is flying into a fit of rage like my brother Appu when he doesn't get his way.

Ayah uses her fists on the wooden door.

"It's me Ayah. Let me in. Come on, open up."

There is only silence. Lakshmi is not yelling anymore. Everyone is quiet and waiting.

"I'll call the police, if you don't open the door," Ayah yells.

The door swings open. I work my way to the front of the crowd and look into the dark interior of the house. At first I can't see anything but as my eyes get used to the gloomy darkness I see there are pots and pans all over the ground. Clothes and newspapers are scattered. It looks like a huge wind storm had come through the house and blown everything around. In all this mess I almost don't see Gopal on the ground. He doesn't move. I hear Lakshmi crying in the kitchen doorway.

"Your anger will kill him one day," I hear Ayah scolding.

"I didn't mean to hit him so hard. But he makes me so mad," Lakshmi says. "He just never answers back."

Ayah comes back out.

"Shoo, everyone go. There is nothing to see here. You little miss, go find your mother and bring her back."

I turn around to get my mother but she is already crossing the road and soon comes into the house.

"Oh, oh....Not again. Will they ever learn," she mutters as she walks by me.

I walk into the house behind her. She and Ayah lift Gopal's head and place a folded blanket under it. His forehead is all red and swollen. There is blood streaming down his face. I watch them clean and bandage the cut.

"I think this cut needs stitches," Ayah says.

"Let's get the doctor," my mother agrees.

She turns to me, "Go and see if Raman and Bhojan are still in the cowshed and ask them to come help carry this old man."

I run all the way to our house. I hear her ask a man from the Lane to go call our family doctor, Dr. Sampath.

Soon, Gopal is resting on an old mattress in the storeroom, right next to our kitchen. Dr. Sampath comes in and shakes his head. I'm sent out of the room while the doctor examines Gopal.

"These people never learn," I hear him say to my mother.

My mother is not happy. I can see her lips are pressed together very tightly.

"Just send the bill to me Doctor. Thank you for coming."

"Yes, yes. Keep him quiet, and if he has a headache or sees double, send him to the government hospital tomorrow morning."

I ask my mother to make some special tea stall potatoes for Gopal. The next day I take a plate of potatoes and glass of hot tea to Gopal who is sitting up on in his mattress.

"Thank you Meena. You are kind and loving just like your mother," he says in a strange wobbly voice. "Don't ever change."

A week later, Gopal is able to walk slowly.

"I'm ready to go home, little mother. Thank you for taking care of me," he says to my mother.

"Be careful Gopal."

"Don't go back," says Ayah.

"You know I can't stay here forever. My home is with my wife."

"She'll kill you one day," Ayah says.

"No, no. She is irritable, but she won't really hurt me."

I watch Gopal walk down our driveway and out of the front gate. He's going back to his house on the Lane. I turn to Ayah and ask, "Why did he get hurt Ayah?"

"Because Lakshmi hit him little one."

"But why?"

"Because she is a mean old lady."

"But why does he let her hit him."

"People do strange things and we don't know why, little one."

"Doesn't Lakshmi love him?"

"I think she does in her own way, but she can't take good care of him."

"If someone hit me, I would run away."

"That old man doesn't have your sense, little one, even though you are just twelve years old. Never let anyone hurt you."

I nod and feel so sad that I start to cry.

"I wish he could have lived with us," I sob.

Ayah hugs me. Mother lifts me onto her lap even though I'm almost too big to fit on her lap. I hide my face in her neck and cry for Gopal's pain.

Mother's Tea Stall Potatoes

2 Russet potatoes, washed and cut in half
5 tablespoons vegetable oil or ghee
Pinch of asafetida (Hing)
1/2 teaspoon cumin seeds
1/2 teaspoon mustard seeds
1/2 teaspoon turmeric
1 tablespoon finely minced or grated fresh ginger
1/2 teaspoon salt (adjust to taste)
1-2 teaspoon lemon juice
1 tablespoon chopped cilantro
Optional additions: ½ cup minced onion; ½ cup fresh or frozen peas; 1 small green chili chopped and ½ cup minced red sweet pepper.
Garnishes: Fresh minced coriander leaves.

Preparation: Boiled the potatoes until they are soft and let cool. Peel and coarsely mash the potatoes. Heat the oil in a frying pan on medium high. Add mustard seeds and wait for the seeds to stop popping. Add cumin seeds and asafetida. (Add any of the optional vegetables and cook them) Add turmeric, potatoes, minced ginger, and salt. Stir-fry for a few minutes, until the potatoes are a uniform golden color.

Add lemon juice and cilantro.

The potatoes should be slightly moist not dry.

Serve hot with Indian bread or wheat tortillas.

Chapter Fourteen

A Thief in the Night

• • • • • • • • • •

"As a toddler Lord Krishna was very mischievous and always getting into trouble. One sunny afternoon, he woke up from his nap and went to look for his mother. She was in the kitchen, getting ready to churn cream into sweet butter. Krishna asked for a snack and she told him she would get him the snack as soon as she was finished with the churning. "Can't I just have a taste of the sweet butter?" he asked his mother. His mother gave him a small handful of the fresh butter and Krishna liked the taste so much that he asked for more. But his mother told him that the butter was not quite ready and to go outside and play with his cowherd friends. Little Krishna went outside and decided the goats needed some exercise. So, he untied all the goats and the creatures ran around the yard, tearing into the garden and the clean laundry that was hanging out to dry. Krishna's moth-er, Yasodha, ran outside to see what all the commotion was about and saw the goats racing around her garden. It took her a long time but finally she was able to catch all the goats and tie them up again. But when she came back into the kitchen, she found the churn on its

side and buttermilk all over the floor. Sitting on the floor was Lord Krishna, his face smeared with sweet butter. Yasodha was angry to see her buttermilk on the ground but she had to laugh at Krishna's smile. She picked him up and hugged him and called him "her little butter thief."

—as narrated by Muthi

"Why is every cup dirty? Didn't you wash the dishes last night?"

"I washed and dried everything little mother. I know I did."

The loud voices wake me up and I jump out of bed. It is still early in the morning and I shiver as my bare feet touch the cold cement floor. I hurriedly push my feet into a pair of rubber flip-flops and head toward the kitchen. I can clearly hear my mother's voice. I make my way to the kitchen from the third bedroom which I share with Ayah.

My mother is standing next to the large wooden table. Devi is right by the table with a cup in her hand. Her face is red and she looks upset.

"I'm telling you little mother, I washed all the cups and saucers before going to bed last night," Devi says, waving the cup in the air. "I don't know why there was milk left in the two cups."

"These are the two good cups we used yesterday afternoon," Muthi says, holding up the other delicate green cup.

"What exactly is the trouble?" my mother asks, "You'll wake up the four-year-olds with all this yelling."

"Alright little mother, I'll tell you what happened," Devi begins in a calmer, softer voice. "This morning as usual I came over from my house a little after the first rooster crowed."

"It was about six in the morning," Muthi interrupts. "I heard her opening the kitchen door so I got up to have a warm cup of coffee."

"I turned on the light in this room," Devi uses her hands to gesture toward the outer room of the kitchen. "I nearly stumbled over a foot stool in the way. I stopped and put it to the side and came into the kitchen and started the fire going."

"I came in right behind her," Muthi says. "The cups and saucers were draining on the table. So I thought I'd put them away before Bhojan and Raman come in with the milk.

"I started to put the cups away when I noticed two of the cups were sitting in their saucers."

"I know I put them down to drain," says Devi, her voice starting to rise again with emotion. "I can't imagine leaving dirty dishes on the table."

"What happened next?" my mother asks Muthi. "What did you do?"

"I looked at the dirty cups in the light and there was a sticky residue on the bottom of each cup. It looked like dried milk and sugar."

"Well, we served the priests tea, not milk and sugar," my mother says.

Fifteen Hours Ago

It is late afternoon and we have some unexpected guests. The two Franciscan monks are the whitest men I have ever seen. They wear long brown robes with hoods and have knotted ropes around their waists. Their long pale toes stick out from beneath their flowing robes.

"We are the newest members of the Franciscan community," one the priests says in a soft voice. "So sorry to drop by without any warning, but we had no way to get in touch with you except in person."

"Please come in," my mother invites the two men into our living room. "Meena, go ask Ayah or Muthi to make some tea and snacks for the visitors."

"Please sister, we don't want to be a bother. We just came to say hello and bring our good wishes to your twins on their fourth birthday," the other priest says. He is a large man with a big belly that sticks out from under his brown robes. He wears glasses and his eyes behind them are large and filled with fun. He looks like a man who loves to laugh and eat.

"It's not a bother at all," my mother assures him. "We always enjoy visits from the Franciscan brothers."

The two men sit on the wooden sofa in the living room and I walk away to find Muthi or Devi.

"Little one, before you go, here is something for you." The fat priest holds out a brown bag. The bag appears like magic in his hands. Where had he kept that package?

I eagerly reach for the bag.

"Thank you sir for the present. What is it?"

"Wildflower honey from our bees," the younger priest answers. He, like his companion, has a thick, full beard. He looks very serious, but there is gentleness about it that I like.

"This year the honey is flavored with the local eucalyptus blossoms. Usually, the orange trees have the strongest flavor," he says. "We also brought you a loaf of brown bread."

"Did you make the bread too?" I ask, holding the strange shaped loaf in my hand. The loaf is round and very brown, not like the square white bread we buy from the bakery in Mahagiri.

"Oh yes, Meena. We bake the bread every few days. We also grow or make everything. You and your mother and the twins should visit our monastery. The gardens are beautiful and even St. Francis would be impressed at how many birds visit our orchards."

"Who is St. Francis?" I ask.

Before the two men can answer, my mother reminds me to go get some tea for the visitors. I reluctantly leave the room with the honey and loaf of bread. I find Devi in the kitchen and she agrees to make some tea.

"Kutty, look in the pantry and see if we still have some banana chips or cashews to serve with the tea."

I find a bag of each and bring them to Devi. She has taken down our fancy china cups and tea pot. I am not allowed to drink from these fragile cups because they are so delicate. I run a finger around the rim of the cup which is a pale green and reminds me of a jade statue I have seen at a neighbor's home. There are deep purple flowers painted on the outside of the cup and dark green leaves and vines all around the handle of the cup and the saucer.

Devi fills the matching tea pot with a mixture of tea and hot milk. She places a small silver cup with sugar cubes, plates of cashews and banana chips and the cups and saucers on a large wooden tray.

"Come with me and help serve the snacks," she says over her shoulder to me.

We enter the living room and the conversation stops while we serve the hot tea.

"Aren't you drinking anything Meena?" the fat priest asks me.

"I'm not allowed to drink from those cups," I say.

"Really Meena, you can have a sip of tea if you want," my mother says. "You can also tell them the reason you aren't allowed to drink too much tea."

I blush. "I talk too much when I drink tea." I murmur looking down at my toes. "I'm not allowed to drink from china cups because I dropped one last time and it broke into bits."

"Devi, can you go bring a stainless steel tumbler for Meena and a glass of buttermilk for me?" my mother asks.

A few minutes later, I am sipping the tea, sweetened with three sugar cubes.

"Well, Meena, we are waiting to hear you talk," the young priest says with a smile. "Has the tea kicked in yet?"

I laugh. "I would like to hear more about St. Francis."

The fat priest laughs too. "She knows how to keep us talking. One of my favorite St. Francis stories is about him and the birds. One day, St. Francis was walking with his companions and he noticed there were a lot of birds flying around in the valley. He stopped and looked at the birds and started talking to them. Then, something wonderful happened. The birds stopped flying around and chirping and came and sat on St. Francis's shoulder and all around him to listen to the saint's voice. St. Francis told them about God's love and the birds listened.

"Our gardens at the monastery are filled with all kinds of animals. We have deer, rabbits and many varieties of birds. There is a stone statue of St. Francis in our vegetable garden and everyday we find many birds sitting on the statue's arms and shoulders, even his head," the priest laughs again. "St. Francis would have liked Mahagiri and south India because people here are so kind to animals."

I am enthralled and want to hear more about this gentle saint. "Tell me another story."

"One day, St. Francis found a rabbit caught in a trap. He stopped and released the rabbit and told him to be more careful and set him free but the rabbit refused to go back to the woods and wanted to stay close to the saint."

I want to ask for another story, but we hear Appu's voice. He is awake from his afternoon nap. Soon Thangam will be awake too. The brothers leave soon after, promising to return.

Present day

"Now, I remember, we only served them tea," Devi says, her voice bringing me back to the present. "I also remember I showed Meena how to wash the cups."

"That's right Amma, Devi did show me how to rinse the cups and turn them upside down on the saucers so that they would dry," I pipe up.

"So it seems like we had a mysterious visitor who came to drink milk," my mother says.

"A thief?" Muthi asks in disbelief. "One who comes to drink milk? I have never heard of such a thing."

"Devi, make sure nothing is missing from the kitchen. Was the door locked when you came in this morning?"

"I can't remember little mother, but from now on I'll make sure I lock the door at night."

Devi finds that nothing is missing from the kitchen. The pan with the day-old milk, usually stored in the pantry cupboard, is almost empty and the sugar bowl needs to be filled again. It looks like our thief just wanted a sweet drink.

For the next few days, Bhojan sleeps in the kitchen. He curls up in front of the hearth on a thick blanket and waits for the thief, who never shows up. I am excited and a little frightened to think a thief is wandering around our house at night, mixing sugar and milk in the best china cups and drinking it down. I refuse to go the bathroom alone after dark and insist someone accompany me to the bathhouse. I jump at sudden noises and see spooky shadows in every dark corner. I don't like to feel unsafe in my own house.

Every morning about 11 o'clock, our mailman arrives with the day's mail. He wears a khaki-colored uniform and carries a huge cloth bag on his shoulder filled with letters, newspapers and magazines. He walks from Mahagiri and his first stop is our house. When he gets here, he goes into the kitchen for a cup of hot tea or cool buttermilk. He sits down on the wooden bench and chats with Devi or my mother. Besides the letters, he also delivers the latest news and gossip. Sometimes he stops by at the end of the day for a snack and to pick up any letters my mother needs mailed.

This Tuesday morning, he is very excited and can hardly wait to talk to my mother.

"Little mother, I just heard some disturbing news," he says, patting his forehead with a white cotton handkerchief. "The Nelsons down the street had a break-in last night."

The Nelsons are two British women who live a short walk from us. Grace Nelson and her sister, Faith, live in a small, stuffy bungalow that is filled with cats. Their cats are allowed to roam around the house, sit on tables and sleep on the beds. My mother says I can have a pet kitten the next time one of the Nelson cats gives birth.

"Are the sisters alright?" my mother asks.

"They are fine. It is a strange story," the mailman says. He takes a sip of cool buttermilk before continuing, "They said they walked into the kitchen yesterday morning and found someone had come in at night and eaten slices of bread and butter. They usually lock everything in a cupboard to keep the cats from getting into it but the lock in the cupboard is broken and they hadn't fixed it yet. They knew the cats hadn't eaten the bread because a knife was used to cut the bread. It's a puzzle."

Later that day, we hear that the sisters have called in the police, but the local police constable doesn't have any clues about the puzzling theft of bread, butter and a few spoonfuls of pear jam.

"That thief must have been hungry," Grace Nelson tells my mother when we see her at the local market. "We've started locking the doors and making sure we put all the food away at night."

There are no more incidents reported and everyone begins to forget about the strange thief. I still find it hard to sleep at night and lie awake listening to the night noises. To help me feel safer, my mother suggests I invite Kumari for a sleepover. So the next Friday night, my friend and I spend a pleasant evening dressing up in my mother's old saris and jewelry. We admire the heavy silk saris and try on all the bangles on my mother's dresser. Kumari likes the glass bangles and the way they tinkle on her skinny arms.

After dinner and a bath, we sit in my huge bed reading out loud from a story book with colorful illustrations. Ayah comes in with a tray and two steaming stainless steel tumblers.

"Here is some hot almond milk to help you sleep. There's plenty of honey in it for sweet dreams."

Hot milk, flavored with ground almonds, a slight hint of vanilla and plenty of wildflower honey is one of my favorite bedtime drinks.

"Ayah, is the honey from the St. Francis garden?"

"Yes it is little one. It also has a little bit of vanilla."

The soothing drink warms me up, right down to my toes. Kumari and I sigh with satisfaction at the sweet taste of honeyed milk and giggle at our milk moustaches.

"Rinse your mouths and then turn off the light and go to bed," Ayah says. "Don't forget to use the restroom. You don't want to have to get up at night."

We walk to the adjoining bathroom and rinse our mouths and come back to bed. We pull the heavy quilt over our heads and try to go to sleep. Sometime later we know Ayah is asleep because she starts to snore.

"Doesn't she sound like a train," Kumari whispers.

"Not a train, she sounds like a lorry horn that is broken," I whisper back.

We stop giggling when we hear a thud.

"What's that?" Kumari says, clutching my arm.

I sit up and stare out of the half open doorway, "Shh…it's probably Devi leaving for the night."

"What if it's the burglar?"

I tremble at the thought. "It can't be."

We hold hands and sit as still as we can. Even Ayah has stopped snoring and the night is very still and dark.

"Do you want to walk to the store room and look across the courtyard?"

"No," Kumari says.

"Come on, we'll be inside the house and we can see the kitchen door through the windows."

Kumari refuses to come.

"I'll be right back," I say and get out of bed. I carefully step over Ayah and slip out through the half open door. My feet are cold but I don't want to put on my sandals and wake up Ayah. It is dark in the hallway and I slowly make my way into the storage room. The door swings open without a sound. The bags of rice and bunches of bananas are clearly visible in the pale moonlight. This storage room has a big glass window that overlooks the inner courtyard.

The storage room is partitioned off on one side and this small area is used as place of worship. Here my mother and Ayah or Muthi light oil lamps and incense, and pray to the statues of gods and goddesses. The air still carries a hint of burnt oil lamp and fragrant incense. I stop in front of the pooja room doorway and mutter a prayer to lord Ganesha to keep me safe from the thief.

I step over an old pillow and stand on a roll of blankets to peer through the glass window. I feel something soft touch my elbow and I nearly lose my balance. I'm about to scream when a voice whispers, "Sorry to startle you." Kumari is beside me. "I couldn't let you go alone."

My heart is thudding and I hang onto her in relief. Both of us stand on the pile of blankets and look out onto the courtyard. The kitchen courtyard is bathed in bright moonlight. We gasp and hug each other when see a shadow make its way to the kitchen door. The door is apparently locked and the figure is fiddling with the lock. We turn around and this time we run inside, not caring if we wake up Ayah.

"Ayah, wake up, wake up!"

Ayah makes groggy noises and opens her eyes.

"What's going on?"

"Someone is trying to break into the kitchen," I say, dragging on Ayah's arm.

She gets up, muttering under her breath about 13-year-olds and their wild imagination.

"It's true Ayah. We saw someone," Kumari says.

"You girls wait here. Bhojan is sleeping in the hallway and I'll get him."

Ayah walks stiffly out to the main hallway. We hear voices and a shrill scream. Kumari and I walk down the hall. All the lights are ablaze in the hallway and kitchen and we can clearly see Ayah and Muthi in the doorway. Bhojan is struggling to hold someone. It is a boy and Bhojan has twisted his hand and is kneeling on the boys' back.

"Girls, move out of the way and let me see what's going on," my mother says. She pushes us side and walks into the kitchen. "Bhojan? Who is this?"

"Ayah came and woke me up and told me that the girls had had seen someone breaking into the kitchen. When I came down the hallway, I found this thief trying to break in."

"I'm not a thief," the figure on the ground says. "Let me go."

"Bhojan, let him stand up," my mother says.

When Bhojan removes his knee, I can see he is a young boy with a defiant and angry face. He is skinny and dressed in a ragged pair of shorts and a thin undershirt.

"I'm not a thief," he says again, looking at my mother and rubbing the shoulder Bhojan had twisted.

"Then what are you doing sneaking around at night?"

"I'm hungry so I came to get a little something to eat and drink."

"Why?"

"Because…because I have no place to go and I'm hungry. Please, mistress, don't call the police. They will take me away to jail and lock me up."

"You should have thought of that before sneaking in and stealing," Muthi says angrily. "Did you sneak into other homes too?"

"I had to eat. I didn't want to beg. I tried to ask for work but no one wanted to hire a teenager. Once I got a job in another town pulling weeds. But after working all day the woman refused to pay me and I had to leave with nothing."

My mother doesn't say anything and I lift my head to look at her. Her face is set and stern, but I can see a little softening in her eyes. I look back at the boy and want to tell him everything is going to be all right. My mother will take care of him. The boy looks scared and his face is streaked with dirt and angry tears. I feel sorry for him. My mother has a thoughtful look on her face.

"Alright, Bhojan, take him to the bathhouse and get him cleaned up. There are some old clothes in the store room for him. Muthi, please go find him some leftovers and something to drink."

"Muthi can you please make more almond milk for us?" I ask in my most pleading voice.

Muthi looks down at me and smiles. "I suppose I can find some milk for you."

The boy, Jaibal, becomes a part of our household. After he apologizes to our neighbors for sneaking into their homes, the Nelson sisters hire him to take care of their cats. When my mother learns that he is only 16 years old, she enrolls him at the local government school. A few years later when my mother buys an old car, Jaibal fixes it up. He keeps it running and officially becomes our driver. He also learns how to make the most delicious almond milk, grinding the sweet nuts and mixing it with warm milk. His almond drink becomes a bedtime routine in our household.

Almond Honey Milk

¼ cup blanched almonds
2 cups milk
¼ teaspoon cardamom seeds or 1-inch piece of vanilla bean
3-4 tablespoons honey

Preparation: Place nuts in a blender or food processor and pulse until finely chopped. Add about 2/3 cup milk and process until smooth. Pour this mixture into a heavy-bottomed saucepan and add the rest of the milk. Heat over medium heat, stirring constantly, and bring to a full boil. Remove from heat; add cardamom seeds or vanilla bean. Boil once more. Remove from heat and add honey. Heat again to a boil and strain the mixture using a strainer. Pour milk back and forth from the pan to a cup so that the mixture is frothy. Serve immediately.

Chapter Fifteen

Trouble

• • • • • • • • • •

When Kumari's father comes to pick her from after our pajama party, he is a little upset to find out that my mother has not arrested Jaibal.

"Really Sudha," he says. "You shouldn't be so lenient with the boy. He will grow up to be a hardened criminal."

"That's just the point Colonel, he is not a hardened criminal and I wanted to give him a chance be something else," my mother says.

"That's all very well and good but once a thief, always a thief. Just like those bloody gypsies, camping out at the Maidan."

The Maidan is a large grassy meadow a short distance from our house and is used by many local cowherds as a grazing area for their cattle. Kumari's father and other men were trying to convert the meadow into a golfing range and to keep out the cattle.

"There are several cartloads of them right now and I wanted to inform the local police about them," the colonel says.

"Usually the gypsies only stay there for a couple of days before moving on," my mother says. "Perhaps you should just let them stay. After all, if the Maidan becomes a golf course, then they won't be able to camp there."

"I suppose," he agrees. "In any case, I'm going to stop by the camp and warn the buggers that I'm keeping an eye on them."

I'm going to spend the day with Kumari and after saying good-bye, we climb into her car. Everyone calls Kumari's father the colonel because he is an officer in the Indian Army. His job takes him far away from home for long periods of time. Soon he plans to leave for the Kashmir region in north India.

Today, Chelappan has the day off so Kumari's father is driving the car. When we arrive at the Maidan, he pulls to the side of the road and shuts off the car.

"Girls, please stay in the car. I'm just going to have a few words with the leader of this gang," the colonel says, closing the door with his elbow.

I can see the green meadow is dotted with a half a dozen brightly painted caravans. Several mules and horses graze on the nearby grass. Women in colorful robes are tending to a fire and the smoke rises in a blue-grey column. There are several small children running around between the caravans. The men wear bright green, blue and orange turbans and long black jackets over their white trousers.

I roll down the car window and peer outside. We are parked by a thick hedge and I hear a rustling in the bushes. I open the car door a crack to get a better view.

"Don't go outside," Kumari says in an urgent whisper. "My dad will be mad."

"I'm not going outside," I say. "I just want to look at something."

I open the car door a little wider and nearly close it again in surprise when I see a pair of bright eyes peering at me from between the branches of the hedge. A thin brown hand reaches out from the bushes and parts the leaves and I see a brown face peering at me.

"Have you come to chase us away?" a soft voice asks. She speaks in the local dialect that I use to speak with Bhojan and Kashi.

"No," I say. "Who are you?"

A girl about 10 years old emerges from the hedge and shakes off the dust and leaves from her brown hair. She is smaller than me and is painfully thin. She wears a bright green and pink skirt that is embroidered with little bits of mirror and a matching blouse. I can see her smooth belly when she lifts her arms to untangle her hair. She has many shiny bangles and bracelets on her arms that jangle when she moves.

"My name is Priya," she says with a shy smile. "Usually people stop to ask my mother to read their palms or to shout at us to go away."

"Why do they shout at you?"

Kumari leans over my shoulder and says, "Who are you talking to Meena?"

I move aside so that she can see Priya.

"People are scared of gypsies because they think we can curse people and make them go mad."

"Can you do that?" I ask.

"Of course not, silly," Priya giggles. "We are gypsies and we don't live in one spot for long. We camp at different places so that our animals can eat and we can make some money to buy food."

"You mean you don't live in house?"

"No, we wander all over the country. I like it best high in the hills because there aren't as many people who yell and chase us away. My father says one of these days we'll go back to the land of our ancestors but for now we are wandering gypsies."

"I think it's silly to wander the land," Kumari says over my shoulder. "My father says gypsies are all thieves."

My new friend clenches her small hands into fists and I can see an angry blush on her cheeks. "We are not thieves. We never take what doesn't belong to us. The sun and air are free."

I don't want them to fight, so I say in a soothing voice, "Priya where did you come from?"

Priya's face is still flushed but she looks at me and says, "We traveled up the mountain. The plains are hot and dusty right now and we wanted to find a cooler place to stay until the rains come in winter."

I want to hear more about Priya's travels but there are raised voices near the campfire.

"I better go now," Priya says with a frightened look.

"If you ever need help ask for Meena and little mother, that's my mother, at the Big House," I tell her. But I'm not sure she heard me because she has disappeared into the bushes.

We look over at the campfire and see Kumari's father is talking with angry gestures. The man he is confronting is smaller but his large moustache is bristling and he looks like he's ready to attack the colonel.

"We must do something," Kumari says in a worried voice.

I lean over and press down on the car horn as hard as I can. The loud noise surprises everyone and when the man turns away, Kumari's father runs over to the car.

"Are you girls all right?" he asks with an anxious look.

"Papa, we should go now," Kumari says.

The colonel turns back to the crowd of gypsies and yells, "If I hear of any thefts in this neighborhood, I'll call the police constable to arrest the whole lot."

We don't hear what the gypsy leader has to say because Kumari's father gets into the car and we drive off.

It is late that evening when Chelappan drives me home. We pass the gypsy camp and I can hear laughter and music. The camp fires cast an eerie glow in the meadow and I wonder if Priya is enjoying time with her family.

I hear nothing more about the gypsies for a few days until our mailman arrives one morning.

"Little mother, I tell you there is going to be trouble on the Maidan," he says, accepting a cup of hot tea from Devi.

"What do you mean?" my mother asks.

"It started yesterday when a woman from the dhobi village complained that several of the cloths she hung out to dry were missing. She ran around complaining and it turned out the silk sari that was missing belonged to colonel Sen's wife. He of course went and brought the police to the meadow and they ransacked the caravans and made a mess. The gypsies are threatening and the dhobi village is considering retaliating."

The dhobi village is a small community of washer men and women who live across from the maidan on the banks of the Mahagiri River. They wash soiled cloths in the river and beat them on the rocks to get them cleaned. By midday the rocky hillside is a mosaic of colorful clothes drying in the sun. Usually the dhobi villagers keep to themselves, leaving the village only to collect bundles of dirty laundry and returning with piles of neatly folded shirts, saris and bed sheets.

"Please Amma, can you help the gypsies?" I ask. "I know there are not thieves."

"And how do you know this Meena?" Devi asks, bringing my mother a cup of hot tea.

"I met a gypsy girl named Priya. She lives in a caravan with her family. She says they travel from place to place and they only take things that are free like sunshine and air."

"Humph," grunts the mailman in disbelief. "All gypsies are born thieves and liars. They never stay in one place because they rather steal than live like honest men and women."

I can tell my mother is annoyed by her frown that wrinkles her forehead. "Really, Ram, you should be careful about calling people thieves and liars without knowing anything about them."

She turns to me and says, "I'll send a message to the chief constable and see what is going on."

That evening just as the sun goes over the horizon and the first stars twinkle in the twilight sky, I am in the front yard, gathering the last of the rose buds for our nightly pooja ceremony when I see someone rattling the front gate.

I peer through the metal spaces and see that one of two figures is my gypsy friend Priya.

"Priya, is that you?"

"Oh Meena sister, please help us. This is my older brother Shiva and we need your help."

"Wait here and I'll get my mother."

I drop the blossoms on the grass and run inside to fetch my mother. She and Muthi are giving the twins their evening baths.

"Amma, my friend Priya is here and says she needs our help."

My mother looks up and wipes her wet face with end of her cotton sari which is also sopping wet.

Muthi looks at my mother, "You go little sister. I can handle these children."

My mother wrings the end of her sari and smoothes her hair. We go to the front yard and my mother lifts the latch and opens the gate.

"Priya, this is my mother and she can help you."

"Oh little mother, I didn't know what to do," Priya sobs.

My mother bends down and draws the girl into her arms. She looks up at Shiva who is standing still. His jaw is clenched tight and he looks angry.

"Can you tell me what happened?" my mother asks him.

He takes a deep breath and says in a grim voice, "Yesterday morning the colonel came with a group of policemen. The y tore through our caravans, saying they were looking for stolen goods. The chased our horses and destroyed many of our belongings. One of the caravans belonged to my grandmother. She is old but fie rce and she tried to stop a policeman from entering her caravan when he pushed her down. My grandmother fell down and hit her head on a rock."

He had to stop to clear his throat, "My father tried to protest and help my grandmother but the colonel and a policeman took him away. I saw one of the policemen hit my father in the stomach."

Priya places her hands on my mother's shoulder and says, "Please little mother, you have to help my father. He can't be locked up for something he didn't do. I know who stole the silk sari."

Shiva looks at his sister in surprise.

"It was the lady who complained it was stolen. I was watching her beat the silk sari on the rocks and when she started to spread it out, there was a huge tear in it. She took the sari and bundled it up and threw it behind some bushes. I can show you where she hid it."

My mother stands up and I can see she has a determined look about her.

"Meena, go get Devi and ask her to go to the village and fetch Bhojan to come here as quickly as they can."

When Bhojan and Devi come in a little later, my mother sends Bhojan to borrow a car from our neighbors, the Nelson sisters.

"Meena, you need to stay home and help Muthi with the twins. I'll be back soon."

I want to protest but I know she is going to help my friend and her family.

"Can I wait up for you Amma?"

"All right Meena, you can do that. Stay in the kitchen and I'll come back as soon as I can."

A few minutes later, she leaves with Priya, Shiva and Bhojan.

Muthi, Devi and Ayah keep me company in the kitchen. Devi has cleaned all the dinner dishes and Muthi has swept the kitchen. The twins are in bed and the place is quiet and still. The hearth gives off a comforting heat.

It is past midnight when my mother finally comes home. She looks exhausted and Devi gets busy, lighting the kerosene stove and making my mother a hot drink.

"What happened?" I ask her.

"Well, we stopped by the Sens and picked up the colonel and we all went to the police station. Sure enough, Priya's father was locked up in a cell. After the policeman called up the chief constable and he came over, I explained everything. Meena, your friend was right about the sari. We found it behind some bushes and when the constable confronted the dhobi woman she confessed. The colonel apologized to Priya's father.

In fact, he agreed to pay for the damages to the caravan."

"Amma how is Priya's grandmother?"

"We tried to get her to go the hospital but she refused. I'm sure she will be all right. Now, you better get to bed Meena."

The next morning Raman comes running to the kitchen. He's carrying a bucket of fresh milk that is only half full.

"Little mother, come quick and see what is going on the lower land."

The lower land is expanse of ground that lies just beyond the cowsheds. It belongs to us and every summer it is turned into a huge garden filled with potatoes, cabbages, radishes, carrots, tomatoes, peas and beans. Right now, the garden has been tilled but nothing has been planted. My mother was thinking of selling the land and so had not planted a garden.

Now she smiles at Raman and says, "Is the garden filled with painted caravans and gypsies?"

Raman gapes at her. "How did you know?"

"That's because I invited them to stay there."

"What is going on Amma?" I ask.

"Well, Meenakutty, I didn't quite finish my story but the dhobis and the gypsies were about to get into a fight and I didn't want Priya to get hurt. So I invited her family to come stay on our land. I guess a few of her relatives joined her."

I tear on some clothes and sandals and rush down the path to the lower garden. Sure enough the entire garden area is covered with caravans, gypsies and their horses. One of the gypsy women sees me and beckons me.

"Come here child," she says. She has a bright yellow kerchief covering her head and forehead. Her teeth are stained red with betel juice and she has an earthly scent of fresh soil and drying hay. She takes my palms in her rough hands and studies them intently.

"Little one, you will change many lives," she says with a smile.

"Is that good?" I ask.

"Most of the time but sometimes you can get hurt so be careful."

"Meena, you came to see us," a voice shouts out. I look over the woman's shoulder and see Priya running toward me.

"That's my friend," I tell the gypsy woman and tug my hands out of her grasp.

She smiles again. "Of course she is your friend. You have made many friends, a tribe of friends. You are changing things little one, just as I predicted."

Priya chatters excitedly about the night's activities.

"Your mother is so brave Meena," she says. "She wasn't scared of the colonel or the policeman or the dhobi woman. I want to be brave like her when I grow up."

I smile at my friend, "I predict you will. Amma says you can come to the house for a meal and I hear Ayah is making her famous coconut rice."

"I've never eaten coconut rice and I've never eaten inside a house," she says with excitement. "Come on and I'll race you up the hill."

Coconut Rice

1 cup basmati rice
2 cups water
1 teaspoon salt
3 tablespoons ghee, unsalted butter or vegetable oil
1 teaspoon brown mustard seeds
1 small onion, minced, about ½ cup
½ cup coconut, unsweetened, shredded.
1 tablespoon minced cilantro, for garnish
¼ cup dry roasted cashew bits-optional

Preparation: Wash and drain the basmati rice. Bring water to boil, add salt and washed rice. Cover and simmer on low heat for about 15 minutes. The rice should be tender and the water fully absorbed. If necessary, let rice simmer an additional 1 to 3 minutes. Set aside.

Heat the ghee in a saucepan with a lid. Add mustard seeds and cover. Listen for the mustard seeds to pop. When the popping sound starts diminishing, add minced onion and bell pepper, and sauté for 2-5 minutes. When the onions and peppers are soft, add shredded coconut and cook until the coconut turns a light brown color. Add cooked rice to coconut mixture and fold in until the rice is thoroughly mixed. Fold in cashews and cilantro. Serve hot or warm with plain yoghurt.

Chapter Sixteen

Festival of Lights

• • • • • • • • • •

"Long ago in the kingdom of Ayodhya there was a king named Dasaratha who had four sons. Although, he was the father to the four boys, they had different mothers. His oldest son was named Rama and when the king was ready to retire, he decided to choose Rama as his heir. But his wife Kaikeyi pleaded with him to choose her own son, Bharata, rather than Rama as the next king. She reminded the king that he had promised her two wishes. For the first wish she wanted Bharata to be crowned king and for her second boon she asked that Rama and his wife Sita be banished to the forest for fourteen years. The king was heartbroken, but he had to keep his promise to Kaikeyi. So Rama, along with his brother Laksmana, and Sita were sent to live in the forest. They enjoyed their simple life in the forest, until one day a demoness saw Rama and fell in love with him. When she tried to win Rama's affection, Laksmana protected his brother by cutting off the demoness' nose. The demoness fled to her brother, the wicked Ravana, the ruler of the island kingdom of Shri Lanka. To avenge his sister, Ravana kidnapped Sita

and took her to his island palace, but Rama and Laksmana with the help of an army of monkeys defeated the demon king and brought Sita back home. At the end of 14 years, Rama, Sita and Laksmana returned to the kingdom of Ayodhya. His brother Bharata was waiting to welcome Rama. Everyone was delighted their King Rama had returned so they lighted many lamps and lined the roads and streets of the kingdom with hundreds of clay lights. That's why we celebrate Deepavali because King Rama has finally come home."

—as told by Ayah

The cool November nights mean it's time to celebrate Deepavali, the festival of lights. The twins and I look forward to the sweets, fireworks and new clothes.

The mornings are cold and Bhojan comes to work in a woolen coat with a thick scarf wrapped around his neck. When Devi hands him a bowl of warm water, he gratefully washes his hands in the hot liquid.

"Ahh, that feels much better," he says, flexing his numbed fingers. "It's going to be a bitter winter if November is already so cold."

"I can feel the chill in my hands," Ayah agrees. "We are in for some very frigid weather."

The adults complain about the wintry weather, but the twins like to watch me blow my breath out so that it comes out like a puff of white smoke. I pretend to be a dragon and chase them across the yard. Soon we are breathless and hot and don't feel the cold at all.

One morning after breakfast, Devi asks us, "Little ones, would you like to go to the riverbed with me?"

"Is it time to celebrate Deepavali?" my sister is happy at the thought.

"In just a few days, we'll light the lamps and welcome the night."

Later that morning, bundled up against the cold, we are on our way to the riverbed. Raman joins us at the banks with a small shovel and pick. We walk down the well-worn path. It hasn't rained in a few months so the river is just a small trickle now. As soon as the monsoon rains fall, the little stream will become a roaring creek. The damp dirt along the banks of the river is soft and easy to dig and soon Devi and Bhojan are busy. Appu is wearing big rubber boots and tries to jump in the small mud holes. Thangam is trying to keep her shiny black boots from getting muddy. I wear a pair of old shoes and try to keep Appu from falling in the muddy patches.

"Can't you stay still for even a minute," I ask my six-year-old brother, who just laughs and wriggles out of my reach.

Thangam holds my hand and walks very carefully across the slippery river bed. I have to watch the twins and can't help Devi and Raman dig up the mud. I wistfully remember last year when the twins were too young to come to the river bed and how much fun I had helping Raman with the digging. Soon Devi and Raman have dug up enough mud to make many oil lamps.

I carry a shovel in one hand while Thangam clings to my other. Appu is too busy skipping ahead to help. He stops in his tracks when we hear a loud boom from the valley behind us.

"Sounds like the boys are already setting off firecrackers," Raman says, shaking his head. "They start the celebrations earlier every year."

"Raman, do you think Amma will let me come to the village and watch the fireworks?" Appu asks his eyes wide with excitement.

Raman stops and turns around to look at him. "I don't think it's a good idea, little one, to go to the village at night. The fireworks aren't lighted until late at night and you will be tired after playing with the fireworks at your own house."

I know that Appu wants to argue with him but I keep urging him on and he has to concentrate on climbing up the hill to the main road. When we reach our house Devi and Raman dump the moist mud on a bamboo mat in the courtyard. Ayah and Muthi are ready to knead the clay and take out any rocks, pebbles and pieces of wood. Thangam squats beside Muthi and watch her fingers move through the clay. They look like worms digging in the mud.

"Can I help?"

"Of course, you can. Just remember that sometimes there are unpleasant things in the first mud."

Thangam makes a face and moves away from the clay. But Appu is eager to get his hands in the clay. "What kind of things?"

"Well, sometimes I find a worm or dead bug. But this clay looks very clean."

"Can I keep the worm if I find one?"

Ayah shakes her head and peers at him. "You want worms? What for?"

"I think they are very nice and perhaps I can keep one as a pet," he tells her.

"Appu, you can help knead the clay after it has been cleaned," I tell him. "I'm sure Muthi and Ayah will save you the worms."

He sits back and watches Ayah transfers handfuls of red clay from one corner of the mat to another. Soon, there is a second pile of "clean" clay and she says, "It's alright for you to knead now."

I sit down beside Appu and dig into the mud which is cold and squishes through my fingers. Thangam leans on me but doesn't want to try to stick her fingers into the damp clay. I enjoy the feeling and start rubbing and rolling the clay with my palms. Devi and Ayah also mold and roll the clay until it looks like soft bread dough.

"We are ready to make the lamps," Ayah says.

I stand up and stretch my tired back and legs. Ayah and Devi transfer the firm clay into two wicker baskets and carry them to the front gate. We follow them to the three-foot stone fence that surrounds our property. Here we are going to build small clay lamps all along the top of the fence. On Deepavali night, all the lamps are filled with oil and cotton wicks.

Devi takes a knob of damp clay and using her palms makes it into a round ball. Then she presses a hole in the center of the clay ball with her thumb. Her fingers smooth and shape the round lump of clay into a perfect little lamp with a thumb print depression for the oil and wick.

"Here Thangam and Appu, let me show you how to make a lamp," Ayah presses a round ball of damp mud into the twins' palms.

She shows them how to make a depression using their thumbs and then smooth the edges so that oil will stay inside the lamp. The twins' lamps are a little lopsided, but Ayah and Devi place them on the stone wall and press them onto the rocky surface. The lamps will harden and dry in a few days. I'm very careful and only finish two lamps but I think each one of mine is perfect, so round and smooth.

"Let's hope it doesn't rain like it did two years ago," Devi says, pressing another lamp onto the wall.

I giggle, "I remember the wall was like a big mud puddle and we had to go buy candles to light."

There are no clouds in the pale blue sky and even though it is not very warm, the sun is shining. I can see some of the lamps are already drying out, some have small cracks in them, and Devi goes back and smoothes out the little wrinkles in the mud lamps.

A few days later, my father arrives in time to celebrate Deepavali. He brings Thangam a special present.

"Here, do you know what this is?" he hands her a bundle wrapped in a green banana leaf.

I can see that she's very excited, thinking it is a special holiday sweet, and then she lets out a disappointed sigh at the handful of dark green leaves.

"Do I eat these?"

My mother and I laugh along with my father. "Of course not, little one. This is mylanchi for coloring your hands."

Later that day, Muthi grinds the henna leaves into a thick paste that smells like fresh grass. Using a toothpick and piece of cloth, she draws designs on our palms. She paints dots, little stars and squiggly lines on our palms and fingers.

"Now sit very still until the henna dries," she says. "We'll wash it off with some coconut oil and you will have beautiful hands for Deepavali."

Thangam has a hard time sitting still. Her nose starts to itch and she lifts her hand to her face, but I stop her and patiently rub her nose until the itch is gone.

Muthi looks down at our palms. The green henna has dried to a dull grey. "Looks like you can wash your hands now."

Muthi helps us wash my hands in warm water and then she pours a few drops of coconut oil on my hands and scrubs the last of the dried henna off my palms. When I dry my hands, I see that the coils, swirls and stars form a bright red pattern on my palms.

That evening Devi, Ayah, Muthi and my mother get ready for the festival of lights. The house is cleaned, dusted and swept. The concrete floors are washed and wiped dry. My mother uses a rice paste and draws a complicated design on the floor of the pooja room. In the center of the design she places a brass oil lamp. She also paints a similar design in front of house. She uses colored sand to fill in the pattern of a large pink and green lotus flower. She then arranges small clay lamps all around the design.

Meanwhile, Devi is busy in the kitchen frying, sautéing and steaming. There are paper-thin noodles that taste of sugar and almonds. Small orange balls made of garbanzo flour and flavored with spices and sugar crystals. Milk fudge filled with almonds, pistachios, cashews and cinnamon. My favorite is the pink coconut candy that is so rich and flaky that it melts in my mouth. Devi has mixed freshly grated coconut with sweet butter, sugar and milk. The coconut candy is flavored with cardamom powder and is colored a delicate pink shade.

The kitchen smells like a sweet factory and I'm slightly sick from tasting all the goodies. Devi arranges all the different kinds of treats on silver trays. Tomorrow my mother and I will go deliver these sweets to neighbors and friends.

Ayah insists we take oil baths. Oil baths are not Appu's favorite because it takes so long. First Ayah warms coconut oil in a small saucepan and adds a handful of rice and a few peppercorns in hot oil. The rice sizzles and the pepper corns crackle. The aroma of oil and toasted rice and pepper fills the kitchen. Ayah then lifts the saucepan off the flame and carefully pours the hot oil into another container. She gives us a few grains of rice to munch on and I like their toasty taste. The peppercorns make my tongue burn.

Next, Ayah rubs the fragrant oil into my hair and my neck and shoulders. She also massages the mixture on my legs and feet and we wait for the oil to soak into my skin. I love the feel of her warm hands on my feet and neck. I wash off the oil with sandalwood soap. Afterwards, I dress in a new silk skirt and blouse. My mother braids my hair and entwines it with a strand of fresh jasmine blossom.

In the front hallway, my mother gets ready to light the first oil lamp. Devi and Ayah light all the oil lamps in the hallway. My father and Bhojan have strung tiny electric lights on the pear tree and it glows eerily in the mist. We walk up to the stone fence and Devi fills each lamp with oil and a cotton wick. My father, Bhojan and mother hold a match to each wick and soon the row of lights blaze along the wall. I help my mother and make sure the twins don't get in the way. Finally, all the lamps are lit and I can feel everyone's excitement.

The evening sky is dark lavender and the first stars can be seen high above our heads. A faint evening breeze stirs the leaves of the jacaranda tree and the flames flicker and dance in the darkness. My father carries out a bag filled with a variety of fire-crackers. He hands each of us a sparkler and I hold it out, away from my face, so that my father can light it with a match. The twins copy my gesture and hold out their sparklers. The stick sizzles and snaps in my hand and the twins gasp with delight. Bhojan lights a spiral shaped firecracker and we all step back as it starts whirling and twirling. The light from the firecracker is reflected in all our eyes.

"This is called the eye of Shiva," my father says. "See how it twirls and looks like an eye in the middle."

Bhojan lights a cone-shaped firecracker and it bursts into a fountain of light and sparkles. I love the colors and the sizzling smell of the chemicals. I cover my ears when the loud firebombs go off. My father lifts Appu into his arms and he snuggles close to him. I put my arms around Thangam and we watch the rock-ets fly into the night sky and burst into a million pieces of light. Before I know it all the firecrackers have been lit. It is now time for bed. Appu tries to protest but he's too sleepy to argue. Ayah helps me change into more comfortable clothes before I slip un-der the warm covers. As I fall asleep I can hear the faint boom of the firecrackers from the village. I sigh and burrow into my soft pillow.

Coconut Candy

1 cup freshly grated coconut or 1 1/2 cups sweetened coconut flakes. Omit the sugar.
¾ cup sugar
1 cup whole milk
2 tablespoon ghee/oil
½ teaspoon cardamom powder
1 tablespoon ghee
Few drops red food coloring (optional)
A greased 9-by-9 pan.

Preparation: Heat the ghee or oil in a heavy bottomed sauce pan. Add the coconut and toast it until the flakes are lightly browned. Add sugar and milk. Bring the mixture to a boil, stirring continuously to prevent it from sticking and burning.

Continue cooking until the mixture becomes thick and starts sticking to the bottom of the pan.

Add the cardamom powder and stir in a tablespoon of ghee. Stir in food coloring if using. Pour mixture into a greased pan and spread evenly. Let it cool and slightly harden before cutting into squares.

Makes about a dozen pieces of coconut candy.

Chapter Seventeen

A Wedding

• • • • • • • • • •

"Long ago in ancient India there was a beautiful princess named Savithri. Her father was a wise and powerful king and he wanted to arrange his daughter's marriage. But Savithri wanted to travel the kingdom and find a husband for herself. So along with her father's best warriors, Savithri wandered the land looking for her soul mate.

One day she reached a forest where an old king, his queen and son lived. The king had lost his kingdom and was now old and blind. His son was a handsome man named Satyvan who made a living as a woodcutter and took good care of his parents. Savithri fell in love with Satyvan and wanted to marry him. Savithri's father was not happy with his daughter's decision especially when he heard that Satyvan was doomed to die within a year after his marriage. But Savithri was adamant and the couple was married. Savithri lived with her husband in the forest and was very happy. On the last day of the year, she rose early and insisted on accompanying her husband to the forest. Satyvan was happy to have her company and picked wild flowers for her to string into garlands. About noon Sa-

tyvan felt a little tired, and so he came and lay down resting his head in Savithri's lap. Suddenly the whole forest grew dark, and Savithri saw a tall figure standing before her. It was Yama, the God of Death. "I have come to take your husband," said Yama, who looked down at Satyavan, as his soul left his body.

Savitri ran after the Lord of Death and pleaded with him to take her along with her husband. Yama replied, "Your time has not yet come, child. Go back to your home." But Savithri refused and finally Yama said he would grant her any boon, except the life of her husband, if she returned to earth. So Savithri asked for many sons fathered by Satyvan. "So be it", replied Yama. Then Savitri said, "But how can I have sons without my husband, Satyavan? Therefore I beg of you to give back his life." Yama realized he had been tricked but had no choice but fulfill Savithri's wish. Satyvan came back to life. He slowly woke up from the stupor and the two gladly walked back to their hut. Even the God of Death cannot stay in the way of true love and determination."

—as re-told by Ayah

I never know who will be waiting to meet me after school at the bus stop. Today, I see Kashi is by the tea stall to meet me. The bus hisses to a stop and the conductor, Hanuman, waves me off the bus. I watch Kashi walk toward me. She looks particularly pretty this afternoon in a pale pink skirt and blouse. She has a black and pink scarf tucked into the skirt and draped modestly over her left shoulder. Her hair is pulled back into a thick braid and the gold bobby pins in her hair catch the rays of the late afternoon sunlight.

"Meenakutty, why are you staring me?" she asks, taking the lunch box from my hand. "Do I have a smudge on my nose?"

I laugh, "No Kashi, I was just thinking you were looking so pretty in your pink half-sari."

She blushed, "You think so? This is a new skirt and blouse because today Raman is coming to see your mother."

"Why are you wearing new clothes because Raman is coming to see my mother?"

"Oh kutty, sometimes I forget you are just 13 years old," Kashi sighs. She grins at me, "Raman is coming to see your mother to ask my hand in marriage, you silly..."

I stop in my tracks and look at Kashi who is grinning at me. "You want to get married to Raman? But I thought you never wanted to get married."

"I changed my mind. Raman is not like Thimban. He is strong and young and will take care of me."

"Oh I'm sure my mother will take care of you," I say with a smile.

"Your mother has taken such good care of me for the past five years. I don't know what I would have done without your mother, Meenakutty."

Kashi pushes open our gate and we walk down the driveway and into the kitchen which is filled with activity. The twins rush to greet me with cries of "chechi is home." The twins attend a local elementary school and are home a little before me. Ayah who is quite old now, likes to sit by the warm hearth. Today she is kneading bread dough by the fire's heat. Muthi is busy churning cream into butter and my mother is stirring something on the stove. The smell of toasting nuts, frying onions and baking bread is mouth-watering.

"What are you making, Amma?" I lean on her for moment. She looks up at me and her eyes are sparkling. "I heard I might have some guests for tea so I thought I'd make some poories, masala potatoes and spicy nuts."

Kashi giggles behind me and Devi comes in with a tray of clean silverware.

"Little mother, I'll take the twins and keep them busy," she says as she places the tray on the table.

"We don't want to go," Thangam says with a pout. "We want to stay and see the guests."

"Appu and Thangam if you both go and change into some nice clothes and come back with Devi, you can see the guests and maybe even have tea and poories," my mother says, gesturing the twins to follow Devi.

"Meena, please go wash up and change out of your school uniform and you can help serve tea," she says to me. "Kashi, you sit down and wait in here until we call you."

Muthi has arranged the flaky bread, tangy potato and peas and the spicy cashew nuts on silver platters. She starts making tea. First she boils water in a saucepan and when the bubbles rise to the top, she pours in five heaping spoonfuls of black tea leaves into the boiling water. As soon as the water comes to a boil, she adds two cups of milk into the tea water and lets the milky mixture come to a boil again. Once, the milk is hot and the tea is seeped, she strains the hot tea into the tea pot.

I change into a deep green skirt and blouse. I look in the mirror to make sure my bindi dot is on my forehead matches the color of my skirt. I dab a bit of rosewater behind my ears and tuck a lace handkerchief into my waistband. I'm ready to greet Raman, Kashi's bridegroom.

I hear voices coming from the formal living room and stop and peek through the half-open doorway. Raman dressed in a snowy white dhoti and a colorful red and white shirt is standing near the sofa.

"Raman, today, you are not my employee but a visitor, so please sit down," my mother is sitting in the big rocking chair. "You too, Mala, please sit down."

I walk into the room and my mother gestures to join her. I sit by her side on a small wooden stool.

"Mala is Raman's older sister," she says to me.

Mala is a large woman, dressed in white Bhadaga robes. She has a big gold nose ring and her face is dark with tattoo marks that cover her forehead and cheeks. She smiles at me and her teeth look very white against her dark skin.

"My brother has told me a lot about you Meenakutty. He didn't tell me you were so pretty."

I blush and look down at my toes. Raman perches on the edge of the sofa and his sister sits down next to him.

"Meena, can you go and ask Muthi to bring in the tea and snacks?"

"No, little mother, we don't want to be any trouble," Raman is up again. "We just want…"

My mother holds up her hand and Raman stops speaking. "Really Raman, you need to be more gracious. Today, you are the groom visiting your bride's family and I want to take care of you and your sister."

Raman sits back down. I help Muthi with the heavy tray of food and tea. After we serve the tea and snacks I sit back with a cup hot tea. I sip the milky tea and stare at Raman from under my eyelashes. He looks very nervous. We had just finished the snacks when Muthi comes back with Kashi, who stares down at her feet.

"Mala and Raman please meet my adopted daughter, Kashi," my mother gets up and leads Kashi to another sofa. Both of them sit down and Kashi's face is all red.

"You are a beautiful child," Mala says to her. "If you want to marry my brother, Raman, I would welcome you as my little sister."

Kashi looks up at my mother and I can see tears in her eyes. My mother pats her on the shoulder and turns to Raman and Mala, "As Kashi's family, I would like to know how you will manage to support her."

Raman looks at my mother with a twinkle in his eye, "Well, I have a wonderful employer and I think she will give me a raise as a wedding present."

My mother smiles and I laugh out loud. Even Kashi relaxes her shoulders and smiles.

"I also have one bull and two cows that I will give to Kashi as her dowry. I have my own house and I hope to add another room to the house soon," Raman says looking at my mother.

My mother nods, "Then you can marry my daughter Kashi with my blessing."

She turns and looks at Muthi, "Muthi can you please go call Bhojan."

Kashi looks at my mother in surprise but she doesn't say anything. When Bhojan enters the room both Kashi and Raman stand up to greet him.

"Bhojan, as the father of the bride, I hope you will bless this union," my mother says to him.

Both Raman and Kashi move closer to Bhojan, who hesitates, and looks at my mother, "Little mother, if you are happy with the match, then I'm happy too."

"Oh, Appa, thank you," Kashi cries and runs to her father and bends down to touch his feet. Raman also bends down to touch Bhojan's feet.

"Get up, my daughter, I only want your happiness," Bhojan raises Kashi by her shoulders and blesses her and Raman.

* * *

After many more meetings and consultations, the day of the wedding is finally scheduled. On a cool September morning, Muthi and I make our way down the path to Kashi's village to attend the wedding. My mother and twins will join us later for the feast.

I wear a beautiful pale green silk skirt with gold threads and a red border. The blouse is made of the same material and I wear my gold earrings, necklace and bracelets.

My mother braids my hair tightly and ties green bows on the end of the each braid. She powders my face and neck with perfumed talcum powder. It smells like a flower garden and makes me sneeze. Finally, she places a bright red bindi mark on my forehead.

"You are pretty as a bride," Muthi says when she sees me.

"Here," she holds out a string of fresh jasmine buds. The blossoms smell sweet and she tucks them in my braid. I look at myself in my mother's tall mirror and like what I see.

We take the path behind the cow shed. The worn dirt trail is easy to follow. There are raspberry bushes alongside the pathway and I stop to pick a ripe berry. The juicy berry squishes in my eager hands and I lick dark fruit juice off my fingers.

The footpath curves down a steep incline and is shaded by huge eucalyptus trees. It is like walking in a quiet green cave. I pull my skirt up and walk on my toes so that I won't make any noise.

The walkway ends at the bottom of the hill. Suddenly we are in the bright sunshine. We walk past the meadow dotted with yellow mustard and purple wild flowers and I squint against the harsh sunlight. As we reach the village, I hear film songs on the loud speakers. The central courtyard of the village is hung with colorful banners and flags. The red and yellow pieces of cloth flutter in the early morning breeze. A group of village children are playing hide-and-seek around the gnarled old tree in the center of the square.

The wedding is going to be held in the square, right near the temple.

Muthi and I enter the small whitewashed building. After the bright sunshine, the inside of the house is dark and cold. I move closer to Muthi. We walk through the small front room. There is a wooden table and two chairs. I take off my sandals and place them next to a pair of pink flip-flops. There are many pairs of shoes and slippers arranged in a straight row, as if standing guard. We step into another dark room and hear voices singing and laughing in the back of the house. The voices are coming from a small bedroom which is bathed in a mellow light from the three oil lamps in the room. In the golden lamplight, Kashi looks like a dainty fairy dressed in white. She wears traditional Bhadaga robes and the white cotton cloths are wrapped tightly around her waist and chest. She wears a thick gold necklace around her slender throat and large gold rings in her nose. Her forehead and upper arms are covered with fresh black tattoo marks. Her eyes light up when she sees us.

"Meenakutty, you look so pretty. Come sit down beside me."

There are a lot of women in the small bedroom and all of them are talking, laughing and making a lot of noise. The noise is deafening in the enclosed room.

She pulls me along and we start to sit on the bed.

"Time to go, time to go," someone says.

The women begin filing out of the room, still laughing and talking. I stand and watch Kashi get up and arrange the cloth around her. We walk out into the blinding sunlight.

Rows of steel folding chairs have been set up outside. Muthi and I sit down in the front row. Kashi is lead away by Mala to join the wedding procession. Raman looks handsome in a fancy turban. His teeth glisten as he grins at all of us. Kashi looks small and delicate next to him. I know she is probably smiling too but I can't see her face because her head is bowed.

The ceremony takes place inside the simple temple. We wait in the hot sun for the bride and groom to come out after exchanging wedding vows. Soon Kashi and Raman walk out of the temple wearing bright orange garlands of marigolds around their necks. They both look so happy that I can't help smiling at them. We follow the wedding party to a large cottage. The wedding feast will be served in this house for the wedding party. We walk farther down to another dwelling for our meal.

Before entering the residence, Muthi bends down and washes her hands, using an orange plastic jug to scoop up water from the brass vessel. I do the same thing and we go inside the house. This cottage has an expansive entrance hall and most of the space is taken up by long wooden tables. On either side of the tables, there are bare benches and mismatched stools and chairs

We find a place to sit on the sturdy bench. A boy who looks like he's just a few years older than me comes in with a stack of banana leaves and quickly places one in front of us. Muthi lifts the glass tumbler and pours a small handful of water in her cupped palms. She sprinkles the water on the banana leaf and wipes off dust and dirt on it. I do the same.

"Chechi, we are here," little Appu says running into the room.

My mother and the twins come and sit down next to us. Muthi and my mother help the twins clean their banana leaves. Thangam wants to do it herself and ends up using too much water. Muthi leans over and cleans off her banana leaf in one smooth motion and mops up all the water on the table with her white handkerchief.

It's time to eat. A lady enters the room carrying a pot of steaming white rice. She plops spoonfuls on the center of each banana leaf. Another server comes carrying a small pot filled with ghee. The nutty smell of the clarified butter fills up the room as the server carefully drizzles the buttery warm ghee over the rice. We are served a vegetable stew of potatoes, carrots and peas. The thick gravy is flavored with tomatoes and fried spices and I have to gulp down water after a taste of the fiery stew. Rice sweetened with brown sugar and flavored with raisins and cinnamon is served at the end of the meal. I scoop up the sugary brown pudding with my fingers. After the feast, we walk outside and wash our hands. I help Appu wash up and we get ready to go home.

"We'll see Kashi later," my mother says. "Let's go home."

Vegetable Sambar

1 cup toor dal or yellow split peas,
washed and soaked in hot water for about 30 minutes
½ teaspoon turmeric
1 teaspoon salt
2 ½ cups water
Assorted vegetables, cut into bite size chunks, about 2 cups. Suggestions: potatoes, carrots, a tomato, an eggplant (peeled) or pumpkin or pearl onions.
1 red onion, chopped into small chunks
1-3 dried red chilies, depending on how spicy you want the dish
2 tablespoons tamarind concentrate or a lemon size lump of tamarind soaked in ½ cup hot water.
1 teaspoon turmeric powder
1 teaspoon mustard seeds
2-5 curry leaves or 2 bay leaves
3 tablespoons ghee
½ cup finely ground coconut, soaked in 1 cup hot water
4 tablespoons coriander powder
1/8 teaspoon hing or asafetida powder
1 tablespoon brown sugar

Preparation: Boil the water and add cleaned peas, turmeric powder and salt. Let it simmer for about 30 minutes until peas are tender. Set aside.

Spice preparation: In a saucepan heat 1 tablespoon oil or ghee. Add chopped onion and fry until lightly browned. Add dried chilies, coconut powder and hing. Sauté until the coconut is a light brown in color. Add coriander powder and sauté a few more minutes. Let the mixture cool. Using a food processor or blender, process the spices and coconut, using warm water as needed to make a thick smooth paste. Set aside.

Vegetables: Heat the remaining ghee or oil in a saucepan with a lid. Add mustard seeds and allow them to splutter and pop. Add curry leaves or bay leaves, chopped vegetables and turmeric. Sauté for a couple of minutes, add salt and tamarind concentrate and about 1 cup water. Let the vegetables simmer until barely tender, about 10-15 minutes. Add coconut mixture and peas with about 1/2 cup water. The sauce should be fairly thick but thin enough to pour over rice. Add ½ cup water if necessary. Add sugar and taste for salt. Garnish with fresh cilantro leaves and serve over cooked Basmati rice. Taste for salt and garnish with fresh cilantro leaves.

Chapter Eighteen

Visiting the Animal Preserve

• • • • • • • • • •

The chirping birds wake me. I look out my window and see the day is bright and clear for my very first overnight trip with my father. I'm filled with excitement and anxiety about the upcoming trip.

"Really, Meena you have packed and unpacked your bag three times," Muthi says, coming into the bedroom.

"But Muthi I can't decide if I want to take my silk skirt or not," I say.

"Meenakutty, your mother has already told you that it will be quite cool and even rainy on the farm. You will need to keep your silk skirts here at home."

I know what my mother has told me but I want to look my best when I visit my father's farm. I wait until Muthi's attention is turned away from me and then quickly re-pack the silk clothes laying them flat on the bottom of the suitcase.

My father arrived two days ago and he suggested the trip to my mother.

"I don't know…she's never been away from me," I hear my mother say.

"Sudha, Meena is nearly fourteen years old and quite independent. Besides, she won't be alone, I will be with her and we are taking Muthi too."

"I suppose it will be a fun experience for her and it's only for about a week."

I had been listening to this conversation, hiding behind the half-open bedroom door, and let out a sigh of relief when I hear my mother's words.

The night before leaving I toss and turn, too excited to fall asleep. A cup of warm almond milk soothes me and I finally doze off.

Ayah's snores are now so loud that I have trouble staying asleep at night. But I would never complain and hurt my old nanny's feelings. It seems like I had just fallen asleep when Muthi shakes my shoulder and whispers in my ear, "Wake up Meenakutty. Come get a hot drink and wash your face. We have to be on our way soon."

I groan and sit up in bed, hugging the thick cotton quilt around me. Even in the middle of summer, it is cool in the house. I dress in a thick skirt and blouse and the purple and white sweater my mother knitted for me.

The kitchen is warm and bright with activity. My mother is drinking her early morning coffee by the hearth. The cowhands are in the kitchen, collecting clean buckets for milking. Devi is busy making breakfast and Ayah is sitting in a chair. My sister Thangam is sitting on a mat eating a bowl of sliced mangoes. The kitchen is filled with the fragrance of the ripe fruit. My brother is lying on a bamboo mat, his eyes closed.

"Meena, are you all ready to go with your father?" My mother draws me to her side and hands me a steel tumbler of warm milk, sweetened with honey.

I lean against her and sip the warm drink. "Amma, I'm not

sure I want to go. You will need help with the twins and I will miss my friend Kumari."

"It's going to be alright Meena. Ayah and Devi will help me with the twins and you are going to have so many stories to tell Kumari next week when you come back. Remember, your father has a surprise for you."

At the mention of the surprise I sit up. "I remember his promise. Can I go ask him?"

My mother laughs. "He's having a bath and will be here soon. Finish your milk and have a bite to eat."

Devi hands me a plate filled with fluffy rice dumplings. The melting butter has formed a warm yellow puddle on each warm iddli and the white sugar sparkles on top. I'm putting the last bit of iddli into my mouth when my father walks in bringing with him a scent of sandalwood.

"Acha, can you tell me what my surprise is now?"

My father laughs his booming laugh and sits on a stool next to Ayah.

"You never forget anything do you, Meenakutty? I was going to wait until we were in the car to tell you but I can share the surprise with you and your mother right now. On the way to the farm we will pass a wild life nature preserve. I have made arrangements for us to stop there tonight and go on an elephant ride tomorrow morning."

"A wildlife preserve with real jungle animals?" I ask. "What kind of animals?"

"Well, there are supposed to be water buffalo, deer, all kinds of birds and even tigers," he says, accepting a cup of coffee from Devi.

"Tigers? Are the animals in cages and far away from people?" Thangam asks.

Devi giggles at her worried tone and even my father smiles. "No, kutty, the animals live in the wild but Meena and I will be safe on top of an elephant. When you are older I'll take you and your brother to see the wild animals."

I open my mouth to ask another question but my mother places a hand on my shoulder. "Meena, please go brush your teeth and wash your face and bring your suitcase to the front hallway."

A little later Muthi and I climb into the Ambassador car, along with my father and our driver Jaibal.

I hug my hug my sister who looks like she's about to cry, "It's all right little one, I'll bring you back a surprise."

"A surprise? One for me too?" Appu asks.

"Of course, something for both of you," I say.

"You will have a great time Meena. Don't worry about us," my mother says, hugging me back and kissing my forehead.

I watch them through the rear window until I can no longer see them. I sigh and sit back and roll down the window. The fresh morning air is soothing on my warm cheeks. I brush away a tear and take a deep breath. The sun is still low on the horizon but already the sky is streaked with orange and pink. My father turns his head to look at me.

"You alright back there Meena? Do you want to sit in the front?"

I shake my head no and look over at Muthi who has her head back and her eyes closed. She looks like she is ready for a nap.

The car journey is tiresome and long. We bounce along and seem to hit every hole in the road. The rolling hillsides look like a green ocean of tea plants. The green slopes are dotted with bright red, orange, yellow and blue as workers, dressed in bright colors, busily pick the tender tea leaves.

We arrive in the town of Great Mahagiri which is a bustling city unlike little Mahagiri, the sleepy hamlet where we usually go to shop. Jaibal brings the car to a stop at the busy bus station.

"Meena, Muthi, do you need to use the restroom?"

"I do Achan."

Muthi wakes up and is re-tying her hair into a knot at the back of her head. We get out of the car. The air here is much warmer now and smells of diesel fumes. The bus station is a central stopping place for trucks, cars, taxis and huge buses.

The restroom is a stone building, overlooking a slow-moving creek. There is rubbish scattered all over the place and I am careful not to step in any of the brown liquid on the ground. The stench in the public bathroom is horrendous and I hold my nose. The diesel filled air outside the restroom actually smells good after the public bathrooms.

My father waits for us with a long strand of creamy white jasmine flowers.

"Here, this will get the smell of the bathroom out of your nose," he says.

I bury my face in the sweet, fresh scent of the flowers and let their sweet fragrance fill my nostrils.

When we are back in the car my father passes me a paper bag.

"The Greater Mahagiri bakery has the best bread and rolls," he says.

I pull out a flaky round roll. The varkee roll is crisp and a perfect combination of sweet and savory.

"Chai, sweet fresh Chai," a boy comes by holding a wire tray with steaming glass tumblers of milky tea.

My father rolls down his window and buys each of us a glass of tea. The tea is hot, sweet and milky and tastes delicious with the flaky rolls. My father returns the glass tumblers to the boy who looks at me with curious eyes. Jaibal starts the car and we are off again.

The road is much steeper now as we make our way down the mountain. The sharp hair-pin turns make me woozy. I lay my head on Muthi's lap and doze off.

I awake up when the car comes to an abrupt stop. For a moment I'm disoriented. I look out the car window and remember that we are on our way to my father's plantation. We have come to a stop because a herd of lowing cattle are crossing the narrow road. The driver of the car in front of us is leaning hard on his horn but the noise doesn't ruffle the placid cows who take their time. The coconut palms on the side of the road are so tall that they look like they are trying to reach the sky with their bushy long arms. On the limb of a shorter palm tree, I spy a little monkey. His bright eyes dart around as he peels a small yellow banana. I roll down the window to get a better view when a small furry face suddenly peers inside the car.

I scream in surprise. "Close the window, Meena, there are many monkeys here and most of them aren't afraid of humans," Muthi says, leaning across me to roll up the window. The monkey has disappeared as quickly as it had appeared.

The cows are finally across the road and we take off again. We are on a narrow road with a deep gully on one side and a steep, rocky mountain on the other. The gully or deep valley is covered with dark vegetation and huge trees. I can make out the blood-red flowers of the Flame of the Forest tree. I imagine the gorge, dark and impenetrable with vines and dark leafy bushes, is filled with monkeys, snakes and even tigers. I shiver at the thought of all the wild animals, just a few feet from our car.

It is warm and humid and I take off my sweater. Jaibal turns on the car's air conditioner. We make our way down the mountain and the final hair-pin bend. Suddenly the road straightens out and is smooth and well-paved. The rows of trees on either side of the car are just a green blur.

"Are we almost there Acha?"

"Just a few more minutes and we'll be at the nature preserve. We'll check into our cabin and find a place for lunch," my father assures me.

I'm ready to get out of the car. It is early afternoon and we have been driving since dawn. I realize now this long and tiresome trip is the reason that my father visits us only once a month.

A sign on the side of the road reads, "Welcome to South India's Largest Nature Preserve."

I see another one, "Please do not litter. No plastic bags allowed inside the Preserve."

Jaibal turns off the main road and we bump along on a smaller, unpaved street. We come to a stop at a closed gate. There is a small guard house next to the gate and a uniformed guard comes out and pokes his head in through the open window.

My father leans over and says, "Good Morning. We have reservations at the main cabin in the name of Unnikrishnan."

The guard goes into the gate house and comes back with a pink slip of paper.

"Please have this on your windshield at all times. The front office for reservations is to your right. Please park in front of the office to unload your luggage and then follow the path to your cabin. Thank you for visiting Mountainside Nature Preserve."

The guard bangs his hand on the roof of the car and we drive to the nature preserve lodging. The front office is a large wooden building and as we pull up to the front, another uniformed guard hurries over to open my father's door. My father turns around and says, "Wait here until I get us checked in."

I roll down the window and lean out. The air is warm and thick. There is a dirt parking lot on one side of the office building and a winding trail on the other side. The trail is closed off by a small wooden gate and behind the trail the foliage is thick and green. I hear the scream of some wild creature and realize the jungle is not very far away. I don't think I'll be taking any night walks in this place.

"We are all set. Muthi and Meena you can come with me to the cabin and Jaibal can take the car around. A porter will bring our luggage to the cabin," my father says.

I get out. It feels good to stretch my legs and back. Muthi climbs out of the car and immediately takes my hand. I guess she isn't too thrilled with the dark jungle surrounding us. Her warm strong fingers are comforting even though I think I am a little too old to hold hands.

We follow my father down the dirt path and he opens the wooden gate and waits for us to pass before closing the gate. The jungle has been cut back to make room for about a dozen little cottages. Each little cabin is a white washed structure with a tiled roof the color of red clay. The cabins all have small front porches, each with a wooden bench of a different color. The path leading to each cabin is lined with bright red and orange flowers.

Our cabin has a bright green bench on the front porch and my father uses a heavy iron key to open the matching green cabin door. The door opens directly into a small living room with a wooden table and two chairs. Another doorway leads to the bedroom which has a double bed with a plaid blanket draped across it. The only furniture in the room is a small chest of drawers with a mirror at the foot of the bed. A door on the right side of the bed is partially open to reveal a little bathroom with a miniature sink and a toilet. There are two orange buckets and jugs in one corner of the bathroom. "Property of Mountainside Nature Preserve" is stamped on each bucket.

"Meena, you and Muthi will sleep here and Jaibal and I will be next door. Muthi, here is the key to the cabin. Make sure you lock the front door when you leave."

He hands the fancy looking iron key to Muthi, who immediately ties it to the end of her dhoti cloth.

"Are you hungry? Or do you need to rest?"

"I'm starving," I say.

"Alright Meena, lets find the dining room."

There are several other families in the dining room. The waiter leads us to a table by the window.

"Please don't open the window because monkeys like to reach in," he says, handing us menus.

After much discussion we order the thali rice plate. The thali plate is a feast with rice, gravy, vegetables, crispy rice wafers, spicy mango pickle and sweet pudding. I am hungry and scoop up handfuls of rice and spicy coconut gravy.

When we finish we walk out through the lobby. "Excuse me sir." A man dressed in a black pants and maroon jacket, stops us. "We know that you had reserved an elephant ride for tomorrow morning."

"Yes, I did. Is there a problem?"

"No problem sir. We just had an elephant evening excursion available and thought you might be interested."

"You mean going on an elephant ride this evening instead of tomorrow?"

"That is correct, sir."

"I know the dawn rides are good for viewing but are the evening ones as good?"

"Many of the animals come out at twilight to the watering hole and the likelihood of seeing animals such as tigers is greater at night than at dawn."

Father looks down at me. "Well, what do you think Meenakutty? How about we go for our elephant ride now and then we can get an early start to the farm tomorrow morning?"

"Yes, acha, let's go right now."

"Sir, if you come back to the lobby with me I can go ahead and change your reservations."

"Meena and Muthi, you can go to the cabin and see if your suitcases are there and I'll come by as soon as I get our reservation changed," father says to us.

We cross the dirt parking lot and take the path winding around the lot and back to the cabins.

"Let's go down there and back to the cabin Muthi," I point out the path.

Muthi peers down the path. It looks clean and inviting in the warm sunlight.

"I'm sure it's perfectly safe during the day," I say. "The jungle is off to that side and there aren't even any trees near the path."

Muthi nods her head and reaches to grab my hand. "Muthi I want to run down the hill," I say and before she can protest I take off down the path. It is exhilarating to run downhill. I come to a stop where the path starts to go uphill toward the first of the cabins. I wait for Muthi to catch up and we walk up the slope together. My father is already waiting for us in front of our cabin.

"There you are," he says. "We leave for the twilight ride in about two hours. Why don't you go inside and lie down for a while. I've ordered tea to be brought to your cabin around 4 o'clock."

In the cabin, Muthi unpacks our clothes and I take out a book and start reading. After unpacking, Muthi takes a nap but I'm content to read. I'm so caught up in the story about a secret garden that a knock on the door startles me. I close the book and get up. Muthi fixes her dhoti cloth and goes to the living room.

"Madam, your tea," I hear a voice saying.

Almost all the space on the wooden table in the living room is taken up with a silver tray with a steaming tea pot. There are also tiny white china cups and saucers, a small jug of milk, a container of white sugar, and a plate covered with a napkin.

Muthi removes the napkin and looks at the stack of white bread sandwiches. The strawberry jam sandwiches are sweet and tasty, but the sandwiches with cilantro pesto are spicy and burn my tongue. I take sips of the milky sweet tea to soothe my burning mouth.

We finish our tea and Muthi insists I wash my hands and face. She rubs eucalyptus oil on my face, neck, arms and legs.

"Rub it in Meena. This oil will keep the bugs away or you will be eaten alive by mosquitoes."

"Meena, Muthi, are you two ready to go?"

Muthi grabs a shawl and we find my father waiting for us in the living room. He has removed the tea tray and placed it on the front porch.

"Kutty, you smell like you've fallen in a vat of eucalyptus oil," he says with a smile.

"It's Muthi's fault I smell so awful," I grumble.

"You'll be glad of the oil when the bugs don't bite you," Muthi says with a smug expression.

An open-air jeep is waiting for us at the front of the lobby.

"We'll go in the jeep to the elephant ride area," my father says.

The jeep ride is bouncy and I feel my teeth snapping together. The jeep takes us along a dirt path, deep into the dark jungle. The still air is warm and musty.

We stop in front of a mud hut with a thatched roof. On one side of the hut there is a staircase made of wood with a strange looking wooden platform on top. Resting against the platform is the largest elephant I have ever seen. He shifts from foot to foot and is using the platform as a giant back scratcher. A thin man in a dirty dhoti and a plain white t-shirt is standing next to the elephant. He has a bamboo stick in his hand and when he makes a clicking noise, the elephant stops moving and remains perfectly still.

We climb the wooden steps to the platform. I watch my father get onto the back of the swaying elephant. There is a bench made of cloth and blankets tied on its back. The bench is enclosed by a wooden railing and I hold onto the railing and dangle my legs over the side of the elephant. When we were all settled in, the mahout climbs onto the head of the elephant and we take off. The elephant moves at a slow elegant pace. It takes me a while to get used to the gentle swaying motion. The mahout uses his heels and the bamboo stick to direct the elephant. Soon, we leave the dirt path and enter the woods. Tall, stately teak trees surround us in a green embrace. It is quiet except for the sound of the elephant breathing and the clicking of the mahout. I look back over my shoulder and can no longer see the mud hut. We are surrounded by trees on all sides.

The mahout points to my left to a herd of deer standing under the trees. Their coats are spotted with white flecks and they flick their tails nervously. A fawn takes a tentative step toward us but the mother doe urges it away with her snout. A sharp thrill of a song bird shatters the quiet and deer flee, gracefully jumping over logs and stumps. Soon they all disappear into the thicket.

The elephant continues its slow pace, going deeper into the forest. We see another herd of deer with long pointy horns. A lone water buffalo stands in the dappled shade, chewing on grass.

The elephant stops. The stillness is so dense I feel an urge to scream. The mahout holds up his hand and then points to a thicket to the right of us. I almost gasp out loud at the flash of orange and black.

"Is that a tiger?" I whisper. The mahout nods and places his fingers on his lips, indicating I should be quiet. The elephant stands still and patient. I see a deer running across our path. Immediately behind the deer there is a flash of orange and black. The deer disappears into the bushes but a moment later we hear the sound of struggles. I realize the tiger has found dinner.

Even though we go deeper into the jungle, we don't see anymore animals. We make on our way back to the hut. I think I like traveling by elephant better than the bouncy jeep. Back at the cabin, my father has ordered us a light meal of whole wheat bread and roasted potatoes. I enjoy some warm milk before crawling into bed. I can hear the jungle noises outside. I'm glad to be safe and sound inside the tiny cabin with Muthi beside me.

* * *

The next morning, Muthi and I are dressed and sitting on the wooden bench when my father walks over.

"If you are both ready, shall we take off? I know the perfect place to stop for breakfast."

Jaibal is waiting by the car and we load our bags and drive out of the nature preserve. I keep my nose glued to the window, hoping to catch another glimpse of orange and black.

A few minutes later, we are speeding along on the main road toward the plantation.

"Jaibal, remember the little restaurant we usually stop to eat? Can you stop there for our breakfast?"

The restaurant my father has in mind is really not a restaurant at all. It is more like a shack with wooden benches. The cook, dressed in a sweaty shirt, is busy making breakfast over an open fire. There is a huge iron griddle, smoking hot on the flames.

"We'd like an egg breakfast," my father says to the cook.

The man nods his head and I see drops of sweat run down the sides of his face. He has a dirty red towel on his shoulder and he uses this to wipe his face.

"Four egg breakfasts coming up," he yells.

We wash up and sit down on one of the rickety benches. The cook takes out some eggs and expertly cracks them with one hand into a bowl. He adds some chopped scallions, a pinch of salt, a few curry leaves, a sprinkle of chopped herbs and chilies. He stirs the herb mixture into the beaten eggs. He dabs a blob of butter on the hot griddle and pours the egg mixture. As the eggs cook, he takes out a plastic bag from under the table, which contains bread rolls. He places the buttered bread on the griddle. He expertly flips the huge egg pancake and at the same time turns over the bread so that it is toasty brown on both sides, sizzling with hot butter. He cuts the pancake into four pieces and slides these onto four banana leaves. The leaves are placed on four bamboo plates and he plops the pancake and bread roll in front of us.

The omelet or egg pancake is thick and flecked with green herbs.

"You make a sandwich with the bread," my father says.

I watch him place the egg in the middle of the two rolls and take a bite. I do the same and have to open my mouth wide to take a bite. The flavors explode in my mouth. The crunchy roll, the creamy egg and the sharp tang of fresh herbs are delicious. I take a sip of milky coffee to wash down my breakfast.

"This is a roadside breakfast. How do you like it Meena-kutty?"

"I've never had anything so tasty," I want to say but my mouth is too full of eggs and bread, so I just grin at my father.

Road Side Eggs

6-8 eggs
4 scallions, finely chopped, including tender green tops
1 cup chopped fresh herbs (parsley, coriander, dill, or basil)
1 tsp. salt
Fresh ground pepper
2-4 tablespoons butter or vegetable oil
Fresh chopped basil for garnish
4 soft rolls, cut in half

Preparation: Whisk eggs with scallions, chopped herbs, salt and pepper. Can marinate upto 30 minutes.

Heat a large non-stick skillet over medium heat. Add butter or oil. When hot, pour eggs, lower heat and cook until the eggs are set, about 10 minutes.

If you can't comfortably flip the omelet over, slide onto a clean plate and then flip the plate over onto the skillet. Cook for until omelet is brown. Serve warm wedges with toasted rolls or bread. Garnish with chopped basil leaves.

Makes four servings

Chapter Nineteen

At the Plantation

• • • • • • • • • •

Jaibal turns into a long winding driveway as we bump along the rough path that leads to the farm. It is late afternoon by the time we finally reach the plantation and the trees cast their long shadows in the front yard. I step out of the car, glad to get out of the car, and take a deep breath of the warm muggy air. This is nothing like the cool fresh air of Mahagiri. The farm is in Chandur, a small village, surrounded by deep forests and rocky hills. My father lives in a modest house at the entrance of the plantation. The house is a two-story structure and has an open veranda. This porch is surrounded by a low wall that is whitewashed and wide enough to sit on. The concrete veranda floor is so highly polished that I can see the pillars reflected on its surface.

"Meena, leave your shoes on the veranda. I'll show you where you and Muthi will be staying," my father says.

I follow him into a large rectangle room where there is a table, a wooden bench and some chairs and a large calendar on the wall. Instead of dates and numbers on the calendar, there are circles and squares and check marks in different colors. I can make out some of the squiggles that say "picked area 1" or "irr. Area 4" but most of the words don't make much sense to me.

"This is the dining room." My father leads us through a set of wooden doors. The dining room has a large wooden table and six chairs around it. There is a small sink in the corner and a pinkish red towel hangs on a hook by the wash basin. An open window at one end of the room lets in fresh air and the late afternoon sunlight. I follow my father through another set of doors into a small dark hallway. There are several doors in this hallway and my father pushes open the first to show us a bedroom with a large bed in the middle, draped in a gauzy white mosquito net.

"Your bathroom is through that doorway," he says, pointing, "And there is cold water for washing. If you want to take a bath you just let Paru Amma know and she'll make sure you get some hot water.

"Paru Amma's husband is the caretaker of the farm and she in charge of the house. You and Muthi can come outside to the veranda after your wash."

* * *

My father is sipping tea and talking to a man on the veranda when we join him a little later. The man, dressed in shorts and a plaid shirt, has a large moustache and no hair on his head. He stands up and greets Muthi with his palms pressed together.

"Namaste Muthi," he says with a smile that reveals a gap in his front teeth. "Welcome Meenakutty to the farm. Your father says you like to go for walks and tomorrow we'll go for a hike. My name is Murthy and I'm the manager of your father's farm."

"A hike? How far?" I ask. "Can we take a picnic with us?"

Murthy grins and looks at my father. "I see what you mean Unny Sir. She is full of questions and energy."

I blush and look down at my bare toes.

"Meenakutty, we can go to the very top of your father's plantation and look down on the farmhouse. It will be a long walk and of course we can take a picnic. I'll invite my daughter Radha to come along and both of you will have a lot of fun."

A lady walks up the steps of the veranda holding a tray in her hand.

"Ah, Paru Amma, just in time with some tea," my father says. "This is Meena, my daughter and our cousin Muthi."

The lady bobs her head in acknowledgement and places the tray on a wooden table. She wears a bright green cotton sari with the end folded over her head so that it hides her forehead. She has a huge gold ring on her nose and several earrings dangle off her ear lobe. I have never seen anyone with a nose ring that big. She sees me staring at her nose and flushes slightly.

"Did it hurt to get your nose pierced?" I ask her.

Before she can answer her husband Murthy laughs out loud. "This is Meenakutty and she is full of questions," he says.

"It hurt a lot to get my nose pierced," she says, smiling at me. "But my mother said I had to get it pierced otherwise no one would want to marry me. So I didn't cry when the jeweler pierced my nose."

"Did Murthy like your ring?"

Again Murthy bursts out laughing, "Of course, I liked her ring. But I told her that I would have married her even if her nose was not pierced. Her mother didn't believe me."

Paru Amma tugs the end of her green sari over her face and giggles into the cloth. I giggle too.

"Shall I pour you some tea?" she asks in a soft voice. "This is cardamom tea, made from fresh pods grown right here on the estate."

She pours the milky tea into a white cup and saucer and the sweet scent of cardamom drifts up in the steam. I take a sip of the warm tea. It tastes like liquid honey, full of flavor and sweetness.

"This is best tea I've ever tasted," I say to Paru Amma, who beams at me.

"The tea is liquid cardamom," she says. "We peel the seeds and boil them in water and then steep the tea in the spice water. The spice tea is mixed with fresh milk and sugar and served hot. That's why it tastes so good."

The next morning, I accompany my father to the store house to see where all the spices are kept in large bags. There is a large spice drying area just above the store room. Huge wooden trays are filled with pale green cardamom pods, all drying out in the heat produced by an enormous wooden kiln. The drying area is warm and fragrant with spice.

"None of our workers ever get a cold," Murthy says to me.

"Why?"

"Because the scent of the cardamom clears their sinuses and the cold germs can never find a place to grow."

I take deep breaths of the aromatic warm air and feel all the cold germs in my nose dry up.

Later in the morning Murthy's daughter, Radha arrives with a basket on her head. She is a tall girl dressed in a skirt and blouse with a piece of cloth over her blouse to hide her pale brown stomach. She places the basket on the ground and squats down beside it.

"Radha will take you for a walk along the edge of the property. She has some nice things to eat," Murthy says.

Radha smiles at me and her teeth are very white against her pale brown skin.

"I don't wear shoes, but you should wear something on your feet," she says, looking at my bare feet.

I get some sandals and stop to ask Muthi if she wants to come with us but she says she is too tired to go for a long walk.

So Radha and I make our way up a hilly path. The path is very muddy and slippery and I almost slide down the hill.

"See these bushes, Meena? They are cardamom bushes and if you look carefully you can see this stalk all covered with the pods."

I bend down to look at a stalk that is covered with what looks like rows of creamy white pearls.

"They are so pretty and white."

"That's because they are young and as soon as they are ready, my mother and I pick the pods and take it down to the drying shed."

Radha points to the trees and vines covered with pale green pepper pods.

"Your father's pepper pods are fiery hot and so tasty in soup," she pauses. "Meena your father is a good landlord. He gives us all fair wages and makes sure none of us overworks or gets hurt. He has made this small village into a prosperous town."

"What do you mean Radha?"

"Before you father bought this plantation, my father worked for a large landlord. This landlord owned many acres of forests and spices. He didn't live on his farm. He had an overseer who managed the farm. One day, the overseer came to my father and said if he wanted to keep his job he would have to give him baksheesh. But my father couldn't afford the bribe and so he lost his job. He didn't know what to do. Then your father bought this plantation and he offered my father a job as his overseer. My father was afraid that he would lose his job so he came to your father and offered him a baksheesh but your laughed and said his job was safe as long as he worked hard."

My heart bursts with pride at her words. "My mother says my father is the kindest man," I say to Radha.

"Your mother is right Meena because your father has changed all our lives for the better."

"Radha, you would like my mother. She is just as kind as my father."

I tell her the story of the gypsies and my friend Priya.

"Having such special parents must mean you are special too Meena," Radha says. "The gypsy lady is right about you and your family because you all do such good things for people."

We reach the top of the hill and I'm glad to stop for a moment and look around me. The view from the top of the hill is breathtaking. The valley, verdant and lush, is spread out in front of me. The ground on the hill is rocky and bare. The air is thick and heavy with the scent of herbs. Except for the bare hillside we stand on, everything else is budding and flourishing. It seems to be the bushes, trees and shrubs are blooming and growing right before my eyes. The farm is a fertile place of hope and renewal. I look at the country side with new appreciation. This place is my father's legacy and his gift to the people of Chandur.

Radha sets her basket down on the rocky surface and spreads out a blue and yellow cloth. She pulls out a steel Tiffin carrier. The Tiffin carrier is made up of three containers one on top of another and held together by a steel band. Radha unlocks the band and takes each container off the carrier and places them on the cloth. The first container is filled with fragrant yellow lemon rice. The second steel vessel has curd rice, creamy with yogurt, bits of red onion and black mustard seeds. The smallest container has small pieces of bread and spicy mango pickle. Soon, Radha and I are busy scooping up mouthfuls of rice with bread. There is a thermos of tea in the basket and Radha pours each of us a cup of the warm liquid. I sip the sweet cardamom tea and look up to see a fine white mist creeping up from the valley.

"If you are done, Meena we'd better get going. There's going to be a big storm soon and we don't want to get caught up here."

I help Radha put the Tiffin carrier together again and we pack up the blanket. The walk back down the hill is much faster.

I have to keep from running all the way down. The sandals are not much protection against the mud and my legs are tired by the time we reach the farm house. Just as we near the structure, the first fat drops of rain start falling. In the courtyard, I can smell the pungent aroma of the drying cardamom pods. I can't wait to go up to the drying sheds and warm up, surrounded by trays filled with hundreds of pale green pods, giving off their rich and aromatic scent. I wouldn't mind another cup of cardamom tea, either.

Cardamom Tea

4 cardamom pods
2 cups water
2-4 teaspoon black tea leaves
1 cup milk
Sugar to taste

Tea Preparation

Peel the pods and remove the seeds. Bring water to boil and add the spice. Boil for 2 minutes. Add tea leaves and boil for additional 2 minutes. Add milk. Turn off heat. Let the mixture seep for 3-5 minutes and then strain into a warm tea pot. Sweeten with brown or white sugar.

Chapter Twenty

Harvest Festival

• • • • • • • • • •

The story of Onam

Long ago in the land of Kerala there was a king named Mahabali who was a devout worshipper of Lord Vishnu. He was a just and good ruler. But he was arrogant and to teach him a lesson in humility, Lord Vishnu came to earth in the form of a dwarf Brahmin named Vamana. Every evening the generous king gave away clothes, food and alms to the poor and needy. Vamana joined the crowd and when it was his turn, the king discovered all his baskets were empty. In his pride, the king told the dwarf he would give anything he asked, regardless of the cost.

In a humble manner, Vamana asked the king for just three paces of land that he could cover with his short legs. The king agreed, thinking that the dwarf couldn't possibly step too far. But at that moment, Vamana grew and grew into the enormous form of Vishu and his first step covered the entire earth and the second step covered the entire heavens. There was no place for Vamana to place his foot for his third step. Mahabali, a man of principles, was humbled and offered his head for Vamana's final footstep. When Vamana placed his foot on the king's head, he sank underground and vanished. But his loyal followers pleaded with Vishnu to bring back their beloved ruler and Vishnu allowed the king to visit his kingdom, once a year on Onam day. On this special day, homes were decorated with flowers and light to welcome back King Mahabali, a vain but honest king.

—As re-told by Muthi

I've been away for just short ten days but in that time my house and furniture seems to have grown smaller. I was happy to be home but already I was longing to go on another trip. But I didn't have much time to mope because we were getting ready to celebrate Onam or harvest festival.

In Kerala, Onam is traditionally celebrated with the harvest of rice. However, we celebrated the abundance of produce from our garden and orchards. Devi tries all kinds of combinations and cooking methods to use up the fresh onions, peppers, green beans, potatoes, cabbages and carrots that Bhojan or Raman bring in every evening. She bakes the potatoes in the coals and serves them steaming hot with fresh butter or ghee. The potato skins are charred and crunchy and taste smoky. My mother likes the beans, carrots and onions lightly sautéed in oil and flavored with fresh cilantro leaves, served with simple steamed rice.

Besides the vegetables, Raman brings in wicker baskets filled with ripe plums, crisp apples and pears. The yellow plums are sweet and bursting with juice and flavor. They have a mild taste and I can eat them by the dozen. The ruby red plums are tart and the flesh is a beautiful blood-red. We have so many ruby plums that my mother decides to make jam. The kitchen smells of sugar and warm fruit as Devi, Muthi and my mother stir pots of bubbling red jam. Devi doesn't like the tart flavor and keeps adding cup after cup of sugar until the plum turns into red soup. The twins and I lick the wooden spoons to test and see if each pot is sweet and tasty. The thick jars of ruby red plum jam, pretty as jewels, are stored on the kitchen window sill.

The pears from our orchard are crisp and sweet. Each pear is a flawless creamy globe once it's been peeled. There are three pear trees in the orchard and this year they are heavy with fruit. My mother had Devi and Muthi peel all the pears that Raman can pick. She wants to use up this mountain of fruit by making pear preserve. The hot pears and sugar splutter and coat the wall of the hearth with sticky drops. Bottled pale yellow pear jams join the ruby red jars of plums on the window sill.

Besides fruit, there are lots of vegetables to preserve and cook. This year, the tomatoes are fat and red. Each one is perfect, bursting with flavor and thick juice. We have tangy cucumber and tomato relish with every meal.

"The only way to get rid of this many tomatoes is to make chutney," my mother says to Devi one morning.

Soon Devi is busy peeling and mincing onions. Her eyes water as she fills a huge steel bowl with the pungent vegetable. She also chops up shiny green peppers and finely minces gnarly ginger roots.

Mother has been busy immersing fresh tomatoes in boiling water and then peeling them. Ayah helps squeeze out the seeds and dices the red vegetables.

Next, my mother heats a large pan with hot oil and throws in a handful of mustard seeds which start to splutter. Devi hands her the bowl of chopped onions and diced peppers and my mother adds these to the hot oil. The kitchen is warm with the smell of cooking onions and peppers. Finally, the tomatoes and ginger are added to the vegetables. The tangy tart tomato chutney has to simmer for a long time. The right consistency is important.

My father visits us in the middle of the week to celebrate Onam. He brings fresh black pepper, long fragrant pods of vanilla and tender young cardamom seeds. The house is aromatic with the scent of the spices and my mother's cooking.

On Onam morning I get up early and tiptoe out of the house because I don't want to wake the twins quite yet. My mother is already out in front of the house sorting through a giant pile of colorful roses, purple dahlias and orange marigolds. Devi has swept the area of leaves and dirt. Muthi mixes cow dung and water and carefully sprinkles the pungent mixture on the ground. I wrinkle my nose at the smell of cow dung but I know the mixture will help keep the flowers in place.

I squat beside my mother and help her divide all the blooms.

"Meena, let's divide the flowers by color. You can do the yellow and red ones and I do the white, pink and orange," my mother says, pushing the pile of flowers toward me. "You can take the petals off."

Soon the piles of pretty petals are ready. Now, comes the fun part. My mother has drawn up a circular arrangement for the flower petals and I carefully follow the pattern as I begin to lay out neat rows of bright yellow rose petals. Devi and Muthi join us and we complete a brilliantly colored pattern on the ground. My mother places a small mound of mud in the center of the circle. This represents King Mahabali's head rising out of the earth on Onam day. She places an oil lamp with three cotton wicks right next to the king's earthen head. I push in six sticks of sandalwood scented incense into the mound. We light the lamp and incense sticks. The air is rich with the scent of flower blooms and the fragrance of the sandalwood incense. I inhale the familiar smells and turn around to wish Appu and Thangam a happy Onam.

"Come see the bhali." I lead them out to the beautiful arrangement on our doorstep. "Do you think King Mahabali will be happy to see this?" Thangam asks me. I grin at her. "Of course, he is so happy he probably has brought you gifts."

"Let's go get the gifts," Appu yells and races into the house, followed by Thangam.

I take one more look at the Onam flowers and say a prayer in my heart. *Please let all our Onams be such happy ones.*

Tomato Chutney II

About 2 cups ripe tomatoes peeled and seeded and chopped.
Or substitute one 28 oz can of whole tomatoes.
2 tablepoons vegetable oil
1 teaspoon black mustard seeds
1 sprig curry leaves or 2 bay leaves
3 tablespoons finely chopped ginger
1 small red onion or shallot, finely minced
2 cloves garlic, peeled and finely minced
1 teaspoon salt
1-3 tablespoons brown sugar
1 green or red chili pepper, sliced (optional)

Preparation: Heat the oil in a saucepan with a lid. Add mustard seeds to warm oil, cover saucepan and wait for the seeds to splutter and pop and turn grey (about 1 minute or less). Add chopped onion, bay leaves or curry sprig and ginger. Sauté until onions are soft. Add garlic, optional chili peppers and then the tomatoes with juice. Add salt and 1 tablespoon of sugar and let mixture simmer over low heat for about 20 minutes. The sauce should be fairly thick. If the tomatoes are acidic add another tablespoon of sugar. Makes about 1 cup chutney. Serve with rice.

Chapter Twenty One

Celebrating Cow Festival

• • • • • • • • • •

"One day Lord Shiva ordered his mount, the big black bull Nandi, to deliver a message to the people of India that everyone should take an oil bath every day and eat food only once a month. However, Nandi wasn't listening to Lord Shiva's instructions because he was taking a short nap and so he delivered a different message asking people to eat every day and to take an oil bath once a month. Because of the bull's mistake, there was a severe shortage of grains on earth. Lord Shiva wasn't happy with Nandi and ordered the big bull to return to earth and help humans plough the fields. So Nandi and his descendants were doomed to pull the plough forever. But people were grateful to Nandi for his help and when they harvested the grains they decided to honor Nandi and all farm animals with a festival in mid-winter. Pongal or cow celebration takes place every year in honor of all domestic animals."

—as retold by Ayah

Our cows are my pets. I love everything about them from their graceful, swaying walk to their long tails that look so much like my mother's hair in a braid. I like their wet noses and gentle eyes, and I particularly like spending time in the cowshed where it is always warm and cozy.

We have two sheds and both are simple buildings with cement floors and tin roofs. When the rain beats down, it sounds like a hundred horses are running on it. The cowshed closest to the house is used for milking and for housing sick cows. The other one is located at the bottom of a small slope at the very back of our property.

My favorite cow is Shobha who has a creamy white coat and scary-looking curved horns. Shobha is very sweet natured and when I was young she was very patient with me while I tugged on her thick rubbery udder, trying to milk her.

This January morning I walk outside to find all the cows tied up in the yard behind our house. Bhojan is busy washing each animal. I can see the steam rising from their wet bodies in the cool air. The twins are also helping in their own way by throwing water at each other.

"Stop that Appu and Thangam," I say to them. "Can I help you Bhojan?"

"Meena, you can help by taking these two inside," he says, gesturing toward Appu and Thangam who are fighting over a dish rag.

I drag the protesting twins inside with promises that we all could help Bhojan with decorating the cows.

A little later we come outside to find Bhojan mixing various powders. He fills small containers with lovely shades of blue, green, red and yellow dyes. Bhojan then ties a piece of cloth on the end of a stout stick and dips the cloth end into a bowl of dye. He uses this homemade paintbrush to decorate the bull's curved horns.

The twins stand on old overturned milk buckets and paint the horns of the cows. I paint Shobha's horns a bright blue.

"Here's a cap for the tip of the horn," Bhojan says. He hands me a small metal cap with gold tassels dangling from its tip. I fit the cap on the tip of Shobha's horn and she shakes her head at me. The tassels glitter in the early morning sun.

Thangam and Appu helps Bhojan tie a string of bright-colored glass beads and brass cowbells around all our cows' necks.

"You are the most beautiful animal," I say to Shobha. The cow shakes her great big neck making the brass bells tinkle.

Later in the day, Kashi and Raman join us. Kashi strings bright orange marigolds and bold-colored bougainvilleas into long garlands. Shobha looks quite colorful with her flower necklace and blue horns. She stamps her feet on the earthen floor when she smells the sweet porridge.

"Are you ready for some payasam?"

Shobha's tongue is warm and rough on my palms as she gently licks the sweet rice pudding. My mother lights a wick and blesses each animal. The scent of steaming cows, incense and burning oil fill the little building.

"May the cows be part of our prosperity," she murmurs. "May their lives be peaceful and full of good health."

She then hands out small pieces of milk fudge, the pale creamy squares flecked with bits of lime zest, a tantalizing blend of vanilla and citrus flavors. Some of the fudge is flavored with finely chopped almonds and contains bits of dried fruit. The fudge dissolves in my mouth into a creamy puddle of flavor and I savor the taste of nuts and sugar.

Shobha's ears are smooth and I stroke her neck and remember the dramatic night when she was born a few years ago.

Several years ago

We had just finished dinner, when Bhojan comes into the dining room. He is too shy to come in while we are eating.

"Come in Bhojan. What's happening?" my mother asks.

"Little Mother, I didn't want to disturb your meal...."

"No, no, tell me your news."

"It's Gopika. Her labor has started and she may be in trouble, you'd better come and see to her."

His face is pinched with worry. Without another word, mother gets up to follow him.

"Amma, Amma. Please let me come too. I want to help. Please," I plead.

I was about to go on pleading, but my mother surprises me, "Meena, you can come, but you have to stay out of the way. When I tell you to leave you must go without any complaining."

"Oh, Amma, I promise."

"Don't worry about the little one," Bhojan says. "Kashi can keep an eye on her too."

"Well, Meena go with Ayah and get a sweater and some slippers before coming outside."

Ayah and I walk across the yard into the cowshed, which now smells of fresh dung, straw, and animal sweat. Shobha stands in a corner, pawing the straw and grunting.

Ayah walks over to feel the cow's bulging stomach.

"Well, the calf is still alive. Bhojan, did you go inside?"

Bhojan nods, "We need to pull the calf out because she is getting tired."

Just then poor Gopika's legs seem to give way and she tries to lie down.

"Watch out," my mother cries. "Ease her down."

Bhojan massages the cow's leg and neck and my mother murmurs soothing words in her ear. Kashi dips a rag in a bucket of water and wipes the animal's nose and mouth. I want to help too. I walk up to the poor creature and stroke her soft head. Her nose is dry and her eyes are wide with pain.

"It's all right. You'll be fine. You are such a brave cow," I whisper in her big furry ear.

"We need help," Bhojan says. "We need Raman to help us."

"Is he any good?" my mother asks.

"He's the best. He has healer's hands. Kashi, go quickly to the village and ask Raman to come."

The village is a short 10-minute walk from our house and Kashi comes in with Raman right behind her. Raman is the tallest man I've ever seen with long, curly hair with a bright red and blue cloth wrapped around his waist. Raman prefers the colorful lungi cloth to the plain white dhoti that Bhojan usually wears. Tonight he has an olive-green woolen vest over his shirt. His bare feet are broad and hairy.

He removes his vest, rolls up his sleeves, and pulls his lungi over his knees. After he washes his hands in a bucket of soapy water, he squats down and inserts his right hand deep inside the cow. I scrunch my face in disgust and turn away.

A moment later, he takes out his hand, which is all slimy and bloody, and sits back on his heels.

"It's not too bad, little mother. The calf is alive, but we need to help it come out. I'll need some rope."

He washes his hands again. This time grunting with the effort, he puts his arm inside the cow and catches hold of the calf's small feet.

"Quick, give me the rope. After I tie it to the calf, start pulling."

It takes him several tries before he can tie the rope around the calf's foot. Finally, he nods his head. Bhojan, Kashi and my mother pull on the rope. I stand back and watch, careful to stay out of the way. Soon everyone's face is red and sweaty, but finally the calf comes out of Gopika with a slithering pop.

Raman wipes the calf down with a piece of rough cloth and places the small creature in front of the tired cow. Gopika is too exhausted to get up. She looks at the calf in surprise but soon begins to lick it dry.

Within a few minutes the calf is already trying to stand on unsteady legs. I pat her creamy white coat and watch her big ears twitch.

"I'm going to call you Shobha and you will be my very special pet," I say to the restless animal.

Milk Fudge

½ cup unsalted butter at room temperature
2/3 cup confectioner's sugar
1 ¾ cup dry whole milk powder (or as needed)
1 teaspoon milk or cream (or as needed)
A few drops of vanilla, almond or citrus essence
Or 2 tablespoons grated nuts or pureed dried fruit
such as dates or apricots
About 1/2 cup finely chopped nuts

Preparation: Cream the butter and sugar until smooth and fluffy. Use your fingers and add the milk powder and milk/cream until you have a nice soft fudge. Add the flavoring or the nuts and knead until everything is nicely blended together.

Wash and dry hands thoroughly before rolling the fudge into little balls. Roll each ball in finely chopped nuts.

Makes about two dozen pieces of fudge.

Chapter Twenty Two

Growing Pains

• • • • • • • • • •

During botany lesson a classmate of mine, Sylvia, is at the blackboard naming the parts of a flower when I am horrified to see a reddish-brown stain on the back of her pink school uniform. Several of our classmates also notice the stain and begin to giggle. As soon as Sylvia sits down I lean over and whisper, "Sylvia, you have a stain on your back. I think you will have to go to the office."

I see her eyes fill with tears and quickly offer her my sweater to tie around her waist. She doesn't come to school for the rest of the week and when she finally comes back on Monday morning, she's doesn't want to talk about what happened to her. She just thrusts my sweater at me and moves away without a word. Kumari and I have long discussions about Sylvia and her stain. Finally, I decide to talk to my mother about it.

That evening I find my mother sitting by the hearth, talking to Devi. She looks up and her eyes light up when she sees me.

"Meenakutty, it has been a long time since you've come to sit in the kitchen with Devi and me," she says. I sit next to her in front of the warm hearth. I'm too big to sit on her lap so I lean down and hug her shoulders.

Devi gets up to wash her hands and take her dirty plate to the sink.

"Amma, I wanted to ask you about something that happened at school today."

"Of course kutty, you can ask me anything."

"Remember Sylvia, the shopkeeper's daughter, she was sent home last week because she had a stain on her uniform. I know it means she has her first menstruation but Kumari and I were wondering…"

Suddenly, I feel shy, especially when Devi comes back, wiping her hands on the ends of her cotton sari, a huge grin on her face.

"So the kutty is finally growing up," she says with a gentle laugh.

My mother doesn't laugh. Instead she takes my hand in hers and says, "Well, kutty…you know about how a girl becomes a woman and starts to bleed once a month?"

"I remember Amma and what happened when Shanti lied about her bleeding."

"Oh, yes, I'd forgotten about Shanti," my mother says with a sigh. "What a mess that woman turned out to be."

Shanti was a young woman who showed up at our doorstep one evening a few years ago, alone, hungry and cold. She told my mother she was running away from an abusive father and that she had no family to help her. Ayah tried to warn my mother saying that Shanti had the look of a girl who had secrets. But Shanti pleaded with my mother to give her a job, any job, and that she would be happy to be a maid. My mother, who didn't need another maid, nevertheless, hired her to be Devi's helper in the kitchen. She was put in charge of washing the clothes and dishes. Shanti worked diligently for about a week and then started to get up later and later. I had the unpleasant task on weekends to wake her up so that she could help with the breakfast dishes. She was "too tired" to get up and would come into the kitchen around mid-morning, wanting a cup of coffee with plenty of milk and sugar.

My mother became suspicious and asked Shanti the date of her last monthly bleeding. Shanti had replied she was having her monthlies right now and even showed my mother some rags that had reddish brown stains on it.

A couple of weeks later, Shanti was nowhere to be seen. Her room was empty and several of my mother's saris that were hanging to dry in the storage room laundry line were also missing

Our postman brought the news that she had turned up in the next village, pregnant and homeless, and had been taken in by the local convent.

Much later, my mother discovered that the reddish brown stains on the rags were red nail polish and for a long time she and Devi had teased each other that it was the time of the month for red nail polish.

"Well, I don't think Sylvia used red nail polish" I say with a smile at the memories.

"It's not unusual for the first time to be a complete surprise kutty," my mother says to me. "But I don't think it will happen for a while. You are still too young."

My mother was right. It is a year later, when I am nearly 15 that I wake up one morning with stomach cramps and wetness between my thighs. I'm so relieved that it didn't happen at school that I forget to be embarrassed and run to tell my mother.

She and Muthi are sitting in the front room, idly chatting, and sipping on coffee when I burst into the room.

I stop and say in a whisper to my mother, "I think its red nail polish time for me."

For a moment my mother doesn't understand and then she laughs out loud and pulls me down next to her. "Muthi, this one is finally a young woman."

Muthi beams at me. "Come, let's go take a warm bath and I'll tell you about the traditions practiced in the village."

I sit in a huge metal tub of warm water and let the warmth soothe my aching stomach.

"In the village, when I got my first bleeding, it was announced to the entire village. My mother and aunts led me to the woman's hut at the back of our house and I stayed there for four days with other women who were also bleeding. We had a lot of fun, singing, telling stories and laughing." Her voice is wistful. "On the ceremonial day bath, my mother and her cousins led me to the pool for ceremonial bath and I was given new clothes, in-cluding a cloth to cover my chest. That year, our family had a lit-tle bit of money so they hired a horse to carry me home from the temple. All the children ran after us and I was taken home where my mother had made a huge feast. It was just three months later that my husband's family came and proposed marriage."

"What will we be doing here? I hope I don't have to ride around Mahagiri," I say, shivering at the thought.

"Rithumani is a special time in a girl's life and we'll celebrate it but without inviting everyone in Mahagiri," Muthi says.

Muthi helps me out the water and dries my back. I put on clean clothes and tie a rag wrapped with spongy cloths in be-tween my legs. Later my mother shows how to get rid of the spongy cloths and to wash the rag and hang it to dry on the line in the bathroom.

The ceremony is held on a second Saturday and my father is here. A special breakfast feast has been prepared, featuring kichadi, a tasty treat of rice, yellow split peas, cumin, ginger and fresh black pepper. The creamy rice dish is further flavored with pungent cilantro leaves and ghee-fried cashews. Kichadi with creamy yogurt is my favorite breakfast food.

My mother helps me take the ceremonial day bath. She rubs a paste made out of ground up mung beans and fresh turmeric root on my cheeks, forehead, arms and legs.

"You are a lady when you bathe with turmeric," she says to me.

I wash off the yellow paste and dry myself. I wrap a towel around my head and another around me and go into the dressing room to get ready. I let out a gasp of surprise at the beautiful dark blue silk sari. The sari has gold threads on the borders and ends.

"Is this for me Muthi?" I ask, touching the soft silken material. It feels smooth and cool against my fingers.

"Your first sari," she says with a smile.

My mother comes in and helps me drape the sari. She places a bright red bindi dot on my forehead. There are sweet jasmine blossoms entwined in my braid and gold jewelry glisten in my ears and around my neck.

I walk outside and my father is waiting by the doorway. He holds half a coconut filled with red liquid, a mixture of water and red dye. He dips his fingers in the liquid and places a dot on my forehead, below my bindi dot. Next Muthi comes up with a small clay bowl of burning camphor and she chants softly as she circles the flame around me three times. Devi comes forward and dips her fingers in the coconut my father holds. She too places a ceremonial bindi dot on my forehead. My mother leads me to the dining room and I sit down. Appu approaches with a shy smile and gives me a wrapped present.

"What have you got for your chechi?" I ask him.

I remove the wrapping to reveal a piece of beautiful silk cloth, just the right size to make into a sari blouse.

"I love the beautiful yellow color Appukutty," I say and hug him tight.

"My turn," Thangam says, pushing Appu aside. "See, what I got you."

Her present is a set of four different colors of nail polish.

"No red?" I tease her.

Muthi and my mother laugh and Thangam looks puzzled. She's about to ask why we are laughing but my father announces, "Time for kichadi."

Everyone sits down and Devi serves us breakfast. As I take a bite of the smooth and delicious rice dish mixed with creamy yogurt, I look up to see everyone smiling and laughing.

I have to smile too because their joy is contagious.

Kichadi

½ cup dried split peas or hulled mung beans, washed and soaked in warm water for 3-4 hours
1 cup white basmati rice, rinsed and drained.
1 ½ cups water
3-4 tablespoons ghee or vegetable oil
2 tablespoons minced ginger
2 teaspoon cumin seeds
1 teaspoon tumeric powder
1- ½ teaspoon coarsely cracked black pepper
6 cloves
¼ teaspoon hing or asafeotida (optional)
1/3 cup cashews bits
1 ½ teaspoon salt
Pats of fresh butter for garnish
Cilantro or parsley sprigs for garsish

Preparation: Partially cook the beans in about 3 cups of water for 20 minutes. Drain and set aside.

Heat 2 tablespoons of ghee in a large sauce pan with a lid. Add cumin seeds, stirring until the seeds sizzle. Add minced ginger, tumeric powder, cloves and drained rice. Saute until the grains are golden brown. Add beans, water and salt. Bring to boil. Lower heat and simmer the rice and beans until tender, about 20-25 minutes.

Meanwhile, warm a tablespoon or so of ghee is a small saucepan and fry the cashew bits. Season the cooked rice and beans with freshly cracked pepper. Garnish each serving with a pat of butter, fried cashews and sprig of fresh herb.

Serves 2-4.

Chapter Twenty Three

Saying Good-bye

• • • • • • • • • •

When a mother loses her only son, she takes his body to the Buddha and asks him to find a cure and bring her dead child back to life. The Compassionate Buddha agrees and asks the grieving mother to bring him a handful of mustard seeds from a family that has never lost a child, husband, parent or friend. When the mother is unable to find such a house in her village, she realizes that death is common to all, and she cannot be selfish in her grief.

—A Buddha story from the Dhamapada

The summer I am 16 my world turns upside down. The morning dawns clear and bright, full of promise and happiness. School is out for summer vacation and the twins are getting ready to celebrate their "star birthday," a celebration of the time of year of their birth. Their actual birth date is about a month away, but on this June morning we gather to share their joy of turning nine. We watch them open a variety of gifts from new clothes to toys.

As an additional treat, I promise to take both my siblings to a movie later that day. Thangam and Appu are excited to go with their chechi to the movies.

The house is filled with laughter and happiness because my father is here this weekend for the twins' birthday celebration. The mellow June sunshine has warmed all the cold corners of our old house and its life-giving heat has permeated all our moods. My mother is laughing in the kitchen and even Ayah has nothing to complain about because her arthritic fingers aren't as painful as usual on this warm day.

My mother and Devi have outdone themselves in the kitchen. There are mounds of fluffy white rice, fragrant ghee or melted butter to drizzle on the steaming rice, coriander coconut gravy with bits of okra and tomato, spicy garlic broth, crisp rice and bean wafers, aviyal or mixed vegetable stew, tangy injeepully, and milky smooth rice pudding. The aromas of ginger, coconut and cardamom fill the house and add to the festive air. Injeepully, a tangy condiment featuring fresh ginger and tamarind paste, is my father's favorite relish.

"A feast is not complete without injeepully," he says as he licks the sweet sour condiment off his fingers. "Even in the poorest house a simple meal is turned into a feast with a few drops of injeepully. Eating a spoonful of this tangy sauce is like experiencing life. First, you taste the sweet, salty flavor and just when you think this is the best thing you have ever eaten, you bite into a bitter fenugreek seed that reminds you injeepully, like life, is bittersweet filled with loss and sorrow."

I, too, love the sour taste of the ginger sauce but have to usually wash it down with cool water or scoops of sweet rice pudding.

After our meal, my father wanders into the backyard to walk off the feast and then take a short afternoon nap. My mother, Ayah and Devi are busy in the kitchen cleaning up after the big meal. My sister and brother are ready to go to the movies and after promising my mother that I'll take good care of my younger siblings, we are off to wait for the bus.

The afternoon bus is not as full and we easily find places to sit. My brother insists on a seat by the window and my sister wants to sit near the aisle, so I find myself right in the middle. I open my little plastic purse with a blue and white logo of the globe etched with the letters "Pan-am Airlines" and carefully count out the change for the conductor.

"Off to the movies?" he asks, tweaking my sister's cheeks. "You can get the same bus back in the evening."

I sigh. There are no secrets in our little town. Ayah used to say when she sneezed, the entire village wiped their noses. I should have known that the conductor would have knowledge of our plans. I'm sure that Ayah or my mother has asked him to keep an eye on us.

A short and bumpy ride later we are arrive at the movie theatre. The theatre is one of the newer buildings in our town of Mahagiri and is a huge and bright pink structure. Since pink is my favorite color, I like the look of the place, but I have heard more than one adult complain about the garish color of the building. There are a lot of people milling around the entrance of the theatre and I want to make sure I don't lose my sister and brother. I pull each of them along with me to the window that has a sign "First Class Tickets Only." The line here is much shorter than the one for the less expensive second and third class tickets. I hand over several rupee notes and the man behind the counter gives me three yellow tickets. We walk over to the large metal gates and wait for them to open. The early matinee has not finished and we have to wait for few minutes.

"I'm thirsty," my brother Appu whines. "I need to go to the bathroom."

I look down at his face, impatient at all his needs.

"You'll have to wait for a drink until we get inside," I say without much sympathy. "Unless you want to go to the bathroom in the streets like the dogs, you'll have to wait."

He is about to start whining or even cry when the gates suddenly open without any warning and a huge crowd of people surge out of the theatre.

"What a crowd," a grandmotherly looking lady says behind me. "Did they all fit into that building?"

I smile at her, but don't bother answering her question which I think is silly because the building has two theaters and can hold a lot of people. We wait until the last of the people stream past us and make our way inside. I take my brother inside the ladies toilet and hold my nose at the awful stench. Why can't people flush after using the public restrooms? The mess is incredible and nauseating. I'm glad I don't have to use the facilities. I'd rather hold it in than come back in here again.

"Come on, let's go find some good seats," I tell my brother and sister.

"Can we get a Coca-Cola?" my sister asks, her face lighting up with a beguiling smile.

I look at the change leftover in my little plastic wallet.

"I suppose there is enough for one bottle of Fanta. We'll have to share."

"Why can't we get a Coca-Cola? I hate Fanta," my sister grumbles, her smile disappearing.

"Well, it's my money and I like Fanta," I say in a determined voice.

We carry our bottle of icy cold Fanta and paper straw with us into the gloomy interior of the theatre. We make our way up the aisles to the middle of the vast hall. I decide to sit in the middle and hold onto the bottle of soda so that my brother and sister take turns sipping from the bottle. I allow them only a few sips because I have no intention of taking them to the bathroom again.

Chattering ladies pile into seats behind us and the scent of their hair oil fills the air. I'm very sensitive to pungent smells and wrinkle my nose at the aroma of sweat and hair oil. The ladies finally settle down and my nose becomes used to the different scents in the theatre. The lights dim and we watch slide after slide of advertisement. I hate these commercials and almost groan out loud but my brother is enthralled and my sister forgets to ask for a sip of Fanta because she is busy watching a commercial for a bathing soap.

Finally, the movie starts and the three of us are engrossed in the story about a boy who has to watch his entire family being killed by awful bandits. But the boy grows up to be a police detective and finds the gang that destroyed his family and arrests them all. He falls in love with a beautiful girl, marries her, and lives happily ever after. The movie, even though it is satisfying leaves me feeling grumpy and out of sorts. The three of us come out of the dim theater and blink in the bright sunshine.

"I promised Ma that I would pick up some grapes from Mohammed," I say. "So let's go there and then take the bus from his store."

"I can't walk," my brother grumbles. "I'm too tired."

Grudgingly, I give him a piggyback ride down the hill to the fruit stand. Mohammed, the cross-eyed stall owner is happy to see us.

"Here little one, try this big juicy grape," he says shoving a ripe grape in my brother's hand. "Here little miss, you try this piece of orange."

Appu gobbles up the fruit and says it is the sweetest grape he has tasted. Mohammed grins and wraps up a bunch of pale green grapes for me in a newspaper. Thangam sucks on the piece of orange and smiles shyly at Mohammed.

"Tell Muthi the mangoes will be in by the end of the month," he says, placing the newspaper bundle in my arms.

I thank him and we walk to the bus stop. We don't have to wait long before the green and yellow bus pulls up. We wait until the passengers come out like a long line of busy ants and then we make our way to the front of the bus. My brother likes to sit right behind the driver, a jolly fat man named Chandran. Chandran has a handlebar moustache and cheerful eyes. His rumbling laugh is contagious and I have to smile when I hear him. He turns around and winks at us.

"Hey boy, want to come toot the horn?" he asks my brother, who doesn't wait for more than a second before scrambling over me to get to the front of the bus. He is startled by the sound of the air horn at first but then giggles with delight.

"Can I do it again?"

"No, I think we scared that little old lady out there and we don't need to give her husband a heart attack," Chandran chuckles good-naturedly. "Go back and sit down. Almost time to take off."

A few minutes later we are on our way home. The sun is setting and the sky is pale lavender like the jacaranda blossoms. Soon the lavender will deepen to dark purple and then a velvety black. The bus jerks to a stop in front of our house and through the window I can see our front yard is filled with people. Wondering what is going on, the three of us get down very slowly. The bus driver stops the bus and jumps down to follow us into the gate which is thrown wide open. I see Ayah standing to one side, her cheeks wet with tears and her eyes swollen and red.

"What's happened Ayah? Why are you crying?" I ask, suddenly filled with an urgency I couldn't explain to myself. "Tell me what's going on."

I almost shake the old woman. She shakes her head, and dabs at her streaming eyes.

"You poor children. How can I tell you?"

I glare at her and turn to ask someone else when the sound of a car engine blares just behind me. I turn around and see a black and yellow taxi cab, backing carefully into our yard. My sister and brother are clinging to each of my hands and I can't move fast with both of them clutching me. I see several men, including Bhojan and Raman, carrying my father down the front steps. My mother is following them, her face scrunched up and wet with tears.

"Ma!" I shout. "What's happened to Achan?"

She draws alongside me and pulls me into her arms. It is awkward because I'm still holding onto my brother and sister.

"Oh Meena, it's your father. He's not feeling well and we are taking him to the hospital."

I must have looked bewildered because Bhojan comes over and says, "It's alright Meenakutty. Raman and I will go with your mother to the hospital. We'll send the taxi back and you can come with Muthi and see to your mother and father. Now let us go."

I step back from the car and watch my mother get inside the taxi. Soon the taxi is gone, only the swirl of diesel fuel is left behind.

"Come inside children," Ayah says. She has stopped weeping. "We'll go inside and light a lamp for your father's health."

"What happened to my father, Ayah?" I ask again.

She shakes her head. "It was after the meal, the master had gone to take a nap, and little later you mother went in with a cup of hot tea, and found him complaining of heart burn. Your mother called me and I gave him some jeera water to soothe his stomach. We all thought he had eaten too much. But soon he became very pale and then very red. He started to sweat and say he couldn't breathe because his chest was too tight. Luckily, the taxi had come to drop off Thimban's wife and we had Raman go fetch the car. Pray God that the master will be alright.'

I'm silent as I watch Ayah light a lamp and some incense sticks. Even as I breathe in the scent of the burning lamp and the rose-scented incense, I can still see my father's face as he lies in Raman and Bhojan's arms. His face muscles are flax and his jaw is relaxed and open. He did not look like a healthy man. I have a bad feeling that the worst is yet to come.

"Come into the kitchen and have something to drink while we wait for the taxi," Ayah coaxes the three of us into the kitchen.

She and Devi bustle around, heating milk and finding cups and plates for us. My brother and sister were subdued and quiet. They look so sad, I have to bend down and give them a hug. They cling to me and I can feel Thangam's little body trembling against me.

"Shh…It's going to be okay," I murmur against her head. "Achan will be fine."

But I don't believe my own words and I feel a lump in my throat. Devi has uncovered a plate of leftovers and the tangy, familiar smell of injeepully fills the air. The sharp scent of ginger and chilies tickles my nose and brings tears to my eyes. I don't even know I'm crying until I taste the salty tears sliding into my lips.

Injeepully

1/2 cup fresh ginger, peeled and grated or minced
Tamarind pulp about the size of a small lemon
2 cups hot water
5 tablespoons vegetable oil
1 teaspoon mustard seeds
1 teaspoon turmeric powder
2-4 green chilies, washed and chopped
1 teaspoon fenugreek seeds
1-4 tablespoons brown sugar
1 teaspoon salt
1/8 teaspoon hing, asafotida (optional)
2 springs of curry leaves (optional)

Preparation: Soak the tamarind pulp in the hot water for about 15 minutes. Using your fingers, separate the softened pulp and squeeze out the pulp. Strain the tamarind water and set aside. Heat oil in a large saucepan with a lid. Add mustard seeds to warm oil. Cover and let the seeds splutter and pop, about 25 seconds. Add chopped ginger, curry leaves, turmeric powder, fenugreek seeds and green chilies. Let the seeds brown. Add tamarind water, salt, sugar and Hing, if using. Let the mixture come to a boil. Let it simmer on a low heat for about 15 to 20 minutes. Taste for salt. The chutney will thicken as it cools. Makes about 1 ¼ cup. If you use tamarind concentrate, the sauce will be fairly thin.

NOTE: Tamarind pulp is available in small blocks at Indian or Middle Eastern groceries. Tamarind is also available in a paste form under the brand name Tamco. Subsitute about 4 tablespoons of Tamco for the pulp. Hing or Asafoe-

tida is available in small jars. This spice is pungent and a small amount goes a long way. Curry leaves add a wonderful flavor to all south Indian foods and can be replaced by bay leaves (not the same taste, though).

Chapter Twenty Four

Final Goodbyes

• • • • • • • • • •

It's a strange and sad journey down the hill for our family. The four of us are squeezed together in the back seat of the taxi. Muthi and Devi sit up in the front with Jaibal. Bhojan and Raman are accompanying my father's body in another car. We are taking my father's body to his brother's house for cremation and final rites. I still can't believe my father is dead. He has always been larger than life and his booming laughter filled every room of our house. I can't imagine never hearing his laugh and never seeing him again. We begin our desolate trip late in the evening and now night has fallen and I can barely see the view outside the car window. The whole world is as dark as my heart.

A passing street lamp lights up the interior of the car and even my mother's red silk sari looks drab and dark in the artificial light. My brother and sister are asleep, leaning on me and my mother, and their faces look pale and ghostly in the shadows. I stifle a sob and my mother reaches over and lays a soft hand on my cheek.

"It will be alright Meenakutty," she whispers. "Your father's love will never leave the four of us."

I nod but can't speak because there is a huge lump in my throat. I feel tears run down my face. I lean back and close my tired eyes.

I wake up when the car comes to an abrupt stop. I look out and see we have arrived at my uncle's farmstead in Kerala. The sun is a huge orange ball in the horizon and the early morning rays glisten through the palm fronds. The unpaved road leading to my uncle's house is a slushy mess because of the heavy monsoon rains and we bump along unsteadily. I lean over and roll down the window and let in the cool morning air. Soon it will be hot and muggy, a typical tropical day.

The car finally comes to a stop, a few hundred yards from my uncle's farmhouse. A five-foot stone wall surrounds the farmhouse but the gate is wide open in welcome.

"Little mother, the car can't go any further. You will have to walk along the path to the house," says Jaibal.

We wake the twins and all of us stumble outside. Green paddy rice fields stretch out as far as I can see. The emerald fields of rice are inter-connected by narrow mud paths. We follow one of these trails to the main house, trying not to step in the pools of muddy water.

"Jaibal, will you wait here and help Bhojan and Raman with the body?" my mother's voice sounds weak and full of tears.

"Of course, I'll wait here for the car," Jaibal says. "Don't worry about anything little mother. I'll take care of the master."

My mother nods and our mournful procession continue down the muddy path toward the large farm house. We approach the iron gates which are painted a bright red, and I climb up the wide stone steps. My uncle, Damodaran Nair, is my father's younger brother. I have only met him once at a temple festival a few years ago. He is a tall man with long lean limbs draped in the traditional dhoti and a simple cotton vest. He is clean-shaven and his kind brown eyes are bloodshot and tired looking.

"Little sister," he says to my mother. "I'm so sorry. Come inside and have something to eat and drink. Seetha is waiting to take care of you."

My mother starts weeping and the twins and I stand back while she hugs my aunt Seetha. The farmhouse is spacious and the interior is cool and comfortable. The red cement floors are polished and gleaming and the walls are white-washed. There are slow moving ceiling fans in every room.

"You poor children, you must be so tired and hungry," aunt Seetha says to us. She takes us into the kitchen, a narrow room with a long rectangle wooden table. Aunt Seetha is round and plump with a comforting presence. Her smile is gentle and her touch is kind. She coaxes us to eat but I can only manage to sip some hot milk and honey. The twins eat slices of white bread smeared with homemade buffalo butter. My mother looks tired and beaten. She sits at the table with tears silently streaming down her pale cheeks. No one tries to get her to eat or drink because she refuses to answer or look at anyone.

The twins are content to sit with aunt Seetha. Muthi and Devi are also close by to keep an eye on them, so I walk down the long hallway to the front of the house.

"It has been over 24 hours since the death and it is best..." my uncle is talking to a priest and several other men in the front hallway. He stops when he sees me in the doorway and walks toward me, holding out his hand.

"Meena, we were just talking about your father's final rites. I know it will be hard for your mother to make any decisions right now," he says, clasping my hands. But we need to get the body ready for cremation because the day is getting warmer. Can you talk to your mother for me?"

"Yes uncle Damodaran. I can ask my mother but she will probably want you to take care of the details," I murmur. "She is too upset to think about anything right now."

"Very well then, Meena, I'll arrange everything but you might want to let your mother know that the cremation will take place early this evening."

I nod and turn away so that he can't see my tears. The word cremation sounds so final. Later that morning, I try to speak to my mother but she is too upset to listen to me. I find a quiet corner on the back porch of the house and settle down to wait for dusk. My grief is pinching my heart and I have no more tears to shed. In the background, I can hear talk about funeral pyres and oil and wood. The women in the kitchen are busy preparing a huge feast featuring my father's favorite dishes to feed all the visitors that are expected later that day. I allow the conversations wash over me, not really listening to all the words, and soon I fall asleep.

"There you are Meena," aunt Seetha is talking to me. "It is time. Come with me because your mother needs you."

I rub the sleep out of my eyes and go to the bathroom to wash my face and comb my hair. When I enter the living room I see many men and women, relatives and family friends, are lined up along the path of the house. I join the crowd and find my mother. I press close to her and my siblings. She places an arm around me and the twins hug me. We all wait in the late afternoon sunshine. The air is muggy and heavy with the promise of rain.

Then I see them coming. Bhojan, Raman, Jaibal, Uncle Damodaran and several other men I don't know are carrying my father's body. The women weep, wail aloud and beat their foreheads with their open palms. I flinch at the noise, and tears begin to flow down my face. My mother is sobbing by my side. I lick the salty corners of my lips and hiccup. The funeral procession moves slowly down the yard and toward the path into the back orchards. In between the mango and jackfruit trees, I can see a huge funeral pyre of wood and oil has been built. My mother and I, along with other ladies, watch from afar because females aren't allowed at the actual cremation. Soon dark smoke curls into the sky and I know my father's body is melting away in the heat of the pyre.

I lose track of time, but it seems like many hours later that my uncle and the other men return from the cremation site. Their faces are weary and dusty and they smell of smoke and fire.

Now, it is time for the ritual bath after a funeral. We go to the swimming hole to immerse our bodies in the clean water. The pond water is a dull gray and the water is cool and refreshing. I find no solace in the peaceful pool. The four of us slowly head back to the house and change into dry clothes. Aunty Seetha is waiting to lead us to the dining room for the funeral luncheon. Even though these stews, gravies and vegetables are my father's favorites, I can't seem to swallow anything. I can't get any food past the huge lump in my throat.

"Meena, you must try to eat something. How about trying this curd rice?" Aunt Seetha coaxes me to swallow a mouthful of the white rice dish.

The curd rice is a mixture of well-cooked rice, mild yogurt and salt. This particular dish is flavored with bits of red onion, shavings of fresh ginger and mustard seeds. The tangy taste of the mild rice reminds me of my father who loved to eat curd rice at picnics and family gatherings. He could stir together rice, butter, salt and yogurt to form the most soothing and creamy dish. I feel tears running down my face and mingle with the food in my mouth. For days after my father's death, the salty mild taste of curd rice is the only thing that slowly dissolves the lump of sorrow in my throat.

Twilight has come and gone and the smoke from my father's funeral pyre has dissipated. I walk to where my mother is sitting with Aunty Seetha.

"Amma, I want to go see where Achan was cremated."

"Meena, I don't think that is allowed," my aunt says.

Bu my mother looks at me and slowly nods her head.

"Meena and I need to go and say our final goodbyes to her father," she says to aunt Seetha. "Can you keep an eye on the twins until we get back?"

We can hear Aunty Seetha's protests, but my mother ignores her and pulls me along. We hold hands as we cross the yard and walk down the narrow trail to the fruit orchard. Twilight has deepened into early nightfall but we can see the last of the glowing embers of the funeral pyre. We walk to the edge of the blackened mound of wood. This is my father's final resting place, so far from his beloved farm in Chandur and from our shared home in Mahagiri. A wisp of smoke curls up and makes its way to the heavens. I lift my face to watch it disappear into the evening sky when I feel the first drops of moisture on my upturned face.

"Ahhh, they always say even the gods cry when a good man dies," my mother whispers beside me. "Even nature cries for your father Meena because he was a good man, a loving husband and beloved father."

I don't say anything. I just let the rain soak my skin and wash away my tears.

Curd/Yogurt Rice

2 cups well-cooked basmati or other white rice
1 cup mild yogurt (Pavel's brand or Greek style yogurt.)
2 tablespoons ghee or oil
1 teaspoon mustard seeds
1 sprig curry leaves or 2 bay leaves
1 small red onion or shallot, minced (about ½ cup)
1 tablespoon grated fresh ginger
1 teaspoon salt
Fresh cilantro leaves for garnish

Preparation: Heat the oil in a heavy saucepan that has a lid. Add mustard seeds and let the seeds pop and splutter and turn grey (less than a minute). Add onion and sauté until tender. Add curry or bay leaves and ginger. Add salt and then the well-cooked rice. Mix thoroughly until the rice is warm. Remove from heat and add yogurt and mix thoroughly. Taste for salt. Garnish with fresh cilantro leaves.

Serves 2-4.

Chapter Twenty Five

Taking Care of Amma

• • • • • • • • • •

It is hard coming home after cremating my father's body. The house is empty without my father's voice echoing in every room. My sister and brother are subdued and quiet, not wanting to play or leave my mother's side. My mother has the most difficult time coping with her loss. She sits in the house and refuses to go outside. She wears only white saris with an ash mark on her forehead. She does not want to wear the bright silks and big bindi dot. There are no more sweet chiming bangles on her arms nor fragrant jasmine buds in her hair. Her rich dark hair is streaked with grey and it seems like in the blink of an eye she has changed. I'm afraid to say it out loud but my mother looks like an old lady.

Muthi, Devi, Ayah, Kashi and the cowhands take care of the household. Meals are served on time and the cows are milked and the cowsheds washed down, but without my mother, the very heart of the kitchen is missing. I hate the cozy kitchen with its smoky walls and wooden beams. My familiar world has disappeared. I can't stand the sight of the strands of dried chili pepper and drying herbs and onions. The sizzle of cashews frying in nutty ghee or the sharp tang of fresh ginger makes me sick to my stomach. The kitchen is my mother's domain, but every bit of spice and herb brings back painful memories of my father. His memory is everywhere from the cups of sweet milky tea to the scent of fenugreek seeds browning in oil. When Devi fries fenugreek seeds and ginger, the familiar smell reminds me so strongly of my father that I rush out of the kitchen. I flee into my bedroom and fling myself on the bed, burying my head in my quilt. I weep for my father. I cry bitter tears for the fatherless twins, for my widowed mother. I weep for myself because now I will grow up without my father's guidance and love.

"Kutty, you'll make yourself sick crying like this." A hand smoothes my hair and rubs my back. I turn over and look up at Muthi. Her kind eyes are red and bloodshot and she looks weary and old.

"I can't stop thinking about him," I say, sitting up and hugging my knees to my chest. "I miss him so much."

"I know little one. The sorrow of losing a loved one is great. But did you see your brother and sister's face when you ran away and started crying? You upset and frightened them. Come, wash you face and drink some garlic broth and sit in the sunshine."

I know she's only trying to help me so I reluctantly stand up and accompany Muthi to the kitchen. The twins sit next to Devi, sipping on hot milk. I sit on the bench next to them. My brother leans closer to me and I put my arm around him. I feel my sister cuddle next to me. I have been feeling cold and alone but now their little bodies warm me up and I realize I'm not alone anymore.

"Chechi, is Amma going to die too?" Appu asks. His eyes big and round in his narrow face. I hug him tight and say, "Of course not, silly. She is just really sad and misses Achan. We'll have to help her feel better."

"How?" Thangam asks, a milk moustache dotting her upper lip. I lean over and wipe her mouth with my sleeve. "Well, we'll have to go sit next to her and remind her that we still need her. We'll have to keep asking her to eat and drink and take care of herself so that we can be a family again."

Thangam nods her head and for the first time in weeks, her face lights up with a smile. I smile back at her, happy to have distracted her.

"Meena, we have a problem."

I look up to see Bhojan standing in the doorway with his turban unwound and flung around his neck.

"Meenakutty, your mother hasn't been taking care of the milk accounts for the past few weeks and we have a problem," he says in an apologetic voice. "I don't want to worry you but Devi and Muthi thought you might be able to help me."

I stand up and hug the twins. "I'll be right back to have some rice and broth with you," I tell them. "Come Bhojan, lets got outside and you can tell me what is troubling you."

The air is balmy and warm outside and I feel the golden sun's invigorating touch on my skin. I take a deep breath of fresh air and feel the sorrow gripping my heart lessen a tiny bit. I look into Bhojan's worried face. "What's happening Bhojan? Did you talk to Amma?"

"I tried little one but she is not listening to me. I thought perhaps you could talk to her."

I nod. "Perhaps she'll listen to me but she is so full of pain and sorrow that she can't think of anybody but herself. What's the problem?"

"On the first of every month, I take the milk ledger and add up the accounts and then write the amount on a piece of paper and give it to our milk customers. Most of the customers pay me right away when I give them the bill or by the next day. But every month it is a struggle to get Shantiamma to pay her bill.

Your mother usually has to come with me and collect from her. It has been over a week since I gave Shantiamma the bill and she has yet to pay me."

"What do you want me to do?"

"Well, Meenakutty, if you could come to town tomorrow morning and ask Shantiamma for the money, I'm sure she'll pay you."

"Have you tried asking?"

Bhojan looks down at his bare feet and his face flushed with embarrassment. "I usually don't deal with her. It has always been your mother's job."

He's scared of Shantiamma! I can't believe it.

"Maybe she'll listen to me. I'll come with you tomorrow morning."

When the twins hear I'm going to the town of Mahagiri with Bhojan, they plead and beg to come along. Their little faces are bright and hopeful for the first time in weeks. They are even jumping up and down, in their usual pesky manner.

"Alright, alright, stop trying to pull my arm off, you can come with me."

The next morning, all three of us are in the kitchen, sipping warm drinks and waiting for Bhojan to come in with the fresh milk. Muthi, Devi and Ayah strain buckets of fresh milk into tall metal milk cans. Raman pours the strained milk into smaller containers and sets them aside. Each can is labeled with a number to help him deliver the cans to the right customer. The can with the blue number 20 on it contains 20 liters of milk for Woodland Restaurant in Mahagiri. Everyone is working quickly and silently. The only noise in the kitchen is the clanging of the metal cans, the incessant meowing of the two cats that whine and beg for a liquid breakfast and the cracking of the fire. My mother's absence is like a huge hole in the kitchen. My heart aches and I long to see her back in this smoke-filled room taking part in the milking and cooking. I see how hard Muthi, Ayah,

Devi and Bhojan work. I'm filled with determination to bring my mother back to life so that she can be part of this kitchen again. She's needed here.

Bhojan and Raman carry the cans of fresh milk to the front of the house and we follow them. We are taking the milk bus to the town of Mahagiri and there Bhojan and Raman will divide the chore of delivering milk. The sun is just peeking over the horizon and the air is still cool and misty. Appu and Thangam cling to me and I enjoy their warm bodies pressed against my side.

The bus comes to a stop in front of us in a cloud of black diesel smoke. Raman and Bhojan store the milk cans in the back of the bus. This early morning bus is known as the milk bus because it almost exclusively carries cowhands and their cans of milk. We are the only passengers, besides a few sleepy looking villagers.

"Little ones, you are off to an early start." The conductor tweaks my brother's cheek and pats my sister on the head. "Going to sell milk?"

"We're going to collect money," Thangam says. I nudge her with my elbow. "Ow, stop poking me."

Luckily, the conductor has moved on and I don't have to explain what my sister means.

About thirty minutes later, the bus comes to a grinding halt with a squeal and hiss. We wait for Raman, Bhojan and the other cowhands to unload the milk cans. The sun is now low in the horizon and the entire world is bathed in a beautiful golden hue. The early morning mist swirls around us and suddenly I'm glad to be alive. At this moment I can remember my father with happiness instead of despair.

"Come along little ones," Bhojan says. "Raman will take care of the big deliveries and we'll ride in the horse cart and deliver milk to the all the houses at the bottom of the hill."

The twins are excited to ride in a cart but when I see the rickety wooden cart being pulled by a tired old horse I'm not too eager. The driver is an old man with a sleepy face. Most of his head and part of his forehead is covered by a dirty turban. He wears a tattered old sweater and a stained cloth around his waist. He helps Bhojan load the milk cans in the back of the cart and then gets in the front and picks up the reins of the horse. Bhojan climbs in beside the driver and pats the hard wooden bench to indicate that we are supposed to sit next to him. The twins jump in but I'm still a little reluctant.

"Come on Meenakutty, we have to deliver the milk before it gets too late. Customers are waiting for their milk to pour into their morning coffees." Bhojan grins at me.

I sit down on the hard seat. The driver peers at me through bleary eyes and his eyebrows hang over his eyes like huge hairy caterpillars. He clicks his tongue and pulls on the reins and the old horse takes off at a surprisingly fast clip. We wind our way through the quiet streets and enter the residential area of the town. The driver seems to know where we are going and soon pulls the reins to stop the cart. Bhojan jumps out and goes to the back of the cart. A lady emerges from the house with an empty stainless steel pot. She waits patiently as Bhojan measures two cups from the milk can and pours it into the waiting container. Neither Bhojan nor the lady exchanges a word.

We stop at several houses along this street and then turn down a tree-lined street. We come to a halt in front of a large house with an open courtyard. I can hear a dog barking behind the courtyard wall.

"Shush, Chuppa. Be quiet or you won't get any milk today," a familiar voice says. It is our friend Angelina, the lady who sells delicious breakfasts at the Sunday markets. I wave and smile at her. She comes up to the cart and takes both my hands in hers. Her palms are rough and dry, but warm and large. Her enormous brown eyes are swimming in tears.

"Little one, my heart goes to you in your sorrow. How is your mother?"

I squeeze her hands and reply, "My mother is not well, Aunty. She misses my father and cannot stop crying."

"You poor things, you need her now more than ever. Wait here and let me get you something that may help your mother."

Bhojan takes a small milk can and delivers it to the house, walking through the courtyard. He comes back and waits by the cart for Angelina. She walks back out of the house with a small brass container covered with a piece of white cloth. She draws back the cloth, "This Meenakutty is sweet potato cooked and mashed with a little bit of ghee and salt. I then added a bite of ginger, a dash of turmeric, a pinch of pepper and a squeeze of fresh lime juice. The dish is soothing and tangy. Sweet potato made this way heals the heart, soothes the soul and feeds the hunger. When you go home, take some of this to your mother and tell her that her big sister Angelina sent it with her love and blessings. Tell her to eat a bite and let it heal her sorrow and mellow her grief. Share the dish with your brother and sister. Feel the healing power of the dish made with love."

My eyes fill with tears at her kind words and I can only nod and accept the dish. I hold the container of sweet potato magic in my lap. The cart now stops at a smaller house at the corner of the street.

"This is Shantiamma's house," Bhojan says. "I'll go deliver the milk and tell her you are here."

"Wait, Bhojan, don't take any milk. Let me go talk to her first."

Suddenly I'm filled with courage and I know what to say to Shantiamma. As I cross the street, the wooden door opens and Shantiamma stands in front of the house with an empty container, ready for her milk.

"Greetings, big mother," I say with a pleasant smile. The woman is scowling and her eyes are hard and cold. "My mother couldn't come to collect the monthly milk money, so I came instead."

"Where's my morning milk?" she asks in a gruff tone. I gesture toward the cart with my head. "Its right there and Bhojan will bring you some as soon as I have the milk money. In fact, my mother said to give you half a cup extra if you pay today."

"Your mother said that?" she peers at me suspiciously. "Alright, tell Bhojan to bring me my milk and I'll go get the money."

"Here, give me your vessel, big mother, and I'll go get your milk." I tug the container from her reluctant hands and walk toward Bhojan.

"Wait for me to come back before you pour the milk," I hear her say.

Soon she is back with a wad of rupee notes which she slowly and painstakingly counts into my waiting palm. After the last rupee has been counted, she turns to Bhojan and says, "Alright lets see you give me the milk."

Bhojan measures out the milk and looks up at me before pouring an extra half cup into Shantiamma's steel pot.

"Tell your mother I thank her for the milk and next month she doesn't have to send you to collect the money, I'll just give it to Bhojan," Shantiamma's tone is still gruff, but I notice she doesn't look as angry anymore.

"I'll tell my mother."

I climb back into the cart beside my sister. Bhojan smiles at me, "You are your mother's daughter, look at the way you coaxed the old witch to part with her money."

I laugh because I feel full of hope, knowing that things are going to get better soon. The sweet potato casserole bounces on my lap as we make our way down the quiet street.

Angelina's Sweet Potato Casserole

3 well cooked sweet potatoes or yams (about 2 cups mashed)
3 tablespoons oil or ghee
1 teaspoon mustard seeds
1 small red onion or shallot minced (about ½ cup)
1 small green bell pepper minced (about ½ cup)
1 generous tablespoon grated fresh ginger
1 green chili or ½ tsp. cayenne powder
1 teaspoon salt
1 tablespoon brown sugar
Juice from ½ lemon
1-2 pats of fresh butter

Preparation: Heat oil in a large saucepan with a lid with oil or ghee. Add mustard seeds, cover the pan and wait for the seeds to splutter and pop and turn grey (less than a minute). Add onion and bell pepper. Sauté until vegetables are soft. Add green chili or cayenne powder, grated ginger, salt and sugar. Add cooked mashed sweet potatoes and thoroughly mix. Add lemon juice or lime juice. Serve with a pat of butter.

Chapter Twenty Six

New Beginnings

• • • • • • • • • •

"You know, Lord Yama usually visits a household three times in a row," Ayah says. It has been just a few months since my father passed away and the air is already cool with the promise of an early winter. My old nanny is now quite old and she spends most of her days by the kitchen hearth.

"The Lord of Death comes three times," she says again. My mother who is seated at the kitchen table going over the milk accounts looks up with an annoyed expression, "Really Ayah you know that is just a superstition. I wish you wouldn't repeat such nonsense."

Ayah sniffs and holds her swollen arthritic hands to the kitchen fire. I can see a defiant gleam in her rheumy eyes. "You can think what you want little mother but I know what I know."

My mother shakes her head in exasperation but doesn't argue with the old woman. Perhaps that day Ayah glimpsed into her future because a week later Devi found her curled up on her mattress.

"Little mother, I tried to wake up Ayah but I think she's dead," Devi says to my mother. It is a bright December morning and even though the sun is shining it is sharply cold. I'm sipping a cup of milky hot tea and watching Muthi and my mother strain the fresh milk and pour the creamy liquid into large tin cans.

"Here, Meena, can you help Muthi while I go check on Ayah," my mother hands me the large metal strainer and leaves the kitchen in a hurry. She is back in a few minutes with a sad look in her large brown eyes.

"Muthi, it is true, Ayah has passed away. We'll have to start making the arrangements."

Muthi sets the measuring cup down and places an arm around my mother.

"Come little sister sit down. Even though Ayah was old she was part of this family for a long time. Meena, go and see if Bhojan or Raman can come and finish measuring the milk."

I start to walk out the door but hesitate and come back and hug my mother tightly.

"Poor Ayah," I say and feel sadness creeping from my chest into my throat, making it hard to talk.

"Little sister, did she have any family?" Muthi asks my mother.

My mother dries her eyes on the end of her cotton sari and shakes her head. "I'm not sure. Ayah came to live me with almost 20 years ago and she told me that she was alone in the world. But once I remember her mentioning that she had a son. I really don't know anything about her."

Her eyes fill with tears and Muthi is quick to say, "Oh, but you did know a lot about her. She was a gifted healer who took care of you. She raised your beautiful daughters and son. She cared for your sister in her time of need. She took care of me when I had a bad cough a few years ago. All the villagers knew they could ask for her help. You know she was a good friend. She stayed with you all these years because she loved you and your family. She was not just a nanny or kitchen helper, she was part of this family."

At these kind words I can't help crying. I will miss our family confidant and friend. She could be strict but she was always fair and kind to me. The three of us cling together and weep for Ayah.

The rest of the day is a blur of activity. I keep the twins out of everyone's way. At sunset Ayah's body is taken to the local cemetery for cremation.

"Remember how Ayah said that death comes three times in a row?" my sister Thangam says with a worried frown on her face.

"Don't you also remember Amma saying it was all non-sense?" I reply in a sharp tone.

I'm upset with Thangam because I had been thinking the exact same thing and the fear of losing yet another member of our household gives me a stomachache.

"I'm sure Ayah didn't know she was going to be the second person," I say in a calmer voice. "Its all right Thangam, I will take care of you."

Thangam hugs me tight and I try to forget my stomach ache.

All this talk about death and dying makes me sad and I be-gin to realize that things are constantly changing.

"Why are you so gloomy, Meena?" my longtime school friend Kumari asks. "It's really sad about Ayah but she was old. I know your father dying was so unfair and if I had the power to change that I would, but you know you can't change some things."

I shrug, "I know Kumari. I'm sad because I want things to stay the same and I know they won't. I'm starting to realize that even I will die someday."

"Come on Meena, you are just sixteen and we promised to go away together to college next year."

I smile at Kumari's enthusiasm but I still can't get rid of the feeling that things are changing too fast and I can't keep up with all the changes.

A few weeks after Ayah's death, I'm in the kitchen watching my mother and Muthi prepare our evening meal. As I watch my mother's slender brown fingers knead the dough, I realize what I need to do.

"Amma, can you teach me to cook?"

My mother's fingers stop kneading and she looks up. I notice she has new lines on her forehead and around her eyes. Even though she looks older, I can see an inner strength in her. I want some of that and I think I can get it by learning to be more like her.

"You mean you want to help in the kitchen?" she asks with a puzzled look.

"Yes, but I also want to learn how to make all the dishes you cook. I want to know how to make Aviyal and Ishtu and how to knead dough to make soft chapattis."

My mother smiles and her whole face lights up and her eyes are bright and soft.

"Oh, Meena, having you in the kitchen will make me so happy. Muthi, Devi and I will teach you to be the best cook in Mahagiri."

"Not just Mahagiri, but south India," Muthi adds with a grin.

"No time like the present to start," mother says. "Go wash your hands and help me make chapattis."

I feel so light-hearted that I want to skip to the sink. I look around at the smoky walls and make a silent vow to learn everything my mother can teach me. I want to be part of this wonderful place. This is where I belong, in my mother's kitchen, with my mother, Muthi and Devi.

Chapatti

2 ¼ cups flour,
a mixture of whole wheat and unbleached white flours
2 tablespoon ghee or melted butter
½ teaspoon salt
2/3 or more warm water
Flour for dusting cutting board
Melted butter or ghee to brush on bread

Preparation: Mix the flour and salt in a large bowl. Drizzle the butter or ghee on top of the flour and salt mixture. Add a little water at a time and start mixing the flour together. Keep adding water to make soft dough. Place the dough on a cutting board dusted with flour and knead until it is pliable and silky smooth. Cover with a damp cloth and let it rest up to 30 minutes.

Divide the dough into 14 portions and roll each portion into a round ball. Use a rolling pin to roll each ball into a circle that is about 6 inches wide. It is not important that the circle be perfect. Make sure the rolled dough is not overlapping and is covered by a damp cloth to keep from drying out.

Meanwhile, heat an iron griddle on medium flame for about 5 minutes. When the griddle is hot, pick up the chapatti and slap away any excess flour and lay on the griddle. Cook for about 1 minute and turn over. Brush each side of the bread with melted butter or ghee and keep the chapatti warm between layers of tin foil and a tea towel. Cook the remaining rolled out chapattis.

Makes about 14 chapattis. Serve warm with masala potatoes or warm butter and honey.

Chapter Twenty Seven

Seeing Ceremony

• • • • • • • • • •

"Meena!" "Meena!"

The harsh tone of my great-Uncle's voice snaps me out of my daydreams. *Oh great, the tribunal has reached a verdict. Life sentence or just probation,* I wonder.

I stand and brush the cashew shells off my sari. My tongue is thick, coated with the milky taste of the cashews I have been munching on while waiting for my mother and her cousins to decide on my future. My mother and I traveled from our hilltop home to my aunt's house in the nearby village of Kottapali in south India. It is hot and humid here in the village and, as I wait in the shade of the mango tree, I long for the cool breezes of my home.

My great-uncle waits until I enter the dusty parlor before closing the door with a click. I look around at the group gathered in the musty sunlit room. The dust motes dance in the sunbeams and I wish I could drift away too.

"Ahem," my great-uncle clears his throat and peers at me through his black-rimmed spectacles. A retired school teacher, he looks at me now as if I am one of his errant students. His usually kind eyes are hard and glisten like brown pebbles.

"Meenakutty, you are a troublemaker," he says shaking his grey head. "You will have to learn to listen and respect us."

I open my mouth to protest, but he holds up a brown palm, the signet ring on his pinky sparkling in the sunlight. The tropical day is starting to warm up and I can feel drops of sweat prickling my scalp. I finger the letter through the folds of my sari and the feel of the paper gives me confidence to stand up straighter.

"You are much too modern," says one of the aunts. "Your mother has let you run around wild. It is time for you grow up and be responsible."

I glare at her. She has always been my least favorite relation and is known for her constant nagging, the enforcer of rules in our family. Constant bickering has made her face a map of bitter lines. The sunlight brings out every wrinkle on her face. Her expression is as sour as the limes in our front yard.

I glance at my mother, but for once she doesn't look at me with affection. She keeps her eyes on her lap and her lips are turned down in a deep frown.

"Your mother has had a difficult year," she continues, "Who can blame her? Losing a husband is a sad business and having a wild daughter is no help either."

My mother's cousin now pipes in. His mouth is full of chewing tobacco he has to spit into a battered tin can before speaking.

"Not everyday do we get such a good marriage proposal," he says in a tone he thinks is reasonable. "The groom doesn't want money, jewelry, a fridge or a new car. He is ready to marry you as you are."

As he spoke he looks me over as if he can't believe anyone would want to marry me without the benefits of a large dowry.

"You are a reasonably attractive girl," he continues. "But if you argue and disrespect your elders, you will grow up to be an ugly old maid."

"Please uncle, I don't mean to be disrespectful, but all I want to do is finish college before getting married."

"I told you she was modern," my aunt yells. "You are an insolent miss. You should be grateful for the proposal. You had your chance to say no at the seeing ceremony."

The seeing ceremony took place less than a week ago. But it really all started when I was accepted to the local women's college after graduating from high school. My mother was not thrilled with the idea of college, but she agreed to let me attend if I majored in Home Economics. I would have preferred Journalism or Chemistry, but it was Home Economics or nothing.

I can't begin to tell you how much I detested everything about Home Ec. For the past few weeks we had been learning how to knit and I had somehow mastered the task of knitting the start of what looked like a baby bootie. Our instructor, Mrs. Pushparaj, was a stickler for rules. She wore heavy silk saris that rustled as she walked by, checking up on our work. She paused by my desk and peered down at the pale orange bootie dangling from the ends of my red knitting needles. I could smell the scented hair oil she used.

"Meena, what are you working on this week?"

I stood up to answer her question. Any student who failed to get up to answer her question was given a rap on the knuckles or head, depending on what part of the body her ruler could reach.

I looked down at the top of her head and said, "Ma'am, I'm making a baby bootie."

"Again? Didn't you make one last time," she asked, looking up at me, tapping her ruler on the palm of one hand.

I glanced nervously at the ruler. "Yes ma'am I did. But that was another one and my maid's daughter is now wearing it."

"All right then. Continue with your work."

I breathed a sigh of relief when she moved on to her next

victim. I would have to be more careful. It was the same bootie that I worked on last week. I had learned how to make the most of the class I hated by working on the same pair of baby socks. Every week, during class I diligently knitted. Knit one. Purl two. Knit one. Purl two.

Then, just before the next class, I unraveled what I had knitted and began again. My plan was to work on the same baby socks for the entire semester. But now that my knitting had come under the sharp eyes of Mrs. Pushparaj, perhaps I needed to change my plan.

All thoughts of knitting and purling had gone out of my head when I came home to find an unusual visitor in our kitchen. It was matchmaker aunty.

The matchmaker was tall and skinny. She was a widow and wore white or light-colored saris. Her grey hair was twisted into a complicated knot on the back of her head and she had the habit of sniffing or snorting loudly at the end of each sentence. She was never without her trademark bag filled with bits of paper, notebooks and newspapers.

"Everything you need for a good bride or groom is in this bag, (snort)" she would say, tapping the bulging bag on her lap.

She slurped on a cup of sweet tea and munched on a plate of lentil cakes.

"You were not wrong Sudha, (snort)" she said to my mother. "The girl has really grown up (snort)."

I glanced at my mother who was smiling a little too proudly I thought.

"She has nice wheat-colored skin and long thick hair (snort)," the matchmaker said in between sips of tea. "I think she is a little too skinny (snort). How tall are you dear?"

I was waiting for her to snort so didn't think she had finished talking, but she was looking at me so I shrugged and answered. "Not that tall. I guess about 65 inches."

"That is good (snort). We won't have to have to go to the trouble of looking for extra tall grooms," (snort) she said.

I walked over and helped myself to a lentil cake. These were my mother's special recipe. Golden lentils were soaked and ground into a thick coarse paste. My mother added bits of onion, fresh coconut flakes, ginger and green chilies, and then deep-fried them so that each cake was crispy and flavorful. I dipped my cake in a tangy mint sauce and popped the bit into my mouth. Lentil cake and mint sauce was my favorite snack of all time.

The matchmaker watched me eat.

"So (snort)," she said, chewing loudly on the lentil snack. "You know how to cook these (snort)?"

"My mother taught me how to make them," I replied.

"She is the best cook in her home ec class," my mother said. "She has taught the instructor how to make all kinds of food, even foreign foods like noodles."

"But you don't eat that stuff (snort, snort)?" the matchmaker looked horrified at the thought. "Isn't it all impure (snort)? Full of eggs and meat (snort)?"

"No, no. The noodles are just like our sava (vermicelli)," I explained.

The matchmaker wasn't entirely convinced but she didn't say anything more about my cooking, foreign or otherwise.

"So Sudha, I'll leave now (snort). We have set the date for next Friday (snort). Make sure all is ready (snort)," she said, getting up and lifting the cloth bag onto her shoulder.

"What's she talking about?" I asked my mother.

"Now, don't get upset Meenakutty. She has brought a nice proposal from a boy in our village. He sounds like a good man."

The lentil cakes are heavy in my stomach.

"But mother, I thought we had agreed that marriage could come after I finish college," I said.

"No, Meena you agreed. I didn't agree to anything. Now, I've been patient with your ideas about college but since your father passed away I feel an urgency to get you married and secure."

Whenever she brought up my father's heart attack, nearly two years ago, I knew I couldn't argue with her.

"Besides, this is just a seeing ceremony, not the actual wedding," she said. "You can dress up in one of my silk saris, wear some nice jewelry and show everyone how pretty and polite you are."

I did love to dress up and I for a moment I toyed with the idea of wearing her dark purple sari with the pale pearl earrings. But I paused in mid-thought.

"But Amma what happens if the groom likes me and I have to get married. I can't get married yet. I'm only 18 years old," I moaned.

"We don't have to agree to anything. This is just a seeing ceremony," my mother insisted.

I believed her, and against my better judgment, I let myself be pampered, petted and dressed in one of my mother's colorful saris. The soft silk brocade sari could rival the colors of a peacock feather. The iridescent blue and greens glowed richly and set off the gold threads woven along the edges of the material.

My hair was entwined with miniature jasmine blossoms and my mother's sea pearls glowed around my neck and ears.

"You look beautiful, my darling girl," my mother said. She placed an open palm on my head in a gesture of blessing. "What a bride you'll be."

"Remember Amma, this is just a seeing ceremony," I reminded her. "Do you think he'll be all dressed up too?"

"Oh, admit it Meena, you are looking forward to this," my mother laughed.

"No, I was just going to say if he doesn't look like a movie star, I'm not going to marry him," I told her.

She giggled, a girlish sound, I hadn't heard in many months. "Don't be silly Meena. How many men are really as handsome as a movie star? This is real life. Not one of your novels.

I didn't voice my thoughts but I wasn't going to marry a guy just because he proposed. My cousin Kavitha recently got engaged to a man who was a horror to the eyes. He had crooked teeth and even though he was a young man he had a little paunch and an unfortunate habit of adding a hissing sound at the end of every sentence. Kavitha thought he was agreeable, but there was no way I was going to marry a man with crooked teeth and who hissed at you like he was a snake.

"It is time," the matchmaker bustled into the room. "Bring the bride (snort)."

"Keep your head down," she snorted at me.

I walked behind her and stood in the center of our living room, feeling awkward and shy. I looked down at the pink toe nails peeking out from under my sari. I need to paint my big toe again, I thought to myself.

"Look up. No need to be shy," a voice, accompanied by a hand under my chin lifted my head up.

I looked into the beaming face of a stranger. Her face was smooth and round and a huge bindi dot dominated most of her forehead. She smelled of sandalwood soap.

"Come sit by me and talk to me Meena."

I let her lead me to the small sofa at the end of the room and sat down next to her.

She peppered me with questions: Did I like to wear saris? Did I cook the lentil cakes that were served today with tea? Did

I dance? Sing? Play a musical instrument? Did I like to speak in English or was I only comfortable in our native language? How tall was I? Did I usually wear heels?

It seemed like the more I answered, the more questions she had.

"It all sounds good to me," she said. "My nephew, the groom, couldn't come today but I'll give him a good description of you."

She patted my hands and left me to sit by myself on the sofa. I couldn't believe it, I was all dressed in my best and he didn't even show up.

A few minutes later, the aunt and the matchmaker stood up. The aunt walked up to me and took both my hands in hers.

"You are a lovely girl Meena. I'll tell Kumar all about you. I have one more question for you before I leave. Will you agree to marry my nephew?"

I didn't understand her for a moment. She wanted me to accept the marriage proposal before I even had a chance to see her nephew?

"Come on, Meena, tell us truthfully. Are you ready to be married? Just give me your word and it is all set."

"I don't know what to say," I said.

"Just say yes (snort)," the matchmaker said. She couldn't understand my hesitation.

"Is there any way I could see him?" I asked.

"I almost forgot. I have his photograph here. Go look at it and tell me what you think," the aunt said, pressing a photograph into my hands.

I walked over to the window and looked down at it. I don't know what I was expecting to see but it was not what I was holding in my hands. The photograph was of a group of men, balancing precariously in a row boat, holding up what looked like bottles of beer and grinning. The three men in the photograph were not the least bit appealing. The photo was not a close-up so the details were not clear. One of had a heavy beard, the other wore sunglasses and his mouth was open as if he was about to say something and the third fellow was turned away from the camera so that his pointy nose was clearly seen in profile. I wasn't about to marry any of them.

I walked back to the aunt.

"Aunty, which one is your nephew?" I asked as politely as I could.

"Oh, yes. I should have mentioned it. He is turning away from the camera. Doesn't he have a kingly profile?"

The man with the pointy nose. He looked as kingly as the picture of Rumplestilskin in my book about fairy tales.

"Yeees," I said drawling out the word. "I don't think this photo is enough. I would like to meet him in person before giving you an answer.

"Then he can see if he likes me too," I added hurriedly seeing the furious look on her face.

"Now, Meena, I must insist on an answer right now. Is it yes or no?"

I shook my head and said, "I can't say anything without seeing him in person."

Both the matchmaker and the groom's aunt kept insisting that I say yes but I refused. All I could think was I could never enjoy a lentil cake again. The seeing ceremony had spoiled the taste of my favorite snack.

The pair left in a huff and a few days later my mother and I are summoned to our aunt's home for a family meeting.

"Come on Meena, you have wasted enough of our time," says my uncle, the retired school teacher, bringing me back to the present. "Is it a simple yes?"

I notice that now there is no pretense of giving me a choice. I know I can't say yes. All my feelings and pent-up emotion swell up in me and I yell out, "No."

There is a shocked silence in the room and even the dust motes settle down.

"Not acceptable."

"Modern girl, I tell you."

"This is what happens to girls who go to college."

"What will you do now?"

All my relatives and my mother talk at the same time. I try to say something, but no one is listening to me.

"No," I yell as loud as I can.

Everyone stops, and stares at me. I know they can't believe my insolence.

"I have a letter, an invitation," I pull out the wrinkled envelope from the folds of my sari like it is a sword. "It's from my uncle Unny in California. He has sent me a plane ticket and a college application to go study in America."

A second later, my relatives are once again shouting and yelling among themselves, and I quietly slip out of the room, clutching my letter as if it is a lifeline.

Seeing Ceremony Lentil Cakes

1½ cups yellow split peas,
rinsed and soaked in cold water for about 4 hours
2-3 tablespoons of water as needed
1 small onion, chopped finely
2-inch piece of fresh ginger,
chopped into small pieces or grated
1 green chili pepper (Serrano or Jalapeño), minced
1 table spoon fresh cilantro or parsley, chopped
½ teaspoon salt (or to taste)
Oil for frying

Preparation: Using a food processor or blender, grind the yellow split peas into a coarse paste. (It is okay if one or two lentils are still whole, it will add a pleasant crunch to the lentil cake.) Add one tablespoon of water at a time to process the peas to make a thick paste. Stir in the remaining ingredients. Divide the paste into about 12 balls. Place each ball on a clean kitchen towel and flatten into a round shape about 2 to 3 inches in diameter and ½ inch thick. The cloth will absorb any excess liquid and make it easier to handle the cakes.

Heat oil, about ¼ to ½ inches deep, in a wide skillet until very hot. Fry about three or four cakes at a time. The cakes should be light brown and crispy.

Acknowledgements

This story would still be tucked away in a "rejections" folder but for Leslie Browning and Homebound Publications. There is nothing comparable to that feeling of receiving a letter of acceptance for your work. I am still floating! Thank You.

Writers, and especially cookbook writers, rarely write in a vacuum. Thanks to all my recipe testers, including Melinda Zimmerman and Liane and Scott Adler.

Housekeeping took a backseat to writing but there were no complaints from my family.

The book began as a project for *Blue Moon Literary & Art Review* in 2009 and soon took a life of its own. Thanks to Scott Evans and other Blue Moon Writers for their continued support.

Look for the sequel to *My Mother's Kitchen*,
Seeing Ceremony, now available wherever books are sold.

HOMEBOUND
PUBLICATIONS

At Homebound Publications, we publish books written by independent voices for independent minds. Our books focus on a return to simplicity and balance, connection to the earth and each other, and the search for meaning and authenticity. We strive to ensure that the mainstream is not the only stream. In all our titles, our intention is to introduce new perspectives that will directly aid humankind in the trials we face at present as a global village.

WWW.HOMEBOUNDPUBLICATIONS.COM